When Did We Lose Harriet?

Books by Patricia Sprinkle

Nonfiction

Children Who Do Too Little
A Gift from God
Women Home Alone
Women Who Do Too Much

MacLaren Yarbrough Mysteries

When Did We Lose Harriet?

Sheila Travis Mysteries

Deadly Secrets on the St. Johns
A Mystery Bred in Buckhead
Death of a Dunwoody Matron
Somebody's Dead in Snellville
Murder on Peachtree Street
Murder in the Charleston Manner
Murder at Markham

MacLaren Yarbrough Mysteries

When Did We Lose Harriet?

PATRICIA SPRINKLE

ZondervanPublishingHouse
Grand Rapids, Michigan

A Division of HarperCollins*Publishers*

When Did We Lose Harriet?

Requests for information should be addressed to:

ZondervanPublishingHouse
Grand Rapids, Michigan 49530

ISBN 1-56865-550-9

Interior design by Sue Vandenberg Koppenol

Printed in the United States of America

For Sarah Gay Edwards for years of laughter, friendship, and counsel, and for letting Jake and Glenna share your neighborhood

Characters

Harriet Lawson, age fifteen, and her family:

Dee Lawson Sykes, Harriet's paternal aunt, with whom she lives
William Sykes, Dee's husband
Julie Sykes, their sixteen-year-old daughter
Nora Sykes, William's mother
Lou Ella Sykes, William's grandmother
Myrna Crawley Lawson, Harriet's mother
Frank Lawson, Harriet's deceased father
Bertha (Granny) Lawson, Harriet's deceased paternal grandmother
Eunice Crawley, Harriet's maternal aunt

MacLaren Crane Yarbrough and her family:

Joe Riddley Yarbrough, her husband
Jake Crane, MacLaren's brother
Glenna Crane, his wife
Carter Duggins, Glenna's cousin the police officer

Other characters:

Josheba Davidson, part-time employee, Rosa L. Parks Avenue Branch Library
Morse, Josheba's boyfriend
Lewis Henly, director of the teen center
Kateisha, Harriet's friend at the teen center
Dré, Kateisha's brother
Z-dog, Dré's friend
Ricky Dodd, friend of Harriet's who once lived as a foster child with Harriet's grandmother
Beverly White, Ricky's girlfriend
Claire Scott and her mother, Harriet's former neighbors

Foreword

Montgomery, Alabama, is a charming city with big, beautiful homes and the most hospitable people in the world. Natives may wonder why this book set in Montgomery, then, doesn't just deal with charming parts of town and leave out the rest.

It is the nature of fiction that characters have lives of their own. Characters in this story kept wandering in from all over town, and I could not be fair to their story if I didn't let them live where they felt most at home. To those who would complain, "But Montgomery isn't like *that*," I would urge you to sample the rich diversity of your wonderful city. And if you'll let me come back, I'll set a murder on the Shakespeare Festival grounds with your favorite people.

I have taken liberties with the community around Rosa L. Parks Avenue. The teen center in this book does not exist—although maybe it should. The Rosa L. Parks Branch Library does exist, and Teresa Temple and her wonderful staff gave me almost as much help as they do my detective. They also repeatedly told me no librarian could give out the address of a patron, which forced me to come up with a fictitious way around that law.

I want to thank Judge Mildred Ann Palmer, who inspired this whole series. Special thanks to several Montgomery people who helped me with research. Sarah Gay Edwards housed me, fed me, encouraged me and acted like a "mean teacher with a red pen" to help me get the book as accurate as possible. Allison Gore, Craig Cornwell, Kimble Forrister, and the staff at Alabama Arise shared their perceptions of the city. Carol Gundlach and John "Boo" Starling talked in his hospital room about teenagers in Montgomery. The Rosa L. Parks Avenue Branch librarians let me use both their library and their books. Two nice men in Cottage Hill left their truck and reconstruction deliberations long enough to fill me in on some of the characteristics of that neighborhood. Eleanor Lucas at Capitol Book and News recommended the new Chamber of Commerce book on Montgomery just when I needed it. I hope I've been faithful to the help all of you so graciously gave me.

Thanks also to Julie Martens, Gardening Editor, *Southern Living Magazine,* for help with plants that would be in bloom in Montgomery in July, and to Dr. Lee Hearns, Toxicology Department, Metro-Dade Medical Examiner's office, for invaluable assistance on the forensics aspects of this mystery. I promise, Lee, not to tell everything I now know—nor to use it.

Finally, thanks as always to Anne Strahota, Paula Rhea, my agent Dominick Abel, and my editor Dave Lambert, who all read the manuscript and made me redo it until I got it right. Thanks! I could not have done it without all of you.

June

> But little do they know that the dead are there, that her guests are in the depths of the grave. *Proverbs 9:18*

One

The step was steeper than Harriet expected. She stumbled, fell face forward, and caught herself just in time to plunge awkwardly off the bus into the breath-sucking heat that smothers Alabama in June.

She glared down the long sidewalk strafed by the noonday sun, then turned back accusingly to the driver. "This the closest you can get? It's got to be two blocks, and it's hotter'n a stove out here!"

"You can go on a block or two if you like," he said with practiced patience, "but this is the stop you asked for. You won't get any closer."

Outrage in every movement, she shrugged on her backpack and whirled away.

He closed the door. When the bus roared off in a noxious cloud, she felt suddenly, inexplicably abandoned. Raising one fist to her mouth, she coughed dramatically in case the driver was watching. Harriet liked playing to an audience. Still playing, she adjusted her backpack and stomped off in the direction of Oakwood Cemetery—as instructed.

The bus driver, Jerry Banks, caught one final glimpse of her in his side mirror. He was glad his wife Netty couldn't see that kid. Now that their own two were grown, Netty was always bringing home strays. She would know what do to with this one—eyes as gold as a tiger's pelt and a temper to match. She'd scrub off half the makeup and take a hairbrush to the long brown hair. While she brushed, Netty would sweet-talk the kid into losing her black nail polish and half the cheap perfume. The girl would clean up real good.

As he pulled in to his next stop, Jerry felt a twinge of uneasiness. What did a teenager want in that old cemetery in all this heat? He couldn't see her as a faithful daughter of the Confederacy, going up to read the historical marker and check out gravestones of early citizens or Confederate soldiers. He hoped she wasn't making a pilgrimage to Hank Williams's grave—old Hank was buried in the Oakwood Annex. She could have stayed on a few stops for that. In either case, she'd surely be the only person up there at high noon.

But passengers weren't Jerry's responsibility once they left the bus—especially young white passengers. He knew that, and shrugged at his own foolishness. After all, the police station was right across the street from the cemetery.

Jerry didn't know that ivy and kudzu make an effective barrier between the Montgomery police station and Oakwood Cemetery.

He'd guessed right about Harriet's interest in history and Hank Williams, though. She had never heard of Hank Williams. She had no idea the old burying ground *had* a historical marker. And it would never occur to her to be interested in tombstones. Harriet's concern with Oakwood Cemetery was uniquely her own.

The black backpack hung heavily from her shoulders. A vivid bird of prey on her black T-shirt stuck damply to her front. Black jeans hugged her small flat behind. Harriet always wore black. Black sandals. Black lipstick. Black nail polish. She'd dye her hair black if Uncle William would let her. Women looked better in black. That's what fashion magazines said. They never said how hot it was, though. She was so sweaty she felt grimy all over. She had wanted to meet later so she could go back to Aunt Dixie's and change, but the morning caller had been insistent. "I want to see you right now. I can't wait any longer!" The voice was a soft, muffled whisper. Harriet had read her own yearnings into it.

Just remembering made her walk faster, hurrying toward her own particular miracle.

Not that she quite believed it. Fifteen years of living had given Harriet a strong practical streak, and she'd never seen an honest-to-God miracle. She didn't really expect to find one at the end of this hot street.

"But it *might* be her," she argued aloud in a fierce whisper, clenching her fists around hope. "Sometimes . . . in stories . . ."

Stories, to Harriet, meant romance novels, where a secret caller *could* be the heroine's mother coming back after thirteen years. Clasping the heroine close, she'd whisper through raining tears the reason she'd had to leave long ago without a word. Unfortunately, only in her deepest soul was Harriet the heroine of anything.

Perspiration trickled down her back and under her arms. In her sandals, grit stuck to the balls of her feet and crept between her toes. "I'll be filthy before I get there," she muttered. With one hand she wiped her neck, then held her arm out critically. She'd have looked better with a tan.

Anxious thoughts circled like buzzards. Would her mother think her pretty? "You've got great eyes," she reminded herself. Did her mother have the same eyes? Harriet wished Granny Lawson had kept at least one picture.

Mother. Harriet savored the word and regretted she hadn't put on fresh mascara and eyeliner. She'd scarcely spent any time on her face this morning, she'd been in such a hurry to get to the bank.

"What difference does it make?" She could hear her cousin Julie's scorn. "You're such a mess, nobody notices your eyes." Julie the cheerleader, with the perfect figure, red-gold hair, and perfect tan. All Julie and her friends did on weekends was sit by pools and brag about all the boys they knew. Harriet wasn't about to sit around with them and let them smirk at her flat chest, or ask whether *she* knew any boys. Her shoulders sagged, then lifted defiantly. She'd show Julie. She'd show them all!

The cemetery gates were just ahead. Beyond them, irregular lines of white tombstones and a few tall trees marched up a high hill crowned by a grove and a small white gazebo. "At the gazebo," the voice had said.

She squinted against the sun, still afraid to believe. "Probably somebody just puttin' me on," she told herself for the umpteenth time. Anger surged. "But if it is—if they do—" She didn't know how she would punish such betrayal, but it would be terrible.

She felt torn between wanting to dash up that hill and wanting to turn and run. She wished it were yesterday, tomorrow, any minute but now.

Harriet was no coward. "I can leave if I want to. I don't have to stay." Once she'd said it, she said it again. It became a rhythm to march to as she slogged up the narrow road, dogged purpose in every line of her body and a trace of hope in the way she lifted her head to gauge her ascent.

The hill, however, was too steep for heroic entries. Gradually her steps slowed. Halfway up she stopped and swiped her forehead with one forearm, panting for breath and swatting pesky mosquitoes that swarmed around her head. It was so hot that Spanish moss dripped from an ancient cedar like branches melting.

Jerry Banks was wrong again. The cemetery was not quite deserted. One person observed Harriet's slow progress — a person who had parked behind the crest of the hill well before the appointed hour and now stood concealed by the gazebo. A cooling breeze brushed through the shady grove on the hilltop. The mosquitoes weren't quite so thick up there, but from time to time the observer fanned away a few persistent ones and dabbed at a sweat-beaded forehead — keeping carefully out of sight.

Not until Harriet arrived and looked warily about did the observer step out. "Hello!"

Harriet's eyes widened in recognition — then narrowed in suspicion. "What're you doing here?"

"I'm supposed to take you to her. Come on."

Nobody saw them walk together down the back side of the hill.

Nobody heard the parked car start, or saw it leave.

After that, the cemetery was truly deserted.

Be sure of this: The wicked will not go unpunished, but those who are righteous will go free. *Proverbs 11:21*

TWO

Forty miles north of Montgomery lies Lake Jordan, pronounced "jerden" by the well-informed. An hour after Harriet plodded up the road in Oakwood Cemetery, her cousin Julie sat on a dock overlooking Lake Jordan, holding her head in both hands and wishing she were dead. How could she have gotten herself into this mess? It was all Harriet's fault. If she hadn't acted like such a know-it-all …

Julie's stomach churned and her heart beat faster, faster, faster. Would she throw up first — or explode? She had never been dumber in all her sixteen years.

She turned to Rachel Gray, her best friend. Rachel was crying. Julie felt worse than ever, because it had all been her idea.

If it were done when 'tis done, 'twere well it was done quickly. How could she remember Shakespeare now, when she never could on tests? It was a dumb quote anyhow.

How could you tell when something was done? She could see this day oozing out like a wet blot on her entire future, coming back to haunt her for the rest of her life.

Julie laid her head down on her knees and, like Rachel, wept.

In the little community of Chisholm—a cluster of small houses conveniently near Montgomery's northside industrial district—Eunice Crawley and her neighbor Raye Hunter rocked lazily on Eunice's front porch. Raye could tell Eunice was upset about something. Her plump face was flushed, and she kept breathing hard.

"You all right?" Raye fumbled in her pocket, retrieved a sodden tissue, and blew her nose. With all the pollen in the air, her allergies were acting up something fierce.

Eunice fanned flies that hummed a lazy duet with her rocker's steady squeak. "I'm plumb burning up. I guess I oughta go ahead and spend the money to get that air conditioner fixed." She swatted at a fly with her bare hand and missed, as usual. "Seems like if it isn't one thing, it's another. It's hard when a woman has no family."

Raye knew what Eunice was hinting. She thought Raye's second boy, Tom, ought to come look at her air conditioner for free. Eunice liked to hold on to her pennies. Raye dabbed her poor pink nose with the sodden tissue and shifted the subject. "You got a niece. Do you ever hear from Harriet? She okay about living with her other aunt?"

Eunice shifted in her rocker and resettled herself on its sagging cane bottom. "I haven't heard, but I can't have her here, that's for sure, what with me working and all these teenage gangs they keep talking about up here."

Truth to tell, Raye thought uncharitably, Eunice had lived alone so long, she couldn't stand having anybody around. Close Eunice was—with her money *and* her life. They'd been next-door neighbors for nearly twenty years, but Raye never could tell what Eunice would say or do. Take today, for instance. Eunice hadn't gone to work, but she'd left at nine-thirty and been gone well past noon. Raye had come over right after she came back, even missed one of her favorite TV stories, but Eunice hadn't said one word about where she'd been.

One thing Raye was sure of: Eunice never went anywhere or did anything except what suited Eunice Crawley.

What suited Richard Watson Dodd—known to his friends, creditors, and probation officer as Ricky—was to do absolutely nothing. Otherwise, he considered himself an easy young man to please. He didn't mind living in south Montgomery in a mobile home so little you could spit from one end to the other and so close to the airport that planes practically landed on the roof. He'd live happily in that mobile home so long as his girlfriend paid the rent and power bill. Ricky Dodd couldn't do without air conditioning.

Sprawled on the squalid plush couch—which had been a pleasant-enough red before dirt and body oils turned it a revolting blood rust—Ricky flicked the remote control to change channels and lifted his thin bare chest until the air conditioner blew a sensuous stream of icy air across his nipples. "Beverly, bring me a beer."

Beverly, a girl not quite out of her teens, with stringy blonde hair and a slump of despair to her shoulders, plodded obediently to the refrigerator and took a cold Budweiser from the shelf. "Where'd you get these?"

He snickered. "Oh, baby! You don't wanna know." He answered her sharp, frightened look by raising his can. "You gonna make me a sandwich to go with this?"

"I got to get ready for work. Besides, we're out of bologna, and I don't get paid until Friday." She hesitated, then timidly suggested, "Honey, if you could get some work a day or two a week, just to help out a little . . . I heard Buddy's filling station down from us is looking for a mechanic." Beverly clerked in a convenience store. She went to work each day terrified she'd be held up, but more terrified of what Ricky would do if she lost her job. Her terror excited him. To his buddies he referred to it as "Keeping the old woman in line."

He got tired, though, of her constant harping. "Job, job, job. Baby, is that all you ever think about? You know my back won't take the lifting. But I'm getting some money in a little while. Just you wait."

"Ricky!" Her plain face puckered with concern. "You aren't—? If you get caught again—"

He stopped her with a look. "I ain't gonna get caught, and it ain't what you think. I had a little talk with Harriet. She's gonna give me some money real soon. Wait and see."

He'd known that would catch her attention. "Where would Harriet get any money? And why would she give it to you?"

He smirked. "Wouldn't you like to know?" He reached again for the remote control. "Go next door and borrow some bologna. Say we'll pay 'em back Friday, for sure."

In east Montgomery, the famous Alabama Shakespeare Festival is a jewel set in spacious grounds. Since the elegant theater was built in the mid 1980s, it has drawn wealth and prestige like a diamond draws women.

In a beauty salon not far from the Shakespeare Festival grounds, Dee Sykes (nee Dixie Lawson) contemplated her nails. "That looks more purply than it did on the chart. Are you sure it matches?" Diamonds sparkled on her wedding band.

Teri, the manicurist, reached for a magenta belt lying on her table and held it up for Dee to compare. "It's a little darker than the belt, but if it was exact, nobody would notice the polish. I like the contrast."

Dee gave her fingertips one more dubious look. "I guess so." She looked at the clock over the counter. "Goodness, is it nearly two? I must have been at the mall for hours! It took me forever to find a dress, but I wanted something new for the play tonight."

"Well, now you're all fixed up." Teri gave the polish one last check to be sure it was really dry.

"You were so sweet to fit me in when I called." Dee reached into her purse for her wallet. "When I found the dress, it was just perfect, but the polish I had on would have been dreadful with it. I called you before I even wrote my check. If you couldn't fit me in, I was going to get a plain black dress instead."

Teri pocketed a generous tip that almost made up for having to miss lunch. She couldn't help thinking of her own unpaid bills, the cold her three-year-old had caught at day care, and the very real threat that his daddy would come by after work and beat the tar out of her because the kid got sick. "Must be nice to have money," she muttered as Dee headed toward a creamy Mercedes in the parking lot. Sure, Dee complained a lot about her wild niece, her meddling mother-in-law, and how her husband William never wanted to do a thing after work except putter in his yard, but life couldn't be too bad when your mama-in-law was the widow of a rich lawyer politician and your husband sold the priciest furniture in town.

Starting to tidy the table, she saw Dee had forgotten her belt. Dashing out of the shop, Teri caught the Mercedes just before it pulled off the lot. Dee took the belt with an apologetic smile. "Aren't you sweet! I'd lose my head if it wasn't glued on. Thanks." She drove away with a perky little wave.

Dee held the smile until she was half a block down the street, then sagged at the wheel. "Whew!" She expelled the exhausted breath of an actress who's completed a difficult performance. Nobody knew how much energy it took to look happy when you were worried to death. Dee wanted to get home, stretch out on her big, cool bed and sleep until time to fix dinner. At least Nora was at the lake, so she wouldn't be calling with a few more colleges Julie might go to. William's mama could be such a pain!

While Dee's hands were on the wheel, her mind was planning dinner. Lemon garlic chicken and rice. William liked that. Might as well set a place for Harriet. Keep up appearances a while longer. That was all they did anymore, it seemed—keep up appearances.

Nora Sykes stood on her tree-shaded deck and looked across Lake Jordan with contentment. She'd had a very satisfactory day. Her fox-red hair, brushed straight back off her high forehead to curl slightly under at the ends, was lifted by a breeze fragrant with the Russian tea olive she'd planted near the deck. Checking the heavy gold watch on one freckled arm, she saw it wasn't quite two. She needn't go in for a while yet.

William was fond of boasting that "My mama is as pretty today as when Daddy died fifteen years ago." That made people smile, for Nora looked very like her son. However, while they shared bright red hair and emerald eyes, Nora's flawless skin had skipped a generation and shown up in her granddaughter. Poor William was ruddy, freckled, and scarred from a heartbreaking case of teenage acne.

He also suffered from a poor memory. Nora Sykes actually looked better than she had fifteen years before. William Trevor Sykes Junior, called Trevor, had preferred for his wife to stand in his shadow. When he died, Nora got a new hairstyle, trimmed down her figure, and found a personal trainer. These days, nobody would take her for sixty-five. Her honeyed voice—deep and vigorous, like the one Tallulah Bankhead took from Alabama and made famous around the world—rang out in committees and social events all over town. Last year she'd bought a lovely home in Wynlakes, a prestigious community on Montgomery's eastern edge. Her latest enthusiasm was to get her only granddaughter, Julie, into what she referred to as "a quality college." The fact that Dee and William wanted to send their daughter to their own alma mater, the University of Alabama, was merely tiresome.

In an elegant and gracious home just down the street from the big white governor's mansion, Lou Ella Sykes lifted a white linen napkin, dabbed her lips, and surveyed her grandson approvingly. "That's settled, then, William? You talk it over with Dee, and I'll try to think of how to bring your mother around. Thank you for waiting to eat until after my—" she touched the large pearls at her throat, "—meeting." She hoped her grandson hadn't noticed the slight pause, and would never know what she'd been doing before this luncheon. If only she could keep from shaking!

William Sykes nodded absently. He certainly hadn't noticed the pause. William was too busy hoping Lella wouldn't find out how he'd spent his own morning. He couldn't have eaten much before two anyway. He'd had to wind up something very important.

He squirmed in his chair. He couldn't believe he'd done it—but it had to be done. That's all there was to it. It had to be done.

While pretending to listen intently to his grandmother, William was actually wondering why Lella looked so terrible. Sure, she was eighty-four. Her bones no longer carried her frame erect, she used a cane, her once olive skin had faded to a sallow hue, and the veins in the backs of her hands were as thick as the wisteria vine that shaded her dining room window from the western sun. But her voice was still strong, with that faint trace of New Orleans she'd brought to Montgomery as a bride. Usually she was as trim and as elegant as her home. Today, while her gray linen dress was cool and crisp like always, and her iron-gray hair was softly confined in its usual regal twist, she had dark half-moons under her eyes and looked like somebody had taken the helium out of her balloon. Why?

He realized his grandmother was expecting him to say something. At least the gist of her last remarks had gotten through. He sighed. "Lella, why can't you and Mama bury the hatchet and stop pulling me, Dee, and Julie to pieces between you?"

Her smile was frosty. "Your mother and I have had differences since before you were born, William. But this time we won't pull your family to pieces, as you so inelegantly put it, if you'll haul up your socks and stand up to her." She raised her voice slightly. "Irmalene, we're finished in here. You can bring in dessert." She lifted a Waterford pitcher of iced tea to refill their glasses, but her hand shook too hard to hold it. She placed the pitcher carefully on the table and said, to distract her grandson, "Where your daughter goes to college is your business—yours, Dee's, and Julie's. Just because Nora went to Agnes Scott is no reason for her to have a say in the matter."

William had noticed her tremors, but he misinterpreted them. Could Lella be dreadfully ill? He felt terror rise like ice water in his veins. He couldn't bear to think of a world without Lella and her big old house, where he'd taken his first steps and eaten almost every Sunday dinner in his life. Lella's was the only place in all the world where he could truly sit back and relax. In his own house he felt like an interloper. Dee even told visitors as she showed the back room, "This is William's little den"—as if he merely rated a hole in a riverbank somewhere. She and Julie had so completely filled the rest of the house with ruffles, flowers, and lace that it looked like a fancy bassinet. Dee hadn't even given him the den, really. She'd chosen pictures he didn't like, a chair he could never get comfortable in, and curtains in a shade of green that reminded him of one time when he'd eaten too many unripe pears as a boy and vomited up undigested peeling.

Mama's new house—full of thick Chinese carpets, heavy mahogany antiques, enormous mirrors, and gleaming silver—left little room for a man to stretch out and breathe, either. *Someday,* he thought, *I'd like a house with bare wood floors, wooden blinds, no curtains, and very little furniture.* He squirmed in Lella's mahogany chair. What kind of thoughts were those for a man who sold furniture for a living?

As Irmalene trudged almost silently around the table removing luncheon plates and setting down bowls of ice cream smothered by Chilton County peaches, the air conditioner clicked on and whirred softly. William remembered squirming on the very same mahogany chair one summer day when he was ten years old, and the only relief from the thick warm air was a lazy fan above the table. That afternoon, his father had taken him over to Granddaddy's to tell him "how women are."

"You can't ever please 'em, boy," he had concluded, "no matter how hard you try. But don't act like you're gonna run counter to 'em, either, or they'll have a hissy and make your life miserable. The best course is to nod and smile, then go your own way."

Daddy had taken a big puff of his cigar and blown a cloud that made William's stomach queasy in the hot, close room. Then he'd added, almost to himself, "Of course, a day of reckoning will come. They're smarter'n we give 'em credit for."

William's day of reckoning had come. No amount of nodding and smiling was going to settle this new struggle between Lella, Mama, and Dee. *Probably,* he thought miserably, *the only thing that will settle it is death.*

July

> Do not boast about tomorrow, for you do not know what a day may bring forth. *Proverbs 27:1*

Three

My name is MacLaren Yarbrough, and while it's hard to believe now, when I flew from Albuquerque to Montgomery on Monday, July fifteenth, I'd never heard of Harriet Lawson. Furthermore, if anyone had quoted "God works in mysterious ways, his wonders to perform" to me as my plane droned above the inky Alabama countryside, I'd have told them smartly that as far as that particular trip was concerned, God had very little to do with it.

What *God* had done, so far as I could see, was finally get me sent from Hopemore, Georgia – a pleasant little town midway between Augusta, Macon, and nowhere, where I am variously known as the wife of Joe Riddley, mother of Ridd and Walker, and co-owner of Yarbrough's Feed, Seed & Nursery – to our church's national meeting in Albuquerque – where I could say a few things I've been storing up for years. It was my brother Jake who messed things up by having a heart attack smack in the middle of a most interesting discussion on human sexuality.

Jake's timing has been lousy for fifty-five years. He even got born two weeks early, which canceled my tenth birthday sleepover.

I was intrigued, incidentally, by how long some folks can spend discussing human sexuality. I've been married nearly forty-five years, have some good memories and anticipate a good many more, but I never realized how much some people like to talk about sex—particularly people who look as if they aren't getting enough of it.

When I'd told Joe Riddley that on the phone the night before, he'd chuckled. "MacLaren, honey, we both know sex is a lot like eating—sometimes a feast and sometimes just a quick bite on the road to somewhere else—but doing it sure beats talking about it."

By the end of that next week in Montgomery, I'd be delighted that Joe Riddley was still in Georgia where he belonged. As I pressed my forehead to the cold window, though—straining for my first glimpse of Montgomery's lights in the country darkness—I missed him something terrible. I couldn't help thinking that if the plane kept going for another hour or so, we'd be over middle Georgia and could land in my son Ridd's back cotton field. I could sleep in my own bed with Joe Riddley heavy and sweet beside me. Why the dickens hadn't Jake's guardian angel protected him for one more week?

I was grumbling to keep from bawling, and I knew it. There I was with years of practice praying for sick people, and now that it was Jake I found myself reduced to *"Please, God, please, God, please, God!"*

To make me even grumpier, I looked a wreck. I like to look nice, and while I'm no longer the slip of a thing in my wedding pictures, I still have the same big brown eyes and (with the connivance of my beauty operator) keep my hair almost the same honey brown. Joe Riddley even assures me I've grown voluptuous, not plump. He's a very nice man when he wants to be. That night, however, I was about as attractive as a wilty cabbage leaf. If I stopped looking *through* the airplane window and merely looked *in* it, I saw a woman with bags under her eyes, crow's feet radiating to her hairline, and all her lipstick chewed off.

It wasn't just worry over Jake that had me looking that way. Nobody warned me that national church meetings go on day and night. Leaders seem to think that just because God neither slumbers nor sleeps, neither should anybody else. Between lying awake every night for a week ahead planning what to take and what I wanted to say, and trying to stay awake in late meetings, I hadn't gotten any decent sleep for days. When you are on the shady side of sixty, you need your rest. I'd been feeling grumpy even before Jake's wife, Glenna, called to say he was in intensive care. Of course I had to go, right away.

When the plane landed, I could hardly wait for the pilot to turn off the engines and the flight attendants to open the door. I pushed my way almost rudely into the passenger inch-walk down the cabin, and nearly ran toward the terminal. Glenna was waiting just inside. The sight of her fairly broke my heart. How could a woman age so much in one day?

Glenna has never been a beauty. She's tall and bony, seldom bothers with creams and powders, has been gray since she was forty, and doesn't fuss much with her hair—just cuts it to fall straight and cup her cheeks on each side. Her big gray eyes are so kind, though, that I've seen grieving children fling themselves into her arms. She also has something my mother's generation referred to as "breeding"—an easy way of carrying herself and wearing clothes that lets anybody with two eyes know she grew up in a family with enough money and education not to need to parade either one. That night, though, her skin looked like it had been left on a counter overnight when it should have been refrigerated, and her eyes had the same stricken look I had seen in a dog begging to be put down.

She was smiling as I went toward her, but when I held out my arms, her face crumpled.

We hugged awkwardly, both because Glenna is five-nine and I five-three and because we aren't accustomed to touching. Our closeness has always been one of spirit, not bodies.

"Oh, Clara!" Glenna said over and over, clinging like she'd never let go.

I nearly melted in a puddle of tears right then and there. Since Mama and Daddy died, nobody but Jake and Glenna calls me "Clah-ra"—which was all Jake could make of "MacLaren" when he was a baby.

"How is he?" I asked. I couldn't catch a breath while I waited for her answer. So much could have happened in those hours I'd been on the plane.

She averted her head. "Not good, honey." Her voice trembled. "The doctor says he needs bypass surgery, but Jake won't agree. I hope you can persuade him."

I gave my nose a hearty blow. "Durn tootin'." I hoped I sounded more confident than I felt. I saw I was not only going to have to make Jake get his surgery, I was going to have to prop up Glenna at the same time.

"Can I see him tonight?" I asked.

She checked her watch. "It's way past the last visitation, but I told them you were coming and they said they'll let you in for a minute—if you aren't too tired."

"I'm a walking zombie, but I won't sleep until I've seen him. Let's stop by to say hello, then go on home."

As we left the fresh cool air of the airport, I knew I was in Alabama. The night was so hot and thick I could have shaped it in my hands like cotton candy.

Glenna pulled into the hospital parking lot and turned deftly into a waiting space. One of her many grace gifts is that she always gets a convenient parking place when she needs one. In emergencies, I have even gotten a couple myself by chanting, “I am Glenna Crane, I am Glenna Crane.”

In the cardiac intensive care unit Jake was pale, with tubes everywhere and more monitors than NASA. I saw at once why Glenna looked the way she did. The spunk had gone out of old Jake. What little hair he had left was lifeless and dry, his skin was a peculiar ashy gray, and even his voice was a wisp of its usual boom. “Well, Clara, how's this for a way to get you to visit?”

I had to clear my throat before I could answer. I even almost said something polite before I caught myself. If I talked nice, Jake would think he was dying. “Effective, Bubba, but not one I'd recommend. How do you feel?”

“Like an old tire retread. How do you feel?”

“Like somebody who's been on planes all day because her baby brother's being ornery.” I sat down beside him and took his hand. “Glenna says you need a bypass.”

He chuckled weakly. “Not wasting any time, are you?”

“Nope. Why are you?”

“Fundamental chickenism. Besides, I'm not sure that's what I ought to do. I've lived a good life . . .” He had to stop to cough. His monitors jumped around like crazy.

I wasn't about to stay and upset him right then. “We'll talk some more tomorrow. I'm too tired to argue right now.”

“How long you gonna be here?”

“Until you get your bypass and get back home.”

“I'll think about it.”

“You'd better,” I warned, in the tone I used when he was four and I was allowed to switch him if he disobeyed. “Now get yourself a good night's sleep. I'll get you straightened out tomorrow.”

Glenna, who had waited by the door, tiptoed in and kissed him on the cheek. “I'll be back after I get Clara settled.”

He shook his head. "You don't need to come back, honey. I'll be fine."

"I'm not coming just for you, Jake. I'm coming for me. I'll rest better knowing I'm here." She straightened his covers and touched his shoulder in farewell, then motioned me to follow her out.

One of the very few things Jake and Glenna don't agree on is automobiles. To Glenna, a car is transportation. Once she gets one she likes, she hangs onto it for years and gives it just enough maintenance to keep it running. Her current blue Ford was rump sprung and dented, and my suitcases shared the trunk with two bags of clothes she was taking to a homeless shelter and three bags of sanitized cow manure she'd bought for her flowers.

Jake, on the other hand, has always been car proud. He likes new, pretty ones, and treats them more like girlfriends than steel and plastic. This year's red Buick Park Avenue gleamed in their unpaved drive, an Auburn sticker in its back window. It was almost easier to see him in the hospital than it was to see his car in the driveway and know he might never come home to drive it.

Glenna seemed to feel the same, for although she is naturally quiet, she chattered like a squirrel as she lifted the heavier bag from the car. "We haven't had a bit of rain for weeks. I don't know what the yard will do if we don't get some soon. But look! The old magnolia saved three blossoms for you. The rest bloomed earlier, but those waited for you to get here." I peered up the fat old tree. Sure enough, three creamy blossoms glowed in the darkness.

Higher up, from towering pines, came the whir of thousands of tiny motors humming in the night. "The cicadas are certainly having a fling!" I exclaimed. Cicadas are noisy little locusts that hibernate for years, then creep out of the ground, sing their hearts out, lay their eggs, and die. On their jubilee, the whole South gets a bumper crop, but where I live, every year a few rebels come up out of season. This was either a jubilee, or Montgomery's cicadas have the same spirit that made that city the first capital of the Confederacy.

As I waited on the front walk for Glenna to unlock the door, I took a deep breath of thick air scented with honeysuckle, pine, and boxwood, and thought how remarkable she and Jake were. When they'd been married about three years and had just learned Glenna could never have a baby, they bought a comfortable six-room house in Montgomery's South Hull District, a neighborhood of modest brick homes. Their house has a big yard and ceilings high enough so you don't smother, but it also has two small bathrooms and a kitchen Glenna keeps talking about remodeling but never has. Over the years, when a lot of their friends and neighbors moved east to newer neighborhoods with roomy, modern kitchens, enormous bathrooms, and several extra rooms, Jake used to ask, "You want to move, honey?"

Glenna always replied, "Wouldn't you rather put our money in something that really matters, Jake?" Only their family, their church treasurer, and the postman who brings appeals and carries away checks know what matters to Jake and Glenna Crane. I never let them hear me say it, but as far as I know there are no finer people on God's green earth.

Thinking of losing Jake was like a knife in my heart. When Glenna stepped inside and called, "Coming, dear?" I could hardly see to hurry up the steps.

I saw Glenna off for her all-night vigil, kicked off my shoes, and unpacked. After a long cool shower I was padding barefoot across the kitchen's old black and white linoleum tiles for a glass of milk when the phone rang. "MacLaren Yarbrough," I answered automatically, then corrected myself. "Crane residence."

There was a silence on the other end, then an explosion. "Woman, what are you doing there? You are supposed to be in Albuquerque!"

"Joe Riddley!"

I knew I was wasting my charm. He barely paused for breath. "When Glenna called here this morning looking for you, I was stupid enough to give her your number, but five minutes later I wished I hadn't. I just knew you'd do some fool thing like hare off to Montgomery. I never imagined you'd do it so fast, though. What'd you do—sprout wings and fly solo?"

"I got the first plane out, just like any caring sister would."

"Caring, my hind foot. You'll badger that poor man to death."

"I'm not badgering him!" I took a deep breath to fortify myself. Talking to Joe Riddley can be like walking into the Atlantic during a hurricane. You don't make much headway, and you often wind up flattened. Oddly enough, though, he is the mildest man in Hopemore when he's on the magistrate's bench. Did I forget to tell you? Joe Riddley is a magistrate as well as a nursery man. Judge Yarbrough, respected throughout Hope County. Some prisoners—especially those brought in in the middle of the night—ask for him by name, because Joe Riddley never gives them a hard time about being hauled out of bed.

He seldom gives anybody a hard time, except me and our younger son, Walker. He and Walker butt heads because they are so much alike, and he got used to bossing me when I was four and he was six. Joe Riddley's daddy owned the local hardware store (the same one we converted into the Feed, Seed & Nursery when Home

Depot came into town a few years back) and one day my daddy took me there. Joe Riddley looked down, hitched up his corduroy pants, and asked, "Wanna go count nails?" To somebody just learning to count, it was sublime! They kept the nails in bright red bins, and we counted long ones, short ones, fat ones, and skinny ones. I could only go to a hundred, but Joe Riddley could count forever. After that, I begged to go to the hardware store, because I thought Joe Riddley was wonderful. Still do—although I don't let him get away with bossing me the way he did back then.

One day when Daddy called me to go, Joe Riddley looked down at me and said gruffly, "You can't count worth a flip, but you are the cutest little bit of a thing I ever did see." Then he turned beet red.

He's called me Little Bit ever since—as in "Little Bit, don't you go butting into things over there. You hear me?" He often complains that I butt in on people's lives and his cases. I always reply that anybody who's raised two boys and put up with him all these years knows there are times to butt in and times to butt out.

Tonight I said, with the dignity befitting one elected to a national church meeting, "I'm not going to butt in on a single thing, Joe Riddley. All I'm going to do is help Glenna make Jake get the surgery he needs."

His voice softened. "Well, from what Glenna said, he needs somebody to pound sense into his head, and you're the best pounder I know. Tell him I said to go on and get that danged operation so he can get rid of you—then you come on home, you hear me? Don't even think about trying to go back to Albuquerque for that last day or two."

"I won't," I promised, "and don't you worry about things here. I'll keep you posted." I had no idea, at the time, what a whopper *that* would turn out to be.

After he hung up, I got a glass and was just about to finally get my milk when the phone rang again. "Crane residence," I remembered to answer that time. "This is Jake's sister MacLaren. May I help you?"

I leaned toward the fridge, but the cord didn't reach. Jake and Glenna are so old-fashioned they didn't even own a cordless phone. I vowed to send them one for Christmas.

The woman on the other end was courteous, but had whining down to a fine art. "I'm sorry to be calling so late, but I've been trying to reach Jake all day."

While I explained why Jake had been unavailable, I nearly pulled the cord out of the wall so I could finally open the refrigerator. The milk squatted at the back, out of reach.

When she heard about Jake, the woman got real sympathetic, but even that was a sympathetic whine. "Oh, honey, I'm so *sorry* to have to bother you at a time like this. Does the church know? I'll find time to call tomorrow and get him on the prayer chain, then we'll organize some meals, but in the meantime, I just *have* to know about tomorrow, because—"

Living with Joe Riddley, I've had lots of practice wading into conversations midstream. "Meals won't be necessary for a while," I said loudly and firmly. "Glenna and I will be at the hospital most of the time. But I know they'd appreciate being on the prayer chain. Whom shall I tell them called?"

She said her name so fast I missed it, then went on, "Glenna and I are also in the Garden Club together, and the . . ." When a Southern woman starts describing who she is and what clubs she belongs to, there's plenty of time to leave a receiver on the counter, pour a glass of milk, and get back before the other person knows you're gone. I'd drunk half my milk, murmuring "umm's" at what I hoped were appropriate places, before the woman paused for an audible breath. I didn't really start paying attention until she asked, "Do you know who Glenna got?"

"I'm sorry," I said contritely. "I've just come in off a plane, and I'm still getting my bearings. What is it you want to know?"

Her sugar turned a bit sour. "What arrangements Glenna's made about the teen center tomorrow."

"Teen center?" I was totally in the dark, and so sleepy I was having to swallow yawns before they swallowed me.

If I'd had phone-a-vision, I swear I'd have seen her drumming perfect nails. "The teen center! You know, just off Rosa L. Parks Avenue? Run by the Youth Council? Directed by that nice Mr. Henly?"

I opened my mouth to explain I had never heard of the Youth Council or that nice Mr. Henly, but she rippled on. "Jake goes over the first and third Tuesdays, from ten 'til noon. I always call to remind him."

"Well, this time he can't possibly come."

Any decent woman would have hung up right then, but this particular specimen was as persistent as summer's first fly. "We-e-ll . . ." She drew it out into at least three syllables, followed by a meaningful pause—the meaning being, "This is also your problem now, sugar, so you'd better get on the stick and think of something."

I did not say a thing.

After a long pause, she sighed. "I just don't know who I could get this late. Being summer, you know. So many people are out of town . . ." Another long pause.

I knew what was expected of me. Natives of Montgomery fall all over each other being nice and helpful. I, however, long ago learned to live with the guilt of not always doing the right thing. I drank the rest of my milk and still didn't say a word. Finally the woman was forced to come right out and ask.

"How about you? Just this once? Mr. Henly counts on us for Tuesdays."

I simply cannot remember what happened after that. I remember repeating that I was a stranger to Montgomery who had just flown in to be with my brother. I'm pretty sure I told her at least twice I couldn't possibly go to the center. I was so tired I may have given out my mother's maiden name and our bank security code. I would have said *anything* to get off that phone.

Apparently, I did.

By the time I climbed into bed ten minutes later, I'd agreed that the next morning I'd keep the desk (whatever that meant) at a teen center off Rosa L. Parks Avenue (wherever that was), so nice Mr. Henly (whoever he was) wouldn't be disappointed.

"Oh, well," I consoled myself, yawning, "it's only two hours. It won't kill me."

I would live to reconsider those words.

> An inheritance quickly gained at the beginning will not be blessed at the end. *Proverbs 20:21*

Four

I woke early Tuesday morning worrying about Jake. The backyard looked so lovely at that hour that I carried my Bible and a glass of iced tea out to a shady bench, hoping to find a breeze and comfort from the Psalms.

There was no breeze, just a hot waiting morning slowly baking Jake's vegetables and Glenna's flowers, and sunlight streaming between the hackberry trees. I always associate those tall, gracefully leaning elms with Montgomery and Jake's backyard.

When I opened my Bible to the Psalms, the first verse I read was no comfort at all: *My soul is full of trouble and my life draws near the grave.* I couldn't read any farther. Everywhere I looked the yard was full of Jake. Jake building the bench I sat on. Jake crowing over an enormous tomato. Jake bending to carefully place a stone cherub, rabbit, and a miniature St. Francis so they peeped out from the foliage. Jake, calling us all the way in Georgia to brag when bluebirds nested in the little rustic house he built them.

Tears rolled uncontrolled down my cheeks. *"Please, God, please, God, please!"*

Finally I stopped talking and started to listen. As usually happens, the answer was peace. A shaft of sunlight found its hazy way through the tree canopy and pooled just beyond my feet. A mockingbird pierced the morning with its sweetness. A breeze touched my cheek and brought a honeysuckle scent of amazing sweetness. About the time I was beginning to really relax, mosquitoes began buzzing around my ear.

That's life — mockingbirds followed by mosquitoes.

Naturally, I hadn't packed anything appropriate to wear to an inner-city teen center. The closest I could get was a mist green linen pantsuit with a Laura Ashley print blouse — not very close at all. "I'll look nice for Jake later," I assured myself, combing my hair and putting on bright pink lipstick. I often talk to myself. As I tell my family, a person needs intelligent conversation sometimes.

I was pouring out cold cereal when Glenna got home, dead on her feet. Quickly I fetched another bowl. "Let's eat out on the sunporch," she suggested. "It's so pretty this time of year."

The sunporch is a back porch Jake glassed in years ago so they could enjoy the backyard. In Montgomery, between mosquitoes and the heat, a glass room makes a lot more sense than an open porch. Glenna keeps a couple of rockers out there and a small table with two chairs.

She gave a huge yawn as she came to the table. "They said we shouldn't go back to the hospital this morning, because Jake's having tests and we can't see him until after lunch. If you don't mind, I'd like to stretch out a little while."

I didn't bother to mention last night's call. As tired as she was, Glenna would still drag herself down to that center. Jake always claims that if their house was burning up, Glenna would bring the firemen a nice glass of tea. Actually, it was just as well Glenna *was* so sleepy. When I said, "I need to run some errands, so why don't I use the Buick and meet you at the hospital later?" she gave me Jake's keys as pretty as you please. She must have forgotten Jake never, ever lets me drive his cars.

No matter what Glenna said, I wasn't going anywhere that morning without at least one glimpse of my brother, but it was so painful for him to talk and for me to see him trying, I only stayed a second. "See you later, Bubba," I promised, gently squeezing his hand.

"Not going anywhere, Sis." He sank back on his pillow in exhaustion.

Maybe it was because I was so worried about him, but I crossed Rosa L. Parks Avenue three times before I realized it wasn't a new street, just a new name for Cleveland Avenue. Trust city fathers. When they want to honor their cronies, they build arenas and new expressways. When it's anybody else, they rename a street.

The teen center, once I found it, was a small brick building that must have been a school before it got so old and dirty—or maybe that's how it got so old and dirty. The curbs were dirty, too—as I discovered when I got Jake's white sidewalls a tad closer than I'd intended.

Inside, the building was dim and smelled of chalk, old lunches, and much-used bathrooms. The linoleum, which had once been either beige or gray, was now something in between, but somebody had repainted the walls bright yellow. Walking in from outside was like walking directly into the sun. A stuffy, poorly air-conditioned sun.

While a door marked "Office" stood open, its lights were off and the room was empty. "Hello? Hello!" I stood in the center of the hall and called, feeling a bit foolish.

"Hey!" A man hurried from the back of the building, wiping his hands on the seat of clean but well-worn jeans. "I was fixing a toilet. May I help you? I'm Lewis Henly, director of the center."

He was the handsomest black man I'd ever seen except in the movies, and he had a voice like honey—or maybe it was that wisp of mustache under his nose that reminded me of bees. He was around thirty, I figured. His hair was cut short, his smile was friendly, his jeans not only clean but starched and ironed. He was clearly surprised to find me standing in his hall, however. I guess he was expecting Jake or hoping for somebody younger, darker, and thinner. Nevertheless, I gave him my most charming smile. "I'm MacLaren Yarbrough, Jake Crane's sister. I'm taking his place this morning."

He looked at my linen pantsuit, Laura Ashley blouse, purse and flats, and I could almost hear him totting up the price. He raised one eyebrow and waved a slender hand to indicate the grimy hall. "Not your usual part of Montgomery, is it?"

That got under my skin. Jake and Glenna weren't the only people in our family with a social conscience. "I have no usual part of Montgomery," I informed him stiffly. "I live in Hopemore, Georgia, and I volunteered to take Jake's place this morning because he had a heart attack yesterday and can't be here. If you'll just show me what to do—"

"Jake's had a heart attack? For real? How's he doing?" While I described Jake's condition, I had his undivided attention. His concern was so real, I forgave him his earlier unfortunate remark. "Jake's one of our favorite volunteers," he told me. "Tell him we miss him, and to get well soon. Now, shall I show you the ropes? Just a minute." He went into the office and brought back a pink notepad, a battered black notebook, and a pen. "You'll need these to answer questions and take messages. Other than that, all you have to do is talk to kids who come. Do you like teenagers?"

"Not particularly," I admitted. "I've always thought penguins had the right idea—put adolescents on icebergs to float away until they grow up. But I raised two boys and a lot of their friends, so I'm pretty good at not letting that show."

He threw back his head and laughed so hard I could see he had no fillings in his teeth. The way his laugh echoed also made me think the whole building was empty except for the two of us. "The kids will probably adore you," he told me with another chuckle. "They suspect people who like them." He opened a door and beckoned me into a large empty room.

Joe Riddley always says I have the best imagination in the world, and maybe he's right, but I wasn't particularly thrilled to follow a man I didn't know into a deserted room. Not one soul in the entire world knew where I was—except that female who'd called the night before, and I doubted she'd stir herself if I disappeared. However, when I give my word, I try to live up to it, so I followed him. The room was, if possible, even stuffier than the hall.

"This is the lounge," he said, flipping on three high ceiling fans that merely stirred the air like batter. "That scarred monument is your desk, and the black notebook contains answers to almost any question callers ask. If someone wants me, take a message. If they insist on talking to me, send someone to find me—our buzzer is broken. You shouldn't have many kids. Our sports and vocational programs don't start until one, and most kids don't get up this early. But you may get a few who want to get away from bad home situations. A lot go down to the Y, of course, but a few hang out here. Think you can handle it?"

I resisted the impulse to point out that I've put up with Joe Riddley for nearly forty-five years, raised two sons, am in the process of helping to raise four grandchildren, daily supervise six employees, and am still relatively sane. However, when he stopped talking and I looked around, I nearly turned around and went home.

For one thing, the room had that stale ripe onion smell of too much sweat and too few baths. For another, it was filthy. The windows were grimy, cobwebs draped their tops, and the sills were gray with dust. The only furnishings were a few soiled, overstuffed chairs, two sway-backed sofas, and a battered wood desk. Behind the desk sagged the most uncomfortable looking chair I ever contemplated spending two hours sitting on. Beside the desk a wastebasket literally overflowed with trash, and the whole floor was littered with paper scraps and candy wrappers. Heaven knows and my friends agree I am no housekeeper, but I found that much squalor disgusting.

Mr. Henly caught the expression on my face. "It's pretty grungy," he admitted. "We had a woman who used to clean, but she quit a while ago. I keep meaning to find somebody else, but I've been busy— "

"I don't want to insult you, Mr. Henly, but I am incapable of sitting in this room for two hours without at least picking up trash and dusting windowsills. Do you have cleaning supplies? I'll ask some of the kids to help me pick up, sweep, and dust."

The twinkle in his eye made me think he wanted to burst out laughing, but he said, very politely, "If you find anybody willing to clean, ma'am, I can scare up a few rags and a broom. Now, I need to finish that toilet. The term 'director' around here means man-of-all-work." He started out, then stopped. "Oh. If somebody tries to borrow money for a bus or a Coke, don't lend it to them. Under no circumstances. Okay?" He waited for my nod, then left. I was on my own.

I gingerly sat down on a chair as uncomfortable and cockeyed as it looked, and perused the black notebook.

The center's programs were heavy on basketball, volleyball, and car repair and light on academics, art, and music. A drum set, a few guitars, and an old piano would greatly improve the room I was in, and the kids could use a glee club, too. Just in time I remembered: I didn't live in Montgomery. Good thing. I was about to ask that nice Mr. Henly if I couldn't scout up a few instruments and help organize a musical production.

"She doesn't need to learn to say no," Joe Riddley has been heard to growl more than once. "She needs to learn not to jump in with both feet before anybody even asks."

When I checked my watch it was fifteen minutes down, one-and-three-quarter hours to go, and drat! I'd forgotten to bring the morning paper. Without something to read, I'd be swinging from the ceiling fans before noon.

I peered around and saw a bookshelf with one dog-eared paperback, *To Love or to Die,* lying sideways. The cover showed a woman with a long skirt and very little bodice peering up at a darkened mansion. I would have preferred even a seed catalogue, but I'm not a fussy reader in a pinch. This was definitely a pinch.

Inside, the owner had identified herself in adolescent curlicues: *Harriet Lawson.* Within five minutes I had slipped off my shoes and was deep into the adventures of Celeste Brexall. Ten chapters later, poor Celeste had already survived a shipwreck, a fire in her tower bedroom, and the unwelcome advances of Erik, the evil elder son of the family. She was about to fling herself into the arms of the good second son, when—

"That Basil seems okay, but he's not. He's the bad 'un," said a cheery voice over my shoulder.

I jumped halfway to the ceiling. When my heart rejoined my body, I took a deep breath and looked up into the face of a friendly brown whale.

Actually it was a girl—she couldn't have been more than fourteen or fifteen—but she outweighed me by a good fifty pounds and wore her hair pulled into a spout on top of her head. She smirked. "Boy, you don't notice nothin' when you're readin,' do you? I come right through that door and walked straight over here, and you never even looked."

"Is this your book?" I hoped my heart would soon slow to its normal rate.

"Nannh. I don't *like* reading. It's Harriet's. A lot of foolishness, if you ask me. But Harriet told me what it's about, so like I said, Basil's the bad one. Celeste oughta been more careful." She dragged a chair near the desk, draped a bare leg over one arm, and tugged down a purple T-shirt to cover kelly-green shorts. "My name's Kateisha. What's yours?"

I hesitated, but I grew up calling black women by their first names. Fair is fair. "MacLaren. My friends call me Mac. And I was only reading until somebody came. I hope Harriet won't mind my reading her book." Still, I closed it a bit reluctantly. I'd known from the beginning that Basil wasn't what he seemed—which romance writer besides Jane Austen creates bad men who are really bad and good ones who are truly good?—but I hated not knowing what Celeste went through before she found true love.

Kateisha gave a grunt of disgust. "How can Harriet mind? She don't come here no more. I ain't seen her since . . . I can't rightly remember." In an abrupt change of subject, she demanded, "Where's Mr. Crane? He ain't coming no more, either?"

"Oh, I do hope so—" I swallowed a frog that had suddenly jumped down my throat "—but he's sick today, so I came in his place. I'm his sister."

"For real?"

"Yeah. He's had a heart attack."

"No, I mean for real you're his sister? That's cool. I got a brother, too. André. Call him Dré. I come down here this mornin' so's he can sleep." Seeing my bewilderment, she explained, "We ain't got enough beds to go around, so most nights he stays out, then uses my bed in the mornin'. But last night Mama put the TV in that room, so I can't do nothin' but hang out 'til he wakes up. That's why I come on down here early—to see what's doing."

She pulled a pick from her pocket and began to lift the spout of hair several inches from her head, turning her head this way and that so I'd notice her earrings. "I like your earrings," I told her obligingly. They *were* lovely—unexpected, in that place: delicate silver circles laced with silver spiderwebs and turquoise beads the size of pinheads, and with a tiny silver feather dangling from the bottom. When Kateisha tossed her head, the feathers danced.

"They called dream catchers. Me'n Harriet got 'em just alike."

She got up and went to look out the window. "Uh-oh. Here come Cowface and Deneika. I figured they'd be down early, since it's Biscuit's day."

Before I could ask what on earth she meant, two girls came in. One was beautiful—skin like caramels and eyes like violets. She was tall and slender, and swung her shoulders when she walked to show off high little breasts in a skintight pink knit top. Her denim skirt barely grazed her backside, and her legs were superb. I wondered how long it took to braid her hair in that intricate design of corn rows with silver beads worked in.

Kateisha ignored her, and greeted the other—who was small, thin, and drab. "Hey, Cowface." Her blouse was dingy and unironed, her running shoes full of holes, her hair thin and nappy, and her face golden, long, and thin. With those enormous soft brown eyes, she did, indeed, call to mind a worried Jersey cow.

The tall girl looked around the room, passing over me like I wasn't there. "Anybody seen Biscuit?"

"Unh-huh—what'd I tell you?" Kateisha gave me a knowing look. "No, Deneika," she said with elaborate patience, "we ain't seen Biscuit since last week. But since he always he'ps Mr. Henly on Tuesdays, he oughta be here soon."

"Shut your mouth," the girl said bluntly. She sauntered to the desk with a swing that suggested she knew more about human sexuality than most church delegates. "Who're you?"

"That's Mac," Kateisha answered. "Mac, this here's Deneika and Twaniba."

Deneika wasn't listening. She had wandered over to stare out the window with a hungry, waiting look. Kateisha joined her, again picking her hair. Twaniba ("Cowface") slumped down on the sagging sofa nearest the desk and cast a shy look at the book. "You like readin'?" Her voice was little more than a murmur.

"I sure do. Do you?"

"No'm. That there's Harriet's book. She use t'read all the time, but we ain't seen her since—I don't mind when."

The phone rang. A cultured alto asked me to tell Lewis Henly privately—she stressed the word—that Eleanor would be by to see him at noon. Because the woman was so insistent that the message was private, I decided to leave the girls alone and deliver it myself. They'd be all right by themselves for a minute—or so I thought. I returned to find Kateisha and Deneika glaring at one another.

"Get outta my face," Kateisha barked, jaw clenched.

"I was here first," Deneika snarled. "You *move* your face." She shoved. Kateisha shoved back. The taller girl sprawled on the floor with a display of bright red underpants.

I hurried toward them. "Girls, Mr. Henly suggested that the first people here help me clean the room."

That certainly stopped the fight and got everybody's attention.

"Screwy Lewey said we should clean?" If I had suggested they learn to fly, Deneika couldn't have sounded more astonished.

"I ain't much on cleaning." Kateisha lifted one nostril in disdain.

"It won't be bad if we all work together," I said cheerfully, not fooling a soul. "Kateisha, you go ask Mr. Henly for the supplies. You others start to pick up trash."

"Okay." Even Twaniba's voice was colorless. I wondered if she got enough vitamins.

Deneika and Twaniba had each picked up about two slivers of paper by the time Kateisha got back carrying a stubby broom, a dustpan, a plastic trash bag, and three gray rags. I handed out supplies like a drill sergeant. "Twaniba, you dust windowsills and bookshelves. Deneika, sweep down cobwebs. Kateisha, go empty the wastebasket and come right back. We'll have this place clean before we know it."

"What you gonna do?" Deneika demanded.

"She can't clean in them clothes." Twaniba stroked my linen jacket sleeve with the touch of a butterfly.

"If she ain't cleaning, I ain't neither." Kateisha plopped heavily into a chair.

"I'm going to clean," I assured her, looking around for something I could do without getting filthy. "I'm going to pull out the sofas so we can sweep under them, then I'm going to clean out the drawers of that desk. They look like rats' nests."

The girls wouldn't have earned enthusiasm awards, but at least they went to work. After Kateisha bustled out importantly with a bag of trash, I grabbed one sofa to shove it away from the wall. It was heavier than it looked. "I can't move this alone. Can somebody help me?"

"I'm sweeping." Deneika sullenly gave a cobweb a half-hearted swipe. Twaniba drifted over with her dust cloth and gave the sofa a gentle shove. It was like being helped by a wraith.

"Never mind," I told her. "Go on and dust. Kateisha and I'll get it later. Let me give the cushions a good shake first."

I pulled out a seat cushion, and saw why the sofa was so heavy. Beneath the cushions was a hideabed mattress, littered with trash. Tossing off all the cushions, I cleared away several pieces of homework, a couple of wadded candy wrappers, and a filthy blue sweater. A book had fallen down behind, but in order to get my hand between the frame and the back to reach it, I'd have to open out the mattress. Seizing the handle, I tugged.

The bed unfolded with a screech to wake the dead. The mattress was spotted and stained, and as hard as it was to open, I suspected it had been donated that way. Joe Riddley has a theory that our heavenly mansions are furnished with duplicates of whatever we give to the poor. If so, the donors of that sofa might be in for a shock.

Hoping I wasn't picking up a disease I couldn't get rid of—and that Mr. Henly wouldn't appear while I was backside up—I belly-flopped onto the mattress and groped until my fingers grasped the book. *Love Me Wildly, Love Me True.* It was a hardback sister of Harriet's novel, except this one came from the public library. It also had a fat white envelope stuffed between its pages in a way guaranteed to raise any librarian's blood pressure.

I rolled over and sat up, holding the book aloft. "Anybody recognize this?"

Kateisha, coming through the door wearing a plastic bag like a stole, snorted. "What'd we be wanting with a book when school's out? It's probably Harriet's. Or LaToya's. They both nuts about reading."

Twaniba stopped her dusting and flapped her cloth, sending all the dust right back into the air. "When did we lose Harriet? Anybody remember?"

Deneika set down her broom and scratched her neck with an elegant green and gold striped fingernail nearly as long as my little finger. "She come the last week of school, but I ain't seen her after that. Maybe her auntie won't let her come no more."

Kateisha stuck out her lower lip. "If she don't want to come, it ain't no skin off us." She sounded oddly belligerent.

By then, I had looked at the envelope. It was not only fat. It was also blank and sealed. I shoved myself up from the sagging mattress. At the desk, I sat with the envelope hidden in my lap, and gently slit it open. No matter what Joe Riddley tells you, I wouldn't have done that if there'd been a name on it. I figured maybe I'd find a name inside.

Instead, I found a colorful brochure for an acting school in Atlanta.

And thirty pictures of Benjamin Franklin—on one hundred dollar bills.

A kindhearted woman gains respect,
but ruthless men gain only wealth.
Proverbs 11:16

Five

I shoved that money back into its envelope faster than it takes to tell it. My mind whirled with questions. Who'd go off and leave that much money just lying around? Where would a teen—especially one of *these* teens—get three thousand dollars? And why would anybody leave thousands of dollars lying around unless they had to? So whoever went off and left it, *had* they had to?

I looked up and saw my worker bees drifting my way like I was a spot of molasses. I was doing too much thinking and not enough cleaning. Thrusting the envelope into the long middle drawer, I held up the novel. "This is a library book. Who'll volunteer to take it back?"

Deneika twisted her lips in disgust. "It's filthy. Throw it a-*way.*"

"I ain't goin' to no liberry when school's out." Kateisha tossed her head and turned her back before she could get drafted. "Leave it with Screwy Lewey."

That, of course, was the only right thing to do—with both the book and the money.

I would have, too—in spite of what Joe Riddley might tell you—except that by the time we got the room halfway clean and I was ready to leave, Mr. Henly was in his office talking to a thin woman with lovely copper skin, legs like a model, and a beige silk suit that looked like it had come straight from Paris. Her perfume smelled like something they charge you by the minute to inhale, and believe me, Mr. Henly had no eyes for the short white grandmother at his door. He was having enough trouble concentrating on the papers she held. As she said, "According to our budget projections," I seriously doubted that Lewis Henly was thinking about budget projections.

I checked my watch. There was still nearly an hour before Jake's first afternoon visit, and the hospital wasn't far. I'd seen a library on Rosa L. Parks Avenue just down from the center. If I took the book back, maybe they'd give me the address of the borrower. I could return the envelope to its owner later that afternoon. Everybody knows hospitals don't let you stay with ICU patients more than a few minutes every hour or two. I ought to have a lot of free time on my hands, and sitting in waiting rooms is not my idea of a fine old time.

I pride myself on doing things the logical, simple, and efficient way.

I called the hospital before I left, and was told by a nurse that Jake was resting. Reassured, I stuck the envelope back in the book, tucked the book firmly under one arm, and left the center—heeding the advice my seven-year-old granddaughter gave me last year on Grandmothers' Day at her school: "Act casual, Me-Mama."

Nevertheless, I swear I walked five miles from the center to Jake's Buick, and I never saw so many potential muggers on one sidewalk in my life. I fell into the driver's seat, locked the door, and took three deep breaths of relief before I was able to shove that envelope down into a woman's best hiding place.

All the way to the library I felt twice as virtuous as the Good Samaritan. He only rescued somebody. I was returning enough unmarked bills to pay for that Alaskan cruise Joe Riddley keeps wanting to take.

Rosa L. Parks ought to be prouder of her library than of her street. The library was clean, spacious, cool, and cheerful—much nicer than Mr. Henly's teen center. Yet most of the patrons were women or children. The only teenagers in the whole place were two boys sitting at a table in a far corner, engrossed in magazines. I felt a little awkward, being the only white person there, but one librarian bustled right up to ask how she could help, and directed me to the front desk. The desk librarian, busy helping somebody else, greeted me in a lovely contralto. "I'll be with you in just a minute."

I've raised sons. I know exactly what kind of magazine gets undivided attention from adolescent boys—but I didn't think you could get one in a public library. Curious, I rambled over to where the teens were reading. To my astonishment, those boys weren't oogling half-dressed women. They were studying old coins. No wonder they were at the library instead of at the teen center. The kids at the center would laugh them out the door.

Then one of the boys looked up, and I changed my mind in a hurry. Nobody would laugh at that young man and live to brag about it. His hair was shaved halfway up his head and twisted and tangled on top into a mess that looked like bare tree roots. Muscles rippled like vines and oranges on his biceps. And in a face so dark it was almost blue, his dark eyes smoldered like they had looked straight into the pit of hell and remembered.

His eyes held mine and I couldn't look away, until the second boy at the table looked up and gave me a wide smile and a sassy little wave. "Hiya, ma'am. How ya doin'?"

"Fine, thank you." I scarcely noticed what he looked like. I'd just seen that the desk librarian was free.

"Josheba Davidson" was the name on her tag. She was several shades darker than the woman who'd been talking with Lewis Henly, and her African print skirt and white knit top weren't as stylish as that beige silk suit, but she was prettier. Her skin was flawless, her lips full, and her eyes shaped like almonds. Like Deneika at the teen center, she wore braids, but hers were pulled into a crown of loops that swung and danced whenever she moved.

I've said people in Montgomery are the most helpful in the world. Ms. Davidson started out that way, but when I asked for the borrower's name and address, she shook her head. "I'm sorry. It's against the law for us to give out that information about our patrons."

"I don't want to cause any trouble," I pointed out as reasonably as I could. "I just want to return some money to its rightful owner. I can't unless you help me."

My voice carried in the stillness, and I looked anxiously over my shoulder. The other librarians and most of the other patrons still seemed busy about their own affairs. Only the boy with smoldering eyes was looking our way, and surely he was too far away to hear.

"Maybe you ought to take it to the police," she suggested in a low voice.

"I could, but that wouldn't ensure it got back to the right person. Police don't always believe teens come by money honestly. I'd like to give this teen a chance to explain. I can't imagine why anybody would have left money at the center, even overnight. Yet from what the girls said, the person who borrowed this book hasn't been around for several weeks."

The librarian picked up the book, read the title, and turned to her computer. "Let me check on something."

When an answer came up on her screen, she gave a sharp little grunt. "I was afraid of that." She stared at the screen and chewed her lower lip.

"Was the borrower Harriet Lawson?" I guessed.

"Do you know Harriet?" Her voice was almost eager.

"No, but some of the girls at the center thought it might have been her book."

"Well, I'll bend the rules just far enough to tell you it was — and that she owes a fine. If you pay it, maybe the teen center could give you her address so she can pay you back."

I reached for my coin purse and accepted defeat. "I'll be glad to pay her fine, but maybe what I'd better do is just take the money back to the teen center and let them return it. I'd have done that earlier, except the director was busy."

"Be sure to get a receipt." I was surprised at her tone. It sounded like a warning.

While she made change, the librarian asked curiously. "You're just visiting, but you're going to this much trouble? I wish everybody was as honest as you." She bent over the counter to speak even more softly. "To tell you the truth, I've been worried about Harriet. I haven't seen her since — I guess when she checked out this book, the week before school let out. If you see her, tell her to come by to see Josheba sometime."

I was surprised. "Do you know all your patrons by name?"

"No, but we don't get many whites, and Harriet's in here two-three times some weeks. She reads voraciously, but mostly stuff without substance. Yet she's bright — or could be, if anybody took the trouble to encourage her. I've been trying to steer her toward better literature, but she's got her head up in some romantic cloud."

As I left the library, my own head was in a cloud, too, trying to make sense of the fact that Harriet Lawson was white. In my experience, a child who hangs around exclusively with people of another race may be isolated or trying to make a statement. Was Harriet trying to make a statement? To whom? Why?

Joe Riddley often says that once I start asking questions, I nearly die until I get answers to go with them. For once, he would be right.

My chest rustled as I hurried out, and one corner of the envelope was poking a hole in my left breast. I hoped Mr. Henly would be free by now.

If I'd waited and given him the money while I was there, I could already be on my way to the hospital. I was so busy fussing at myself, I wasn't paying attention to anything else. I was flabbergasted when somebody shoved my shoulder and sent me sprawling.

As I fell, I felt somebody grab my pocketbook, then heard thudding feet. I looked up just in time to see someone pelt around the corner. I recognized the tree-roots hair.

By the time I'd hauled myself up and hobbled to the corner, he was out of sight. Nothing was hurt except one knee of my pants and a scraped wrist from where I'd fallen, but when you've been shoved and robbed, the invisible damage is a lot worse. I couldn't seem to stop shaking, and was afraid I would throw up right there on the sidewalk.

I'd never been attacked before. In a town of thirteen thousand people and three magistrates, who'd be foolish enough to snatch the pocketbook of Judge Yarbrough's wife—and risk getting hauled up before him for doing it? I wasn't even sure what I was supposed to do next. I looked around for witnesses, but didn't see a soul. With my heart pounding and my hands shaking, I limped back into the library.

"What happened to you?" The librarians looked as shocked as I felt.

I took several deep breaths before I could speak. "Those boys—" I pointed to the now-empty table. "The one with all the hair—" I wiggled my fingers above my head "—just grabbed my pocketbook!"

The head librarian came from her office to investigate. "I haven't seen them here before," Ms. Davidson told her, "but someone else may have recognized them."

The head librarian raised her voice. "Excuse me, but does anybody know the boys who were reading at the far table?"

You could have heard a stomach growl in the silence. Nobody spoke.

"Let me call the police for you," the head librarian offered.

Another fetched me a cup of hot coffee from their own pot. I needed it. I couldn't remember feeling colder.

"We are so sorry," the librarians said over and over while they waited for the police to arrive.

Ms. Davidson murmured, in a moment of privacy, "They must have heard us talking about Harriet's money." Her dark eyes were kind and concerned.

I tapped my chest. "At least they didn't get that. I've got it right here."

"Good for you!" She shook her head. "There you were, doing a good deed, and lost both your wallet and your keys."

"Oh, Lord!" It was a prayer, not an oath. "I didn't have my keys, I had my brother's—with a Buick emblem on the chain. His was the only Buick in the lot when I came in!"

She and I hurried outside and toward the library parking lot as fast as I could totter.

The car was gone. If Jake's heart attack hadn't killed him, this certainly would.

Have you ever tried reporting a stolen car without letting the police officers know the owner would throttle you if he knew you'd been driving it?

I kept telling the two policemen who came that they didn't need a lot of details—they could find that car in a minute if they'd just go out and look for it. Instead, they kept pestering me with silly questions I couldn't answer. "Year of the car, ma'am? Model? Tag number? Insurance company?" They made me so nervous that after a while I could scarcely string words into a coherent sentence.

I tried calling Glenna to get some of the information, but she'd already left. Finally I admitted it was my brother's car, and gave them Jake's name, but warned them, "Get what you need to know from your computers. If you call him at the hospital, you could kill him."

When they started giving me more guff about needing to talk with Jake, I lost my temper. "Look," I told them, "it's a new red Buick Park Avenue with red leather upholstery, and it can't have gotten far. Just go out and start looking up and down the danged street!" If women ran this world, there'd be more reliance on common sense and gumption, and far less on procedure. I can tell you that for a fact.

Finally they tracked down the tag number and promised they'd do their best to find the car without bothering Jake. By then, though, they'd wasted so much time I figured the Buick was halfway to Birmingham. Before they left, one tried to make me feel better. "Your pocketbook may turn up, ma'am. If it was kids, sometimes they just take the cash and toss the wallet and credit cards in a dumpster."

That's when I realized I'd have to call Joe Riddley to cancel all our cards. I could tell you exactly what I knew Joe Riddley would say, but I don't use that kind of language.

Starting a quarrel is like breaching a dam; so drop the matter before a dispute breaks out. *Proverbs 17:14*

Six

I hope it won't confuse you to hear from someone else, but poor MacLaren was so upset by the time the police left, she's asked me to tell about what happened next. We were all on a first-name basis by then.

I am Josheba Davidson—the assistant librarian who couldn't give out Harriet's address. I felt real bad about that, because I'd been wondering what happened to Harriet. She was always real prompt about bringing books back, and I'd expected to see a lot of her that summer. I won't say it worried me, exactly—I'm going to graduate school these days and only work part-time, so she could have come in while I was off—but I'd asked some of the other librarians if they'd seen her around, and nobody had. I found that puzzling. Harriet read all the time. What could make her give it up for the summer?

Anyway, when the police finally left, another librarian brought MacLaren some coffee and I offered to call her a cab. "I can't pay for it," she pointed out apologetically, "unless my sister-in-law has some cash with her at the hospital." For just an instant her brown eyes twinkled. "Which she almost never does. She's one of those women who let their husbands carry the money." I suspected MacLaren Yarbrough carried her own. She looked pretty feisty to me.

Our head librarian had another idea. "You're due to go off-duty in a little while anyway, Josheba," she said to me. "Why don't you leave now and run Mrs. Yarbrough to the hospital?"

I glanced at my watch. My fiancé was leaving for a week's white-water rafting trip that afternoon, and I was due to drop by his place and kiss him good-bye. Morse is a big teddy bear most of the time, but he's more like a Kodiak if his plans get messed up. I didn't want to make him late leaving. Still, it was earlier than I'd thought. Morse wasn't expecting me for nearly an hour. "Sure, I'll be glad to," I told Mrs. Yarbrough. "Just let me finish something I was doing at the computer."

Stepping out of the library into the midday sun was like leaving a refrigerator for a steam room. The seats of my Honda were as hot as an ironing board after a hard day's work. "I'll get the air conditioning going in just a minute," I promised.

As my passenger reached to fasten her seatbelt, something crackled under her blouse. Harriet's money, I suspected. I gave her a sideways look. "I could get fired for this if anybody finds out, but if you want to, I can run you by Harriet's on the way. I looked up her address, and it's just off Martha Street, right up the hill. I hate for you not to get rid of that money after all you've been through trying to deliver it."

"Me, too," she said fervently. "I'd really appreciate it."

It seemed so simple at the time.

Although the community around our library is black, at the top of the hill is a small, old, mostly white neighborhood, Cottage Hill. It's houses are generally one-story bungalows with big high windows and ample porches. I'd guess the neighborhood was built around 1900, but some of those oaks were around when my great-great-grandparents were slaves. Cottage Hill's been gentrifying for a long time, so most of the houses either have been or are in the process of being restored.

The house we wanted was shabby, with scaffolding to the roof. Mac—we'd hit it off so well by then that she'd told me to call her that—asked me to come to the door, since I already knew Harriet. As soon as she rang the bell a baby started crying. A moment later a young woman in jeans answered the door with an unhappy infant on her hip. She informed us she'd just moved in in June and didn't know anybody named Lawson. "Maybe one of the older neighbors would know something." She gestured across the street to a blue house with cream shutters and a yard full of flowers. That neighbor was certainly older—older than God. In a straw hat and pink cotton dress, she was busily watering black-eyed Susans and trying to pretend she wasn't watching everything that was going on.

We headed across the street.

The old woman was so bent over she was several inches shorter than she used to be. Unconsciously I straightened my own back and saw Mac do the same as she said, in a friendly tone, "Good afternoon. Did you know the Lawsons, who used to live over there? We're looking for Harriet."

Beneath wisps of white hair escaping from her straw hat, the woman's eyes were a bright suspicious blue. "What you want with Harriet?"

"I found something of hers this morning and wanted to return it," Mac told her.

"Harriet moved right after her granny died." With a gnarled hand ropy with veins, the woman brushed away a fly from her cheek. "Went out to live with her aunt, Dixie Lawson. Dixie Sykes, she'd be now. Mrs. William T. Sykes the Third. Lives out in McGehee Estates somewhere. They're in the phone book. He has a store."

"Well, you're finally getting somewhere," I told Mac as we gratefully sank into the Honda and turned on the air.

She sighed. "Yeah, but it's getting more complicated than I ever imagined. I think after I've visited with my brother a little while, I ought to just take the money back to the center and let Mr. Henly return it to Harriet."

I hesitated. I'd only met Mr. Henly over the phone, but our dealings hadn't been too pleasant. I'd approached him about doing a summer reading program at his center, and he'd been real curt. Said he "was concentrating on sports that summer and would rather not scare kids away from the center its first summer of operation." A man who talks that way about reading—well, I wasn't sure he'd really get Harriet's money back to her now that she'd moved across town. He might spend it on volleyballs. "Why don't you call Harriet yourself when you get time?" I suggested.

Mac picked up right away on what I was hinting. "You don't trust him? Why?"

"I don't want to say more than I really know," I told her, "and it's more of a gut feeling than anything else, but Lewis Henly is a bit of an enigma. Blew into town from nowhere and got to know a lot of important people real quick. If I had money belonging to Harriet, I think I'd take it back to her myself."

Mac decided to follow my advice. It still sounded so simple.

After that we headed toward the hospital, exchanging the little details women use to weave friendships. I told her I'd cut back at the library to part-time while pursuing my Masters in Business Administration from Auburn at Montgomery. She told me about her family store, her husband, two boys, and four grandchildren.

"Do you have family here?" she asked.

"Not at the moment," I told her, trying not to feel jealous that she had so much. "Daddy died when I was nine and Mama just last year. Now I rattle around in my house all alone. I hope to change that this fall, though," I couldn't help adding. "I'm thinking about getting married over Christmas."

Before I knew it, Mac had me telling her all about meeting Morse. "Last April I went to watch my friend's son wrestle in a high school match, and Morse was coaching the other team. I recognized him immediately. He was the champion wrestler on the Alabama State team the year I won a second in track. We got to talking about college, and one thing led to another. We went out to dinner and discovered we like the same music and food. We've been dating ever since." I tried to sound casual, but I suspected my face was flushed with happiness. "He's big and handsome and athletic and looks like nothing would faze him, but he had a rough childhood. Underneath he's a hurting little boy who needs somebody to take care of him—which reminds me. He's leaving this afternoon for a week's trip with some of his buddies. I ought to call from the hospital to see if he needs me to pick up toothpaste or something."

"Would it be possible to stop by my brother's?" Mac gave me an embarrassed smile. "I hate to ask when you've already been so nice, but it's not far from here, and I could freshen up while you make your call. After two hours in that center and my nosedive on the sidewalk, I sure could use a wash."

I thought about telling her I was supposed to be at Morse's very soon, but since I hadn't mentioned that already, I didn't like to make her feel worse than she already did. Besides, she certainly needed to fix herself up a little. One knee of her pants was slightly torn, and her makeup and hair were wilted from the heat. She'd want to look nice for her brother. There was one thing, however, I thought I ought to mention. "At the risk of bringing back painful memories, how will you get in without a key?"

"My sister-in-law hides one in the toolshed."

Her sister-in-law hid it well. By the time Mac found it, she wore every spiderweb in that shed.

She showed me a phone in the master bedroom, and while she went to wash and change I called Morse—aware that by the time I got Mac to the hospital it was going to be past the time I'd said I'd stop by his place. He was disappointed, of course, but so excited about the trip that he didn't fuss. He said he'd try to get his buddies to wait until I got there. "Gotta kiss my baby good-bye." His chuckle sent nice feelings up my spine.

I heard Mac padding to the bathroom for a wash. We'd have a little time to talk before she was through. "By the way, Morse, I found out about my dance. It's Saturday a week. You'll be back before that, won't you?"

"No problem, honey. We'll be back Sunday, I think. Is this the dance where I'm supposed to wear a monkey suit?"

"Sure is. Do you need me to call about renting one?"

"Would you do that? Tell them I'll pick it up the day of the dance." He rattled off his sizes and I felt downright wifely writing them down.

"Are you all packed?" I asked, putting off the time when we'd have to hang up.

"All except my blue shirt. My favorite one, remember? I couldn't find it in that laundry you left here yesterday."

I couldn't believe what I had done. "Oh, Morse, it's in my ironing basket! I left it in the dryer too long, so it's got to be ironed. I meant to do it this morning, but I ran late—"

"How could you have left it in the dryer too long, Josheba?" he demanded. "I told you to take it right out as soon as the dryer finished."

I gave an embarrassed little laugh. "Yeah, but you know what an airhead I am when I'm working on a paper. I got to writing, and I just plumb forgot."

"You forgot? Well, imagine that."

His voice was mild and flat, but I started to tremble and felt a little sick. Like I said, Morse can be a Kodiak when he's riled, and when he's riled he always starts out slow, easy, and sarcastic.

Sure enough, words began to pour through the line like hot lava. Angry words. Insulting words. I couldn't bear to hear them. Even though I held the receiver away from my ear, a few reached me anyway. ". . . stupid . . . if you really cared . . . Why can't you do what you're *told?*"

The awful thing was, he was right. Maybe he was being obsessive about a shirt, but he *had* told me to take it right out of the dryer, and I had forgotten. "Morse," I interrupted, my voice thick with tears, "I'm dreadfully sorry. I'll run by the house and iron it and bring it right over. Just wait thirty minutes, honey. I'll be there as soon as I can."

"I thought you had to take that woman by the hospital."

"Yes, but— "

"Never mind, baby. We're leaving. See you when I see you." He slammed down the receiver. I called him right back, but he didn't answer.

It's dreadful when you have disappointed somebody you love. It's especially dreadful when that's the only person you have in the whole world *to* love.

The wealth of the rich is their fortified city; they imagine it an unscalable wall. *Proverbs 18:11*

Seven

Josheba left me at the hospital and hurried away. When I got off the elevator at Jake's floor, a woman standing in the waiting room door with her back to the hall turned to go, saying over her shoulder, "I'll see you later, sugar. We're thinking of you."

"Thanks for coming, Nora," Glenna called after her.

She was the kind of woman you hate even when you like her: close to my own age, but still thin enough to wear a full green skirt without looking like a Granny Smith apple. She had also managed to keep her hair a very natural-looking red. It fell straight to curl under at the jewel neck of the prettiest cotton sweater I ever saw—a soft swirl of green, blue, and violet. I didn't have time to think about sweaters, though. As she passed me in a cloud of Chanel, I saw Glenna's face. She looked like she had fallen into a deep freeze and gotten chilled to the bone.

I started telling her why I was late, but for the first time I could remember, she interrupted. "He's worse, Clara. Dr. Watson says he doesn't have a chance without surgery, but Jake won't sign the papers. Says he thinks his time has come. I don't know what to do!"

I hugged her, because I couldn't stand looking into her eyes. "When can I see him?"

"I think they'd let you go in right now for just a minute, but don't stay long."

"Just long enough to tell him to get that operation," I replied grimly.

Jake was so weak he didn't try to smile. It nearly broke my heart to look at him, but I forced myself to sound mad. "Well, Jake, I hear you are being obstreperous again."

He spoke in wisps and gasps. "'s that . . . what they . . . tell you, . . . Sis?"

"It sure is. I won't have it, Bubba." I put on the voice I used to use when he wouldn't eat his carrots. "You sign those papers for Dr. Watson and get it over with. I can't shilly-shally around here forever. Joe Riddley needs me too, you know."

He turned his head restlessly on the pillow. "Need . . . think about it."

"What's there to think about? Get the danged operation and be done with it!" I wanted to holler into his ashen face. But you can't holler at a man who's connected to a hundred tubes and whose entire life is reduced to an irregular little "blip" on a screen.

"It's your decision, of course," I told him, wondering when he'd gotten too big to obey me and why I'd ever let him.

He tried to shake his head, but it was a poor effort. ". . . don't know . . . operation . . . any good." He paused, then said weakly but clearly, "Maybe God's calling me home."

Now that *did* make me mad.

"You don't know that, Jake. If the good Lord's ready for you, he can take you in the operating room as well as here. But if he wants you around for a few more years, who are you to object?" I was getting nowhere fast, and I knew it. Quickly I winged a prayer for inspiration—and remembered a joke. "Maybe this operation's your helicopter. Remember that old story about the man on a roof in the flood? How he turned down offers of help from a canoe, a rowboat, and a helicopter because he thought God was going to save him? Remember? He drowned, and got hopping mad, but God told him—"

I stopped. Jake was already mouthing the punch line. "Hey, buddy, I sent you a canoe, a rowboat, and a helicopter." His eyes softened, then looked pleadingly into mine. "Think this . . . operation's my . . . helicopter, Sis?" he whispered.

"I sure do, Bubba. Glenna needs you a while yet. Me, too, ornery though you are." I reached down and lightly touched his shoulder. "You sign those papers and don't give Glenna any more grief. You hear me?"

". . . hear you, Sis. Lordy," he said with a sudden surge of energy. "How does Joe Riddley stand you?"

"That's Joe Riddley's privilege." Depositing a kiss on his forehead, I tiptoed out.

"He'll sign," I told Glenna.

"What did you do?" she asked, amazed.

"Beat him up a little. Big sisters are allowed."

While Glenna and I waited for them to bring up Jake's consent forms, I reckoned it was as good a time as any to tell her about my morning.

When I mentioned William Sykes, her face lit up. "That was his mother leaving when you came. They're fine people, Clara. If you call and tell them you have the money, they'll probably come get it. You've got such a good heart," she finished warmly.

That made me feel like dirt. I didn't set out to return Harriet's money because I have a good heart. I did it because I thought I could do it faster than anybody else. "If I'd known Jake was getting sicker, I'd never have gotten involved," I said gruffly. I still had to tell her that Jake's car was missing because I'd been so full of my own efficiency.

Once she was past the initial shock, Glenna was far more horrified that she'd forgotten Jake's day at the desk in the first place. "If I hadn't forgotten, honey, you wouldn't have used his car. I'll tell you what. Call Harriet. If she's home, you can borrow my car and take her the money right now. We can't see Jake for a while, anyway."

Harriet wasn't home, and the girl who answered had been well taught not to give information to a stranger over the phone. She never came right out and said her mother wasn't there, but she told me that if I called back after three, her mother could speak with me then. When I asked when they expected Harriet, she was as cagey as a riverboat gambler. "You'll need to ask my mother."

Since I was right by the pay phone, that was as good a time as any to call Joe Riddley about the credit cards. All I can say about that conversation is, confession may be good for the soul, but it sure can be hard on the eardrums.

By three, the weight on my chest was definitely more literal than figurative. That fresh envelope seemed to have a dozen corners. When I wiggled around trying to get more comfortable, they poked me worse. Since I didn't have a pocketbook, I didn't have anyplace else to put it. Jake would never forgive me if I foisted it off on Glenna. "I think I'll just go on out there," I finally told her. "I can explain better in person than on the phone anyway, and if I don't get rid of this envelope pretty soon I'm going to look like that Greek who was pecked to death."

Glenna drew me a map. "You can get there in twenty minutes. Think how good you'll feel to be done with it." She handed me her keys. Since it apparently hadn't occurred to her I didn't have a license, I didn't like to bring it up.

Although Dixie Sykes's neighborhood is now about halfway between downtown and Montgomery's new eastern edge, it was way out on the edge of town in the sixties when it was built. With street names like Edgefield, Fernway, and Farm Road, I figured that the pines shading big furry lawns once shaded pastures. Cows, however, were long ago replaced by Cadillacs, grazing grass with monkey grass.

Glenna's Ford was woefully out of place. Maids in that neighborhood drive better cars.

When I got to the Sykes's, I liked their yard better than their house. Joe Riddley and I live in a big old renovated farmhouse that wanders all over our lot, so I'm not partial to two-story brick boxes with black shutters and tall white columns supporting nothing but a small brick stoop. I sure admired the Sykes's big lawn, though. It looked like something out of *Southern Living* – lots of irregular, gorgeous flower beds, unexpected islands of ivy, even a little humpbacked bridge over a tiny fishpond. A creamy Mercedes sat in the drive beside a bright blue Miata with *Julie* blazoned on its tag.

While I waited for somebody to answer the door, I couldn't help comparing this neighborhood with the one I'd been in that morning. They weren't far apart in terms of miles, but could be on different planets. Joe Riddley was wrong about my imagination, for once. I couldn't picture anybody from the teen center living in McGehee Estates.

If the woman who came to the door was forty, she and her beautician would never admit it. Her hair was fluffy and golden, her face as pretty as cosmetics could make it, and her lipstick could never be that fresh unless she kept a tube right by the door. One look at her matching shell-pink fingernails and I could feel my own breaking out in hangnails.

Yet, pretty as she was, my very first thought was, *This woman is worried sick about something.*

It seemed a shame to make her stand out there in all that heat, so I came straight to the point. "I'm MacLaren Yarbrough, and I'm looking for Harriet Lawson."

Dixie's mouth curved in a bright, welcoming smile that didn't quite reach her eyes. "I'm afraid Harriet's not here right now. Can I help you? I'm Dee Sykes, her aunt."

Dee, not Dixie. The old woman got it wrong. "I'd rather talk with Harriet herself. When will she be back?"

"I'm afraid I don't rightly know. You know how teenagers are." Her eyes wandered to Glenna's old Ford. "Are you a social worker or something?"

Nothing gets my goat like people who judge others by the car they drive. Besides, social workers drive better cars than Glenna's. This wasn't the time or place to get on a soapbox, however. Not with sweat beading my hairline. "No, but this morning I was cleaning behind a hideabed sofa at a teen center just off Rosa L. Parks Avenue—"

Her blue eyes widened in astonishment. "You clean the center?"

That did it. I fixed her with the stare I use to quell the Hopemore Garden Club, and said in a level voice that makes my grown sons quake, "Honey, let's start over. I found something at the center this morning that belongs to Harriet. I'd like to give it back to her, so if you'll just let me leave the phone number where I'll be—"

About then her mental computer finally kicked in and churned up the right data: white female, well-dressed, older, Southern, does volunteer work: *One of Us!* She stepped back with a gracious smile and gestured toward the dim, cool house. "Won't you come on in? It's hotter than the devil's blazer buttons out here."

I followed her, reflecting that life could be a whole lot simpler if churches and the Junior League tattooed lifelong logos on members' palms.

Through an entrance hall tiled in gray slate and past a formal living room with thick white carpet, quality reproductions, and what looked like a few genuine antiques, she led me straight out onto a bright sunroom overlooking a stunning pool.

"Would you like a Coke or something?" she asked.

I forgave her everything that she'd said so far. I could already feel fizzles of cold, frosty drink going down my gullet. I hadn't had any lunch, remember, and just in the time I'd stood on her stoop the elastic in my underwear had permanently bonded to my skin.

"I never turned down a Co-cola in my life," I said honestly. "Real, if you've got it."

While she was in the kitchen, I looked around. This was no converted back porch; it was grand! I loved the white tile floor and wicker love seat, chaise, and glass-topped wicker table with four chairs. I wouldn't have covered the blue flowered cushions with ruffly throw pillows, but my own shefflera and corn plants never looked healthier. Dee must certainly have a green thumb. Beyond the back windows blazed more wonderful flower beds.

"Here we are." Bless her heart, she came back with not only Co-colas, but homemade chocolate chip cookies as well. You have to admire a woman who stocks pretty paper napkins that go with her sunroom cushions.

I took the love seat and she sat down on the chaise like she had nothing better to do than entertain a stranger. The blue flowers on her cushions exactly matched her eyes.

"You've got a lovely home," I told her truthfully, grabbing a couple of cookies and trying not to wolf them down, "and your yard is simply beautiful."

Dee looked around contentedly. "Aren't you sweet? Actually, William does the yard and houseplants. He and his mama both love to play in the dirt, but I'd rather fix up a house. I wanted to be a decorator when I went to college, but then I met William. When you're nineteen, getting married seems more important than finishing college, doesn't it?"

It was a good thing she didn't expect an answer. As my sons could tell you, I can go on about that particular subject for quite some time. And when Dee added, "—and as you know, a woman's house is her life," I could just see Joe Riddley's face.

"MacLaren uses the glacial method of cleaning," he always claims. "She lets piles creep from the corners to the middle of the floor, then calls out the troops to shovel them back a little." Several years ago for Christmas he built me a set of screens, explaining proudly, "They are for parties. Just set them up around your various projects, and how big a party we can have will depend on how much space is left."

I was reaching for a third cookie and about to ask about Harriet again when a woman called from the kitchen. "Yoohoo?" I'd vaguely heard a car in the drive and a key in the kitchen lock. She came closer, still calling. "Hey there! Anybody home?"

Where had I heard that voice? For a minute I thought it was the woman who'd called about the teen center the night before, but as soon as she came in, I recognized the woman who'd visited Jake earlier. She still wore that gorgeous sweater.

Dee looked about as happy as a wet cat, but her voice was sweet. "Hey, Nora! I didn't know you were coming over. This is, ummm—"

"MacLaren Yarbrough." I put out my hand. Since the visitor didn't recognize me, I decided not to complicate things by dragging Jake in.

The woman dropped a shopping bag and a couple of catalogues onto the glass-topped table and stuck out a skinny freckled arm weighed down by three heavy gold bracelets. "I'm Nora Sykes, Dee's mother-in-law. It's good to meet you." She then proceeded to completely ignore me, perching on one of the straight chairs by the table and talking nonstop to Dee. "When William called this morning, he asked for some cuttings. I've left them out by the garage. And here are some catalogues he wanted from that nursery up in North Carolina that sells all those unusual perennials. And while I was in Parisians a few minutes ago, I saw the cutest shorts outfit that just looked like Julie, so I bought it for her to try on. If it doesn't fit, you can always take it back."

From Dee's expression, I suspected she was thinking Nora could jolly well take it back herself. It's hard to be a thoughtful grandmother. We sometimes don't notice when our enthusiasms make more work for our children.

A slim, barefoot teenager spoke from the kitchen door. "Gram? Is that you?" She wore more blusher and eye makeup than I like to see on a child, but was as pretty as could be. Her hair was red-gold, long, and curly. She'd caught it back with clips to swing loose on the shoulders of a peach knit top that exactly matched her nails and lips. Between the top and a minuscule denim skirt, she covered the bare essentials while showing a good bit of honey tan.

Seeing a guest, she paused prettily. "I'm sorry. I didn't know we had company." She tucked one small brown foot behind the other leg. "I didn't put on my shoes."

"I never wear them unless I have to," I assured her.

Nora glowed with pride. "This is my granddaughter, Julie. Julie, Mrs. ummmm . . ."

"Yarbrough," I supplied again.

Nora reached out and gave the girl a proud pat. "Julie's a junior at The Montgomery Academy. Later this summer she and I are going to look at colleges, aren't we, honey?"

Julie squirmed. "I guess so."

She seemed so uncomfortable among us grownups that I tried to draw her out. "I saw your car outside. It's adorable." It must have been all those ruffled pillows. I hadn't used the word "adorable" in years.

It was the right thing to say, though, because Julie glowed. "Thanks. I love it!"

"It's a big help to have it," her mother justified it apologetically. "I used to spend my life driving her places." She turned to both Nora and Julie and explained, "Laura came looking for Harriet." I didn't bother to correct my name. It was a step up from "ummm."

Julie sat down beside her grandmother. "You haven't told her Harriet's split?"

"Split?" I repeated blankly.

Nora gave her daughter-in-law an unmistakable Mother Look.

You know that look. Anybody who's ever had a mother knows it. It's the look that says, "You know very well what you have to do, so shape up and fly right!" I think Jesus himself got one at that wedding where they ran out of wine. Remember? Mary comes and tells him to do something about the situation, and he asks, "What does that have to do with me?" In the very next verse, she turns to the wine steward and says, "Do whatever he tells you." It is my firm conviction that between those two verses she gave him a Mother Look and he capitulated.

That afternoon, I watched Nora Sykes give Dee an unmistakable Mother Look, and I saw Dee cave in. She set down her Co-cola, blotted her lips, and confessed with pink cheeks, "I didn't like to say this at the door, Laura, because you might have been from child welfare or something, but Harriet's run away."

"I'm sorry." I was more embarrassed for them than worried. I figured there'd been a blowup that morning and the child had stomped out. We had times like that with our own teenagers. "How long has she been gone?" I figured they'd say a couple of hours. Maybe, even, overnight. "I hope you won't think I'm prying, but I really do need to see her."

To my astonishment, nobody said a word.

Finally Julie said – seeming to speak her thoughts as they formed, "It must have been right after school let out. We got out on Saturday, because we had to make up a day, then the cheerleaders went up to Lake Jordan. Gram has a wonderful place up there where we all go sometimes – "

"Not Harriet," her grandmother interrupted emphatically. "She was never up there."

"I guess not. But anyway, another cheerleader's grandmother has a house just down the lake from Gram's, so our two sweet, wonderful grandmothers – " she leaned over and gave hers a quick hug " – lent us their houses, and we went up and hung out for the weekend."

"With chaperones," her mother hastened to add.

"Of *course,* mother. Anyway, we were there Saturday night and all day Sunday. Wasn't that when Harriet and Daddy had their fight?"

"Not really a fight." Nora raised one hand in distress. "More of a disagreement."

I had bigger things to think about than whether this family had fights or mere disagreements. Julie was talking about *six weeks* ago! And there sat Dee, doing some figuring of her own. "Harriet was here the day I bought my pink dress, I know, because I'd left laundry on her bed that morning and it was gone when I got back from the manicurist. That was Tuesday, I think." She sighed and explained apologetically, "I'm sorry we can't be more explicit, Laura, but one reason it's so hard to remember is, it didn't happen all at once. Harriet and William had a row on Saturday, and she got furious and stormed out. Several times in the next few days, though, she had somebody drive her out to pick up things. I know she was here Sunday while we were at church, and I think she came at least twice after that. I never saw her, but some of her things would be gone. I didn't really notice when she stopped coming. At first, I didn't even worry. We were going to the mountains that next week, and I had so much to do."

Seeing my expression, she added defensively, "We left a note on the kitchen table telling her to go stay with William's grandmother if she came back while we were gone."

Harriet's money sat like lead on my chest, and I felt like somebody had punched me in the stomach. "So she's been gone since early June? And the police haven't found her?"

I tried to sound as casual as they did, but knew I'd failed when Dee flushed. "William—my husband—refuses to report her missing."

I must have looked as incredulous as I felt, because Nora hurried to explain, "He's not being utterly unreasonable. It was the third time the child had run away in two months. Before, she'd just gone to a friend's and not told Dee or William where she was. William was mortified when the police found her so easily, so this time he's dug in his heels." Her hands clenched and unclenched in tight fists. "But he's wrong. I've told him so a hundred times."

Julie shrugged. "He says she can find her own way home this time."

Dee dabbed at her eyes with a tissue. "But what if she gets—hurt? Or worse?" I couldn't help thinking that not noticing when somebody stopped coming home wasn't real consistent with getting teary-eyed over what might be happening to her. Besides, I didn't see any tears.

"Don't get maudlin," Nora said sharply. "That wretched child worried you to death while she was here, and you know it. But she does need to be found."

"She's probably down at Ricky's again," Julie said, in that irritating tone of utter reason teens use with their parents. "He's the only person she's ever cared anything about."

"Not in a romantic way," her grandmother objected.

"Oh, no. She saved all that for Lewis Henly." She drawled the name dramatically and flung back her hair.

"Julie!" Dee frowned, scandalized. "You know very well Mr. Henly is — " she stopped abruptly. "Have you finished packing?"

"Yes, ma'am. And Rachel called. Her mother doesn't mind if I drive."

"Julie is going down to Gulf Shores for a week at the beach at her friend's condo," her grandmother explained to me. "Why can't Rachel's mother take you all down, honey?"

It was Dee who replied, in almost exactly the tone her daughter had just used, "Her mother's already down there." She turned back to her daughter. "You cannot drive, and that's final. If Rachel's dad can't take you, I will."

Julie wrinkled her nose, but she'd been raised not to argue in front of company.

"Look!" Her grandmother distracted her by holding up the shopping bag. "I bought you a new outfit. See how you like it."

Julie pulled out a turquoise top. "It's gorgeous, Gram. Thanks!" She looked at me and said sweetly, "Would you excuse me? I want to try this on, then I need to go to the mall."

Obviously they all had things to do, and I'd already eaten more cookies than good manners permitted. Since Harriet wasn't likely to be back anytime soon, it was time for me to leave the money and get back to Jake and Glenna.

That's when the funniest thing happened.

I discovered I couldn't for the life of me hand over Harriet's money to people who didn't remember the last time they saw her. I knew perfectly well she could have stolen it from them. Some people do keep that much money around the house. But even if the money was theirs, I wanted to give it back to Harriet. If it was stolen, returning it was her job.

I did, however, want their reaction to the other thing I'd found. "At the center, I found a book and some papers Harriet must have left there. One of the papers looked important. It was an application form for an acting school."

Julie, just at the kitchen door, turned with a superior smile. "That's Harriet, all right. Always expecting to turn from an ugly duckling into a swan."

"Julie!" Dee scolded, understandably appalled.

"I'm going. See you." She left with an airy wave.

"Wasn't William and Harriet's fight about that acting school?" Nora forgot she'd been calling it a disagreement not five minutes before.

Dee nodded. "That and dying her hair. Harriet wanted to dye her hair black and go stay with some of Mama's cousins in Atlanta to take acting lessons all summer. William didn't think it was a good idea. He thought she was too young."

"He was absolutely right, of course." On the table, Nora folded and unfolded the front page of one of the catalogues she'd brought. "A sheer waste of money."

I stood and said lamely, "Well, I'm sorry I missed her. I hope you find her soon. Let me just leave you a number where you can reach me."

Nora frowned in thought. "Do you reckon Harriet *has* gone back to that Ricky's, Dee?"

Dee also stood. "Heaven only knows," she said wearily. "My mother took in foster children," she explained to me, "and he was the last. He stayed nearly three years, off and on, so Harriet thinks of him as almost a brother."

"Some brother." Nora's lips puckered with distaste. "Always in trouble, living in a trailer out toward the airport with a girl he has no intention of marrying—"

"He's been good to Harriet," Dee defended him. "He and Beverly always let her stay with them before. Honestly, Laura," she shook her head in dismay, "you'll think we *beat* the child! But we gave her everything we knew how to give." Her gaze swept the lovely backyard and shimmering pool. "When you came, I hoped you had information about her. I even hoped you'd found her."

I knew it wasn't any of my business, but as Joe Riddley often says, Advice ought to be my middle name. "Have you called Ricky? At least you'd know she was there."

"I tried calling, but he hung up on me!" Dee's eyes flashed with indignation. "I even thought about going out there, but William told me not to. He says it's time Harriet suffers the consequences of her actions."

"Somebody ought to go," Nora muttered. I wondered if she was thinking the same thing I was: *In today's world, some consequences can be deadly.*

Impulsively, I offered, "I'm just here for a few days while my brother is in the hospital, but he's in intensive care, so I have a lot of free time. I could run out to Ricky's one afternoon, just to be sure she's there."

"Why on earth did you butt in like that?" Joe Riddley would demand later.

"Because it looked mindlessly simple," I would reply.

"Little Bit," he would tell me, "when things are really that simple, somebody else does them." He is absolutely right.

That afternoon, however, I was cheered by the way Dee's face brightened. "Would you? I would really appreciate it. Wait a minute and I'll get you his address."

While she was gone, Nora confided, "Dee worries far too much about that child. Of course, Harriet has nobody else. Her mother left when she was barely two, and her father consoled himself pretty soon with a floozy who didn't want a baby around. They hightailed it to Texas, leaving poor Mrs. Lawson with the child when she was well past fifty."

"Poor Harriet!" I exclaimed, appalled.

"Oh, I don't think you miss parents you never knew, and Frank certainly never came back more than once or twice. Then he got himself killed last winter on an oil rig."

"So when her grandmother died, Harriet had nowhere else to go." It wasn't a brilliant deduction, but I was trying to hold up my end of the conversation.

Nora shrugged. "She could have gone to her mother's sister, Eunice Crawley—isn't that a dreadful name?—but she lives up in Chisholm and works all day. On the whole it was wiser for her to come here, although it put a lot of pressure on Dee and William. She requires a lot of supervision."

I couldn't help reflecting that Harriet wasn't getting much lately.

We heard a murmur of voices, then Julie's car started and Dee came in holding a scrap of paper and a bunch of Gerber daisies. She held out the paper. "I'd sure appreciate your going to Ricky's, Laura. Here's the address where he lived last spring, and I guess he's still there. My husband isn't a bad man, but he's not a patient one, and he says Harriet's put me through one wringer too many. If you find her, please tell her we miss her." She held out the daisies, too. "I know your brother can't have flowers in intensive care, but I thought they might cheer you up. I've wrapped wet paper towels around them and put them in a plastic bag. They'll keep until you get home."

She walked me to the car. Before I left she asked anxiously, "You'll let me know what you find out about Harriet, won't you? I'd sure appreciate it."

I'd stayed longer than I intended, so I headed around the first curve going faster than I should have. I nearly ran into Julie, parked smack-dab in the road.

I slammed on the brakes, sending Dee's daisies careening onto the floor, and stopped scarcely a car's length from her bumper. Julie hopped out and ran back to my window.

"I could have hit you!" I said severely, one hand on my thudding heart.

"I was watching for you, and had my foot on the gas in case you couldn't stop. Listen. I had to tell you two things I couldn't say at home. First, Harriet may have gone to live with her mom. My parents pretend Myrna is dead, but I overheard them talking once. I think she's living down in New Orleans—as a prostitute, or something."

I don't like to let on when children shock me, but Julie caught me by surprise. Her lips flickered in a pleased little smile. "Also, Mom said you're going down to see Ricky. I know she says she hasn't gone because Daddy won't let her—"

Oho! I thought. *The child listens at doors.*

She either didn't know she'd given herself away or didn't care. "—but that's not the real reason. Daddy might be furious, but he usually lets Mama do whatever she wants. The real reason she hasn't gone is, Ricky's scary."

"What do you mean, scary?"

"He was in juvenile detention once for robbery and a couple of times for selling drugs. You don't really want to go out there. You could get shot."

Counsel and sound judgment
are mine; I have understanding
and power. *Proverbs 8:14*

Eight

That left me in a perfectly marvelous frame of mind to drive back to the hospital.

I was so upset I made a wrong turn and wound up on Highfield Drive, wherever that is. The name reminded me of one fall when Joe Riddley and I drove around the Scottish Highlands. Their fields were so high, we kept expecting a sheep to roll down and crush us.

From sheep it was a natural progression to that parable about a shepherd with a hundred sheep who lost one. How did it go? Something about leaving ninety-nine to go looking for the one that was lost. I should have known my subconscious was thinking about Harriet all along.

What would happen to that particular sheep, I wondered, if nobody went seeking her? At least ninety-nine dreadful things could happen to a fifteen-year-old on the streets.

"Look," I reminded myself firmly, "you are here to help Glenna. Until Jake's on the mend, you can't spend your time running around looking for other people's lost children."

I was right, of course, but something inside me squirmed. "Okay," I relented, "if I get time tomorrow, I'll run out to Ricky's to see if she's there. How long could that take?"

Not being Glenna, I spent fifteen minutes finding a parking place at the hospital, then had to walk quite a distance in the heat. That, coupled with getting lost, nearly running into Julie, and her cheerful news, made me mad as spit by the time I reached the waiting room. "People ought to have to have licenses to raise children!" I greeted poor Glenna, who was placidly reading an old *Reader's Digest* and munching a candy bar.

She handed me the last half of her candy. "You didn't find Harriet?"

I told her the whole story, grateful she's known me long enough not to believe half the nasty things I say about other people when I'm mad. "I'm glad it's Nora Sykes who's your friend, and not Dee," I finally told her. "She seems like the only one with her head on straight. Dee not remembering when Harriet left really gets my goat. Furthermore," I jerked the damp, wilted envelope from my blouse, "this thing is driving me crazy."

"Why don't you pop in to see Jake again, then go deposit the money in my bank account until you find the child?"

That was so utterly Glenna: simple, practical, and exactly what most people would never offer because they'd worry somebody might sue. Glenna never worries about getting sued. She worries about how she can help.

I didn't stay more than a minute with Jake. He was sleeping, his face a horrid gray that made me sick, and his skin warm and too dry. At least by this time tomorrow it would all be over.

One way or another.

I could not bear to think of that, so I touched him lightly, whispered a prayer, and tiptoed out.

Glenna had filled out a deposit slip while I was gone. I went down the hall and stuck it in with the money, which by now was shaped to my body like papier mache.

"I've got another suggestion," Glenna said when I got back. "I think you ought to call Mr. Henly at the teen center and explain the whole situation. If somebody has to visit this Ricky, it should be him, not you. We've got enough on our plate with Jake."

Why hadn't I thought of that? Joe Riddley claims I'm such a good delegator that he spends a good bit of his life pointing me in other people's direction. It would be wonderful if Lewis found Harriet while I was at the hospital. Besides, I had one more thing on my plate than Glenna did. Once Jake got his surgery, he'd start pestering his doctor about coming home. I needed time to prod the police to find his car.

Lewis Henly started apologizing as soon as he heard who I was. "I'm sorry I didn't get to see you before you left this morning, ma'am. My board treasurer came by unexpectedly and wanted me to go over some figures." I remembered which figure *he'd* been going over. "I want to thank you for organizing the girls, though," he added. "The room looks great."

"Relatively speaking," I amended.

He chuckled. "Point well taken. Say, how's Jake?"

"Not good, but he's supposed to have surgery in the morning. I didn't actually call about Jake. I called about one of your girls. Harriet Lawson."

"Was she around this morning? I didn't see her."

"No, but you do remember her?"

He must have been doing something else, because he paused for a couple of seconds before he answered. "Harriet? Of course I remember her. She comes in the center all the time—or did until her grandmother died last spring. After that she moved in with an auntie, and slacked off some. She hasn't been here much this summer at all. What about her?"

I explained about finding Harriet's things, why I'd taken them with me, and what I'd learned at Dee's.

"She's run away again?" Lewis Henly didn't sound the least bit concerned. "How long has she been gone this time?"

"Her aunt doesn't remember, but it's been about since school was out."

"That's longer than usual, but I wouldn't worry. Harriet's got a history of running away when things don't go her way. Is that what happened?"

"Apparently so. She had a row with her uncle and stormed out, but she came back a few times in the next week to pick up some things. However, they can't remember exactly when she stopped coming. Have you seen her this past month?"

"No— " He spun the word out like it was searching his memory, then repeated it firmly. "No, I don't think I have. What did you find of Harriet's?"

I was tired of hiding it. "Three thousand dollars, in hundred dollar bills."

He whistled. "Where on earth did you find that kind of money around *here?* Even nickels and dimes have a habit of walking."

"I found it while we were cleaning, tucked in a library book behind the hideabed. When I returned the book, it was Harriet's, so I assume the money must be hers, too."

His voice rose in disbelief. "Where would *she* get three thousand dollars?"

"I don't know, but there it was. At first I thought the book might have slipped down accidentally while she was sitting on the couch, but I did a little experiment before I left, and I don't think that's possible. The sofa's pretty tight at the back, and the cushions are so sprung that a book would slide forward, not back. Harriet must have deliberately shoved it down there for safekeeping. I just can't imagine why she hasn't come back for it."

He laughed. "Ma'am, if you figure out why these kids do half the things they do, you let me know. If it was as hard to get to as you say, maybe Harriet's decided our sofa is safer than a bank. I'm not half as worried about why she hasn't come back for it as I am about where she got it."

"It is a lot of money for a teenager."

"You got that right. It's a lot of money for some grownups, even. This one, for instance. And Harriet—Harriet has *nothing*. Where would she ever get three thousand dollars?"

"I hoped you might have some idea."

He laughed without humor. "Believe me, if I knew one of my kids was bringing big bucks into this club, we'd first have a long talk to be sure it never happened again, then I'd watch like a hawk for any sign he or she was dealing drugs. But Harriet?" He laughed at the very idea. "No way. What did you do with the money?"

"I put it in the bank until I can find her." I told myself it wasn't really a lie, just a little story—a time warp, like on *Star Trek*. I was fixing to take the money to the bank as soon as we hung up, and I didn't really know Lewis Henly. I didn't want him robbing me to help finance his center. Like I said before, I have a very good imagination. I should have known, though, that telling even a little story can get you in big trouble.

"The real reason I called," I went on, "is that Harriet's aunt suggested she might be staying out near the airport with a boy named Ricky Dodd. Do you know him?"

"Met him once when he came to pick up Harriet. Know *of* him from both Harriet and the police. Harriet thinks he's a poor boy nobody understands, while the police assure me he's one tough dude. Harriet's stayed with him and his girlfriend a couple of times. It's a good guess she's out there now."

"You wouldn't happen to be going out that way anytime soon, would you? I have his address, but I'm not familiar with the area—" I trailed off, hoping he'd get the hint.

He only got half of it. "Why don't we go together right now?" he said promptly. "I'm almost through here for today."

Actually, that was better than I had hoped for. After Julie's description, I really wanted to see Ricky Dodd for myself—with a big, strong man. Besides, I couldn't see Jake again until after supper, and sitting in that waiting room would drive me straight up a wall. "You'll have to drive, though." I told him about Jake's car.

"The Buick? Lady, when Jake gets up and around, you are going to be in one heck of a lot of trouble. But no problem, today. I can be there in fifteen minutes."

As I was about to leave Glenna handed me her house key. "Go on home when you're done, sugar. I'm going to come back for supper, too. Whichever of us gets there first can find something to fix."

"You'll need a key, if you get there before I do," I objected.

"I have one hidden in the toolshed."

I couldn't believe how dumb I'd been. "No, you don't. I used it at noon and left it sitting on the kitchen counter."

For just a moment a twinkle lit Glenna's weary face. "Jake was a Boy Scout, remember? We keep *two* keys hidden. You take this one. I hope you find Harriet."

I did, too.

Henry Ford would be proud of how well his product takes the years. Mr. Henly arrived in a Ford even more ancient and battered than Glenna's. To my surprise and delight, Josheba Davidson jumped out of the front seat and insisted on climbing into the back.

"How'd you get here?" I asked, fitting my feet in among old magazines and two pairs of gym shoes and hoping I'd soon get used to the smell of sweat, junk food, and old socks.

"I got to thinking about how long it's been since I last saw Harriet," Josheba explained, "and I got so worried I decided to go down to the center to talk with some of her friends. The girls were already gone, but Lewis here was just finishing talking to you on the phone. When I told him about our adventures this morning, he invited me to ride along. Now, you all talk. I'm going to sit back and enjoy this heat."

I saw at once what she meant. Mr. Henly's Ford had lost one facility Glenna's still retained: air conditioning. Even though he drove faster than the law allowed, the breeze couldn't help but be hot on such a day. Dogs lay panting on the sidewalk, looking like they wished they could just curl up and die. Sweat trickling down my bra was soaking Harriet's money so badly that if the ink wasn't waterproof, I'd have Ben Franklin underwear.

Lewis turned left in front of an oncoming car in a way that made me wonder if the next time my name appeared in print, it would be carved in marble. Josheba called from the backseat, "Now you see why I wanted to sit here."

I checked to be sure my seat belt was tightly fastened. "Why don't you distract me by telling me a little bit about Harriet. What she's like, what she looks like, things like that."

"Well—what was your name again?" Lewis asked.

"MacLaren," Josheba told him. "Call her Mac."

"Okay, Mac. Call me Lewis. Now, about Harriet. In the first place, she is white. Most of our kids are black. Harriet wasn't making friends with whites at school, so she teamed up with a couple of our kids and came to the center almost every day. Until she quit, that is."

"Is she pretty?"

"Not particularly."

"No fair!" Josheba called indignantly. "She has pretty brown hair, if she'd brush it. And if she'd wash all that vampire makeup off her face—"

"Well," Lewis said dubiously, "maybe so. But right now? She's a mess. Snarly hair, black fingernail polish, black clothes with lots of heavy silver jewelry, dead white powder, black lipstick, and she's got the personality of . . . what, Josheba? An armadillo?"

"Maybe, but I think that shell's to keep people from getting close. You don't read romance novels if you don't want somebody to love you in a pretty soupy way."

"Maybe so," Lewis still sounded dubious, "but my experience is, ask Harriet a personal question or to do you a favor and she'll bite your head off. If you're up to something she doesn't like, she'll climb up your back and stick like a burr. On the other hand, she's a fighter. When she wants something, she goes for it with all she's got. Coming to the club, for instance. Her granny didn't like it, but she couldn't stop her."

"Maybe she didn't try—figured it kept Harriet out of trouble," Josheba suggested.

"She'd have been right about that. Our kids don't do much, but they don't do much wrong, either. But I think old Granny just didn't want to hassle Harriet. She's one tough cookie about having her own way."

"Unlike the rest of us?" Josheba asked pertly.

On the way to Ricky's we passed three branches of Glenna's bank. Each time, I wished I could ask Lewis to drive through to deposit that money, but since I didn't want to tell him I'd lied, I had to endure hot damp money plastered to my chest.

"Someone told me Harriet has a crush on you," Josheba teased Lewis.

He shrugged. "That's one of the hazards of this racket—ditzy kids following you around. I give them jobs to do. They think they're helping me, while really they're staying out of my hair. Harriet answers the phone during hours we aren't covered by volunteers. She can sit behind the desk reading books and feel real important."

"Is she responsible?" I asked.

"Surprisingly, she is. Or was, until right about the time school let out. One day she came in late, acting very mysterious." He deepened his voice and drew out the last two words. "A few days later I had a meeting and really needed her to take calls, and she didn't come in at all. After that, I don't think she's ever come back. I figured her auntie finally got to her. Put her foot down, or something. Well, here's Ricky's trailer park."

The grass was cut, the roads were in good repair, and many of the mobile homes were landscaped as if the people planned to stay awhile. I especially admired a blaze of white impatiens surrounding a deep fuchsia crape myrtle.

Ricky's address, however, was a dilapidated green and white unit at the back with an old washer in the side yard and no flowers or bushes whatsoever. "You were wise not to come out here alone," Lewis said, as he switched off the engine. "From what I hear, Rick's a great believer in the state motto."

"Which is?"

"We dare to defend our rights."

> Violence overwhelms the mouth of the wicked. *Proverbs 10:6*

Nine

Ricky Dodd had about a hundred words in his total vocabulary, sixty of them vulgar. What they added up to was, "Anything's happened to Harriet, it ain't my business."

He folded his arms across his bare torso, arched his back, flicked back greasy white hair that fell almost to his shoulders, and dared anyone to disagree.

Behind him, framed by a filthy doorjamb, stood a girl who looked like she might die from anemia before we finished talking.

"How long has it been since you saw Harriet?" Lewis pressed mildly. I admired the way Lewis kept his temper, especially since Ricky's vocabulary was also rich in racial slurs.

Ricky turned to the girl for confirmation. "How long's it been, Bev, six weeks?"

"Two months, more like. School wasn't out yet."

"Yeah. Harriet's school," he added, to let us know he had no part in it. None of us would have remotely imagined he had.

"She said she had a letter from her mama back in May," Bev contributed timidly.

"Yeah," Ricky interrupted. "Maybe Harriet split to join her."

"Her mother?" Lewis was skeptical. "I thought her mother was dead."

"Naanh, she just split." Again Ricky flipped his hair. I suspected he practiced that in front of a mirror. My son Ridd went through a stage of practicing tossing his hair—back when Ridd still had hair.

"Where was the letter from?" I asked.

"I dunno. Never read it." As if he could.

It had taken him that long to think of the obvious question. "Why do you care what happened to Harriet, anyhow? She in trouble?"

"Of course not." Lewis acted like he was about to leave, then turned and asked casually, "She didn't happen to mention getting a large sum of money, did she?"

Unfortunately, at the very same time, I said, "I've found something of hers and wanted to return it."

Ricky could at least add two and two. He whipped around to me. "You found money? Where?"

"At the teen center," I admitted uncomfortably. "Hidden."

When he narrowed his eyes, he looked just like a weasel. "Harriet got a pile from her Granny, old Lady Lawson. Left Harriet everything she had." He snickered. "Put her aunt's nose out of joint, I can tell you that."

I'd presumed it was Dee who'd sold her mother's house. Dee hadn't corrected that impression, so I couldn't help showing my surprise. Ricky preened like a peacock, knowing something I didn't. Then he demanded, "What'd you do with that money? Harriet was gonna give some of it to me. If you got it—" He came a step forward. Without thinking, I backed up. He followed.

Lewis caught my elbow protectively. "She hasn't got it with her, and if I catch you bothering Harriet for money, dude, I'll have the law on you."

Ricky whirled and hit his jaw so hard I was surprised it didn't crack. Caught off guard, Lewis stumbled and fell. Ricky crowed brutally. "You and who else?"

Josheba froze, but I hadn't raised two boys for nothing. "Behave, both of you! Ricky, go on back inside. Lewis, go to the car. We've asked what we came for."

"Got more than you came for." Ricky looked like he might even strike *me*!

"Ricky!" the girl squealed from the door. "Stop it! You could get in real bad trouble."

He gave her a glare that would have had me packing my bags if I'd been her, but he must have decided she had a point. Giving Lewis one quick kick in the back, he stomped up his front steps, shoved the girl aside, and slammed the screened door behind him.

Lewis climbed to his feet, nursing his jaw and holding his back, and limped to the car.

"Just a minute!" I called before Beverly could disappear. "Josheba, do you have paper and a pen?" I sure did miss my pocketbook. I'd need to get one as soon as Jake—

I wasn't up to thinking about Jake right then. Quickly I took the pen and a grocery receipt Josheba handed me, and wrote down my name, Jake's name, and his phone number. I held them up to the girl, who stood lumpishly on the top step. "I'm staying at my brother's while he's in the hospital. This is his phone number. Please call me if you hear from Harriet."

She took the paper without a word. Ricky, already lolling on the couch watching television, called, "Fat chance."

Fat chance he'd hear? Or fat chance he'd call me if he did?

[She] who brings trouble on [her]
family will inherit only wind.
Proverbs 11:29

Ten

"I probably asked for that," Lewis admitted as he started the engine, "but that doesn't make me feel any better. Did we learn a blessed thing?"

I felt as dismal as he sounded. "Not a thing."

"Learned not to mess with mean white boys." Josheba leaned up from the backseat and lightly touched his jaw. "Does it hurt real bad?"

Lewis worked it back and forth. "No more than if I'd been hit by a ten-ton truck."

"Come by my place," she offered. "My mama taught me a poultice that'll take your pain right out."

"Don't have time," Lewis mumbled. "I got a date."

"Me too," Josheba said tartly. "A hot date. I was just being nice."

I looked around in surprise. Josheba winked and held one finger to her lips.

During the next few minutes, several thoughts jumbled around in my brain. If Harriet had inherited her grandmother's house, then surely she'd gotten more from the sale than three thousand dollars. Where was the rest? In the bank, probably — but how had Harriet gotten out the three thousand? Fifteen-year-olds can't withdraw money from a bank. Dee must have gotten it for her — but for what? I should have told Dee I'd found the money — except she might not be as worried if she thought Harriet had money to live on. I knew I was more worried thinking she didn't. "Where could that girl be?" I asked the others. "Surely a child can't completely disappear."

Lewis had just pulled onto the Southern bypass, a busy strip of fast-food places and chain motels that utterly lives up to its name: it bypasses every blessed thing that's nice about the South. "See all this?" he waved his hand out his window. "Busy, anonymous, and just like every other city in America. It's easy to get lost in that, and for a lot of kids, it looks better than what they've left behind. Harriet, for instance, gets to choose between living with a snotty cheerleader cousin, or living with Ricky and putting up with who-knows-what."

"Paying his bills, if she has any money," Josheba suggested behind me.

Lewis nodded. "Or going on the streets to pay them if she doesn't."

"Surely not!" I've seen a lot in my time, but what he'd just said made me sick.

He shrugged. "In my business you see brothers selling sisters, Mac, much less foster brothers selling kids they don't give two bits for. I'm not saying Ricky did put Harriet on the streets, but he would've tried in a blinkin' second if he needed bread."

"Why doesn't somebody do something?" I demanded.

"Why don't *you* do something?" Lewis darted through traffic, picking up speed as if driven by anger. "You got any vacant beds in your house?"

"Yes, since our boys are grown." I sure missed Glenna's air conditioner. The wind whipped my cheeks like a fat kiss from an unwelcome lover.

"Why don't you fill them up with neglected children? Then get out there and do something about parents who're too busy to notice what their kids are up to, or schools so bogged down in security and policies they don't have time to teach, or media people whose only interest in kids is how much they can be made to buy."

"You forgot the government who gives kids college loans instead of scholarships," Josheba added sourly, "and banks who practically beg them to take credit cards they don't know how to manage. Seems like everybody is out to screw kids these days." She got so caught up in what she was saying that she came right up against the back of my seat and gripped it with both hands. I could feel her breath on my neck. "I talked to a kid yesterday who's twenty-four years old, up to his neck in college loans, and already maxed out on four credit cards. He won't be out of debt when his own kids are ready for college."

"Preach it, sister!" Lewis said cheerfully.

Josheba flounced back into her seat. "I didn't mean to get carried away, but you pushed my button. But we shouldn't fuss at Mac, Lewis. She's the one who started looking for Harriet in the first place."

Lewis looked over and gave me a smile of apology. "Yeah. And in spite of what I just said, don't get too worked up about her, okay? Whatever she's up to, I don't think she's in any trouble. That girl can take care of herself."

Josheba had been thinking, too. "Maybe she did go to her mother. Did her auntie mention the mother at all, Mac?"

I told them what Nora and Julie had said.

Josheba shook her head. "Unlikely she'd have wanted a grown daughter around if she's working the streets, unless she got sick or something."

Lewis went back to what he'd been saying before. "Harriet's feisty. I'm willing to bet she's struck out on her own—headed down to Mobile or up to Birmingham."

"She had a brochure from an acting school in Atlanta," I told them.

Lewis snorted. "Harriet onstage? Well, if she paid them any money, that is a tragic waste."

"She might make a great actress, with the right coaching," Josheba disagreed. "Maybe that's what the money was for."

"The brochure said the cost of the summer session was two thousand dollars plus living expenses," I informed her, "if paid in full before the session started."

"When does the session start?" Josheba asked. Lewis didn't seem a bit interested.

"It already did, in June sometime. It would be half over by now."

"We could call and see if she went."

"I'll do that when I get home," I promised.

"She wouldn't have gone without the money," Lewis pointed out.

"Don't be a spoilsport," Josheba chided. "At least Mac is planning to do something."

"I'm planning to do something, too," he told her. "I'm planning to sit down with Harriet's friends tomorrow and see if they know anything. Mac, would you rather I took you back to the hospital, or home?"

"Home, please." I could do a lot of thinking in a cool shower. Maybe before Glenna returned, I could even call the police and light a fire under them about finding Jake's car.

"Why don't you drop us both by the center?" Josheba suggested. "I've got to pick up my car, and I can take Mac home. She stays not far from me."

I voted for that—especially since we'd be trading up to Josheba's air conditioning.

As Lewis let us out, Kateisha was swinging down the street licking something from her palm. Lewis called out his window, "Kateisha, you tell Dré we still got room on the basketball team."

"Dré ain't studyin' basketball," she told him bluntly. "Ain't studying nothin' that's good for him." She poured purple powder into her palm from a paper packet and licked it, waiting, while we got out. As soon as Lewis drove away, she ignored me completely and glowered at Josheba. "You Mr. Henly's girlfriend?"

"No *way*," Josheba assured her. "I already got a boyfriend. Lewis, Mac, and I were just checking out something."

"We were looking for Harriet," I explained.

"You and me both," Kateisha said emphatically. "When you finds her, tell her I wants those CDs back I let her borrer. They was my brother Dré's, and he's gettin' ugly." She pursed her lips, then said frankly, "It ain't really Dré gettin' ugly, it's Z-dog." She licked some more of the powder from her palm. "CDs was Z-dog's to start with."

"What's a Z-dog?" I asked.

"Z-dog ain't a what, he's a who. He's Dré's homie."

I was no wiser than before, but at least, thanks to my grandchildren, I knew Kateisha was referring to compact disks instead of certificates of deposit. "Why don't you give me the names of the CDs, and I'll ask her aunt to look for them. Josheba, do you have more paper and a pen?"

Kateisha wiped her hand on the seat of her red shorts and scrawled several names. They sounded more like nonsense than musicians, but I stuck the list in my pocket.

"Let's go," Josheba commanded, getting into her car and putting down all the windows. "It's so humid I feel like we're breathing clouds."

Before I got in the car too, however, I just had to ask once more. "Kateisha, are you sure you don't have *any* idea where Harriet could be?"

Kateisha stuck out her lip and grew sullen. "I don't know and I don't care. I ain't studyin' Harriet. She ain't *my* fr'en' anymore. Like I said this mornin', Harriet ain't come 'round here since school let out, and *I don't care!*" She swung off down the street with her nose in the air and her whale spout bobbing. At the corner, she turned and yelled, "Maybe Miz Scott has seen her. You could ast her." She turned the corner before we could ask who she meant.

"I'll catch her with the car," Josheba said, starting the engine. Just then I saw something red turn into our street from an intersection two blocks away. I gasped and pointed. "That looks like Jake's car! Can you catch it?"

"I can try." Josheba's Honda spurted ahead. As we got closer, I saw an Auburn sticker in the right place. I also saw somebody in the backseat look back, then lean forward. At the next corner, the Buick turned right on two wheels.

"Follow them!" I cried.

"Hold on!" Josheba wrenched her wheel to the right, and I hung onto her side door for dear life.

We followed for several blocks, faster than I would ever have dared drive in that neighborhood. Small children on tricycles and women on sidewalks passed in a blur. But the other driver knew his way better than Josheba. We never got close enough to see the driver, and wound up at a corner with several choices of streets and no sign of the Buick.

"You did a great job of trying to catch them," I told Josheba.

She was breathing hard and shaking so much she had to drop her hands from the wheel to her lap. "Mac, what would we have done with them if I had?"

"I don't know," I admitted, ashamed. I hadn't thought that far. Once again, I'd acted impulsively without thinking of the consequences—which was what had gotten me in this whole mess in the first place. "You really are nice to put up with me," I told her ruefully.

"Well, one thing about being around you, Mac," Josheba said as she put the car back into gear. "Life is never dull. What're you planning to do next?"

"Give the acting school a call as soon as I get home," I planned as I spoke, "then if they don't know anything, maybe after Jake's surgery I'll try to talk with Eunice Crawley, Harriet's mother's sister. If she doesn't know anything, I'll ask Lewis to find out from Kateisha who this Mrs. Scott is."

"Tell me, Mac, why are you going to all this trouble for a girl you don't even know?"

"Well, I'd like to think it's because of the Bible story about a lost sheep—"

Josheba raised one hand to stop me. "Don't give me Bible stories. My daddy was a preacher, of the twice-on-Sunday-and-once-in-the-middle-of-the-week variety. I had enough Bible stories growing up to last a lifetime. Never did him *or* me a bit of good. Killed him, and turned me off religion for life. The way I see it, you are either a very nice lady, or you're just plain nosy. That's all there is to it."

"Just plain nosy, then," I admitted, "and so dad-blamed sure I can finish things up if I talk to just one more person."

When we pulled into Glenna's driveway, I asked automatically, "Will you come in?"

Josheba shook her head. "I've got a big paper due tomorrow, so I'm heading for the library."

"Hot date?" I teased.

She laughed. "Lewis Henly thinks he's God's gift to women. I couldn't let him believe he's the only one with a social life. But don't you tell Morse. He'd flat-out kill me."

I started to get out, then paused. "Can you imagine a single reason why Harriet should have left all that money behind, Josheba? I am increasingly worried about that child."

"You and me both," Josheba said soberly, "but it looks like we're the only ones."

> As a north wind brings rain,
> so a sly tongue brings angry looks.
> *Proverbs 25:23*

Eleven

I'd written down the intersection where we'd lost the car, and Josheba had doubled back so I could jot down where we'd first seen it. The minute I got inside Glenna's house, I called the police.

I'd been pretty rattled that morning, but normally I'm on easy terms with police officers. Joe Riddley has a constant stream of them coming to swear out warrants in the office we share, and if he's tied up on the phone or with a customer, I chat with them and offer them a cup of coffee. I talk to them the way I do my own boys.

Having probably seen Jake's car, therefore, I wasn't shy about ordering the Montgomery police, "Find it. It's in that neighborhood somewhere. Look for a young man with hair like a crow's nest driving a car too big for him, and do it fast. My brother's in the hospital with a heart attack, and I want his car back before he gets home."

Talking big made me feel like I'd done something, even if I knew I really hadn't.

Next I tried the acting school in Atlanta, but they had closed for the night. Finally I could, in good conscience, get that shower I'd been wanting for hours. I can't remember any other that ever felt so good.

Everything I'd taken to Albuquerque was too dressy for hospital visits. "As soon as Jake gets his surgery," I promised myself, "I'll go to the mall and pick up a few things."

What will you use for money?

The question — as clear as if somebody had said it out loud — took my breath away. I'd never before understood what it meant to be destitute. I couldn't buy a dress, a meal, or a ticket home without asking for help. How on earth was Harriet paying for food and necessities, if she'd left her money behind?

At least I had Glenna and Joe Riddley. I even had Harriet's three thousand dollars — although I hoped I'd never stoop low enough to use it. "Poor little rich girl," I chided myself, "stop feeling sorry for yourself and put on your navy linen dress. Without the pearls it ought to look all right for tonight."

Without the pearls I looked like I was ready for a funeral. With them, I looked like I was ready for church. Neither was likely to cheer Jake up very much. I sank into the chair again, defeated. "Never again," I vowed angrily, "will I ever leave home without at least one cotton skirt and blouse in my suitcase."

Just then the phone rang. "Well, Little Bit," Joe Riddley began without preamble, "I've canceled all the durn credit cards, but don't you ever go expecting to get another."

"Don't you dare talk to me like that after the day I've had!" I told him fiercely.

"Jake worse?" he asked, concerned.

"He sure is. He's having a bypass tomorrow morning." Low-down creature that I am, I let poor Jake take the blame for my whole bad mood. If Joe Riddley knew what else I'd been up to, he'd burn rubber getting to Alabama.

"Do you need me to come?"

We both knew he couldn't really come. Not with our big summer sale going on. "Remember what happened the last time you let Ridd and Walker run a sale?"

He snorted. "How could I forget? Walker was so cheap he didn't lower prices enough, so we got stuck with a lot of stuff we wanted to get rid of, and Ridd got so entranced with our new bedding plants he bought them all for his own yard."

"His yard sure was pretty that year."

"Our profits weren't. Okay, Little Bit, I'll stick around here and keep the home fires burning, but if you need me, I'll come in a minute. You know that." For a second, I was tempted to tell him to hit the road.

"Since you can't come," I told him, "do the next best thing. Wire me some money. I don't have a blessed thing I can wear to the hospital."

"I could overnight you a suitcase," he suggested.

"I can just see what you'd put in it. Send cash instead. I'll run down to Gayfers—"

"With poor old Jake incapacitated, you can't be running all over town shopping."

I hoped he would never find out exactly how much running all over town I'd already been doing—and why. "Just send the money, Joe Riddley. Western Union. I don't want some bank holding it up because it's from out of state."

"Will three-four hundred keep you from running around naked?"

"That would be splendid. I probably won't spend it all."

"Spend what you need—I don't want you shaming your relatives. And get something pretty, you hear me? None of that 'I can make do with this' stuff you sometimes pull. But I sure would prefer to send the money to

Glenna's account. I hate to think about you carrying around that much cash."

For once, I didn't say a word.

When we hung up, I bawled. I didn't know if I was crying from missing Joe Riddley, from worrying about Jake, from losing the car twice, from being responsible for all that money all day, or from not being able to find Harriet, but I felt a lot better afterwards.

Then I went through Glenna's closet and found a peasant blouse and skirt she'd bought on a missions trip to Guatemala. The skirt had an elastic waist, so although it brushed my toes, it would work if I didn't breathe or eat.

I wasn't very hungry anyway, and I knew Glenna wouldn't be. Quickly I put together a couple of thick sandwiches from fresh beefsteak tomatoes, lettuce, a Vidalia onion I found in the fridge, and slices of Glenna's homemade sourdough bread. I set the table on the sunporch, because the yard glowed in the setting sun.

As we ate, I told Glenna about our trip out to Ricky's. "I'm going to call the acting school tomorrow to see if Harriet's there," I concluded. "If she's not, I'm going to leave this up to Lewis until Jake's home. We've got enough to do just worrying about him." I noticed her empty plate. "Do you want another sandwich?" I asked.

"No, but that reminds me!" Glenna jumped up and went to the kitchen. "I have to feed the sourdough tonight. Tomorrow one of us needs to start the bread."

"Better you than me," I called in to her. "My family still calls any baking I do 'Mama's Unique Experiences.'"

She came back with bowls of ice cream. As she sat down, she reached over to pat my hand. "You do other things, Clara. My mother used to talk about divine appointments—places we are put or people we meet that we've been given special responsibility for. I keep thinking maybe Harriet is your divine appointment."

"If so, she missed it. There's plenty for you and me to do right now between the hospital and here. Harriet is other people's problem, and it's time Dee reported her missing—whether William likes it or not. I'm ready to take the money back out there and tell them so."

"You still have the money?" Startled, Glenna looked anxiously around the sunporch as if she thought I'd left it lying around.

"It's safe enough. I stuck it in the bottom drawer of my dresser so I could shower." I didn't add that it had been sending out signals ever since. "I've also been thinking about what Ricky said, about Harriet inheriting from her grandmother. I ought to tell Dee that a part of the inheritance has turned up behind a sofa—and let her have it for safekeeping."

Glenna finished her ice cream and folded her napkin. "Then let's leave right now and stop by there on our way back to the hospital."

In the Sykes's yard, a man was taking plants from a wheelbarrow. Only a red pickup sat in the driveway. "Do you want to come with me?" I asked Glenna.

"No, I'll wait here," she said contentedly, leaving the motor and the air conditioner running. "Tell William I said hello." She was smart. Even though it was nearly dusk, heat settled on my shoulders like an unwanted blanket.

That man sure knew his plants. His grass was healthy and thick underfoot, and as I got near him, I found myself asking without thinking, "What is that *marvelous* smell? I'm in the nursery business, but I don't recognize that scent."

When he stood erect, he was not much taller than I—and nowhere nearly as pretty as his wife. His ruddy face was scarred from acne, his red hair was thin, and his eyelashes were a light yellow above bright green eyes. Nobody would take him for the owner of that big house, either. For gardening, he wore a faded Crimson Tide T-shirt with khaki cutoffs, and dilapidated Top-Siders without socks.

If he was startled by a strange woman coming out of the dusk to ask about his flowers, he didn't show it. "Nicotiana," he told me, reaching across gaillardia and blue fringed daisies to break off a tubular flower with a flared mouth. "Pretty, isn't it—like a trumpet?"

I'd heard of that branch of the tobacco family, but we'd never carried it. Joe Riddley said he didn't think a magistrate ought to peddle tobacco in any form whatsoever. I hadn't realized it smelled so good, either. I held it to my nose and could have stood there smelling it all night.

He broke off another, gave it a sniff, then tossed it away. "Comes in white, purple, and yellow, too, but I like the red best myself."

I took one last smell and dropped my hand. "I was here earlier and didn't smell a thing. I wonder how I could have missed it."

"It's nocturnal. Only sends out scent at night."

So far he had shown no curiosity at all about why I was there. Maybe he had women stopping by all the time to ask about his flowers. With that yard, I could see why.

It was time for this woman, however, to get down to business—and I didn't mean nursery business.

When I explained who I was, he wiped his right hand across his shirt and held it out. "Oh, yeah. Dee said you came by looking for Harriet. Work down at that teen center or something, don't you?"

"I was volunteering down there this morning and found some things of Harriet's."

"Well, I'm real sorry Dee's not here right now. She's following Julie and her girlfriend down to the Gulf. I can't see the point of taking two cars, myself—if Julie smashes up, Dee will either crash or watch it all happen—but she wouldn't let Julie drive alone, and Julie pitched a fit about needing a car down there for the week. I'd guess Dee won't be back until late, but I'm about finished out here. Would you like to come in for a drink or something?" He took a plastic Alabama cup from one corner of the wheelbarrow, and I realized that not all the sweetness on the night air was nicotiana. Bourbon was also making a contribution.

"No, thanks. I just came—" I started to hand him the envelope, but he went right on talking. I guessed he might be a bit lonely.

"I'm sorry Dee isn't here." he repeated, taking a big swig from his cup. "She said she told you Harriet's probably staying with a friend down near the airport."

"But she isn't," I told him firmly.

Now I had his attention. "How do you know?"

"I went out there this afternoon. Ricky hasn't seen her. You need to call the police and report her missing."

"I don't think we're quite ready for that yet." He gave a short laugh that was more like a bark. "Harriet's just a rebellious kid who's taken off for the summer. If she gets into a little trouble, it serves her right after all she's put Dee through. But she's pretty streetwise. I expect she's down at the beach having the time of her life."

"How would she support herself?"

"Oh, Harriet's not lazy. She could get a job all right, and she's a hard worker when she wants to be. She's probably lied about her age and is slinging hamburgers somewhere, or taking orders for pizza." He took another swig from his cup.

It made sense. I wondered why I hadn't thought of that myself.

William gave a hoarse whiskey chuckle. "She's sure not taking any back talk, though. Not Harriet." He emptied his cup and thrust his scarred face toward mine. "You may not know this," he confided, "but Harriet's mother took off too, years ago. Dee would kill me for telling you, but who cares? Myrna's no relation of ours. Left poor old Frank holding the baby when Harriet was two, and hared down to New Orleans—where the living is easy and so are the women." He winked.

Because of what Ricky had said, I couldn't help asking, "Have you heard from Myrna recently?"

He stepped back and growled, "What that supposed to mean? Why should *I* have heard from that slut? She means nothing to me."

Up to then I could have given him the money with an easy conscience. He was no drunker than a lot of men on Friday night with their wives away. But alcohol had lowered his manners as well as his inhibitions. Whatever Myrna was, she was family, and where he and I both come from, family *matters*. You might not like them—or even be nice to them in private—but you don't disown them to strangers. I wasn't about to hand him Harriet's three thousand dollars. "Please tell Dee I came back, and that I think you ought to call the police." I headed back toward the car.

He walked along beside me. When we got near the car, Glenna rolled down her window and called, "Hello, William!"

"Why, hello, Mrs. Crane! Are you with her?"

"She's with me. This is Jake's sister, MacLaren," Glenna told him.

He leaned into her window and said sincerely, "I sure was sorry to hear about Jake. How's he doing?" While Glenna told him, I got in the car.

"You didn't give him the money?" she asked as we drove away. She wasn't criticizing, just asking.

I shook my head. "He's had just a tad too much to drink. I decided to wait."

"Oh, dear. I'm sorry to see William drinking. He was such a nice boy. Used to help his grandmother and me with all sorts of projects. Nora, his mother, prefers to give money and attend social functions, but Lou Ella always likes to get right down and *do* a thing. When he was young, William used to help us with rummage sales, children's carnivals, and events for people we tutored. He was such a *fine* young man—devoted to his grandmother." She made a left turn before adding, "Lou Ella and I go way back. We've worked in organizations together since I was a bride. She's slowing down, though. Doesn't get out much except to church. The last thing I remember her doing was play beside me in the bell choir, the night the Olympic torch came to Jasmine Hill . . ." Her voice petered out.

I knew exactly what she was thinking. Last Memorial Day, Joe Riddley and I spent the weekend with Jake and Glenna. Jake had Glenna pack a picnic, and he took us all up to Jasmine Hill, which is a marvelous park just north of town full of authentic reproductions of classical Greek sculpture. As the four of us wandered among the spring flowers, columns, and statues of that lovely garden, Jake kept pestering everybody nearly to death by asking again and again, "Don't you feel just exactly like you're back in ancient Greece?"

Finally Joe Riddley said in exasperation, "Jake, I never *was* in ancient Greece."

At the look on Jake's face, Glenna and I laughed so hard we cried.

We cried on our way to the hospital, too. That's how worry and grieving wear you out. Not just by day-after-day exhaustion, but by sudden catches and claws at memory just when you've managed to forget.

At the window of my house . . . I noticed among the young men, a youth who lacked judgment.
Proverbs 7:6–7

Twelve

Jake was worn out from trying to act brave about his upcoming surgery, so I was ready to go home early. Glenna insisted on staying at the hospital all night, but first she wanted to put on something she'd doze in more comfortably. I didn't try to convince her to stay home. I'd have done the same for Joe Riddley.

As we drove up to the house, she remarked, "It's just as well my car won't be here. Jake had my keys on his ring, too, and he may well have left something in his glove compartment with our address on it." Realizing what she'd said, she gave me a stricken look. "Oh, Clara, they'll have his house keys, too. Why didn't we think of that before?"

"Don't worry," I told her a lot more firmly than I felt. "The doors both have chains, and I'll put chairs under the knobs. I'll be fine." I hoped it was true.

We flipped on more lights than two women needed, but it made us feel better. Then Glenna shut all the blinds and insisted that we hide the money right away. “We won’t want to fool with going by the bank in the morning, and I don’t want to be worried about it.”

Hiding money is a lot harder than it sounds. Every hiding place one of us found looked to the other like the first place any halfway intelligent burglar would look. Finally, I spied Glenna’s ironing basket under the sewing machine. Jake always jokes that putting something in that ironing basket is like flushing it down the toilet. In self-defense, he started ironing most of his own clothes the second year they were married. Mama was scandalized, but I was filled with admiration for Glenna.

In the bottom of the basket I found Jake’s old khaki fishing pants. Shoving the envelope down one leg, I crumpled the pants up a bit and shoved them under all the skirts, blouses, and tablecloths Glenna planned to get around to ironing one day.

When the phone rang, Glenna answered. “Hey, Joe Riddley! . . . Yes, he’ll have it first thing tomorrow morning. The doctor is real optimistic. . . . Aren’t you sweet! And Clara has been so much help to us.”

He asked a question, and because Glenna could not lie, she admitted, “Well, I’ve been there most of the day, but Clara was out a few times trying to track somebody down.”

I managed to pinch her before she told him the somebody was a missing child, but that bloodhound nose of his had already scented trouble.

“Put her on,” he growled. “Who were you trying to track down, Little Bit?”

“Just somebody whose things I found this morning, and wanted to return.”

“What kind of things?”

It was no use lying. He always could tell. “Papers and some money.”

He was onto me like a mosquito onto a bare midriff. "A check?"

"Well, no, it was cash." I frowned at Glenna, who smiled apologetically.

"How much?"

"Oh, three thousand dollars. Listen, honey, I need to say good-bye to Glenna before she leaves for the night."

It didn't work. He yelled so loud I had to hold the phone as far away as I could reach, and he was still clear as a bell. "You been carrying around three thousand dollars? After you'd already been robbed once? Of all the tomfool things! How long did it take you to find the owner?"

He'd find out eventually. "I haven't yet, but don't worry. I'm taking the money to her family tomorrow, and I've found a real good hiding place."

When I told him where it was, he snorted. "Well, Little Bit, let's just hope you don't get a burglar who needs fishing pants."

It was barely nine o'clock, but after Glenna left, I decided to go straight to bed. It seemed like a year since I'd arrived the night before. Had I really never heard of Harriet Lawson then?

Almost as soon as my head touched the pillow, I was asleep.

The brown-haired toddler clung to the gate and shook it with all her might, but the latch held firm. "Mommy! Mommy! Mommy!"

The slight figure on the sidewalk, little more than a child herself, scarcely checked her step. She wasn't going back. No way! No more diapers, no more sticky, messy feedings. No more crying all night.

She gave herself a shake of relief and determination and strode off down the hill, the child's wails propelling her faster and faster toward the bus stop. Reaching into her duffel bag, she put on earphones and tuned in her private music, loud. When the bus arrived, she climbed aboard without a backward look.

Still the brown-haired toddler clung to the gate. "Mommy! Mommy! Mommy!"

I woke gasping, bathed in sweat, my heart pounding so hard I both heard and felt it in my ears. The dream had been so real that the baby's wails still echoed in my head.

I knew I wouldn't go right back to sleep, so I turned on the bedside lamp and took out a mystery novel I'd bought to read during all those long free evenings I'd expected to have in Albuquerque. I hoped it wouldn't be too scary, for in spite of what I'd told Glenna, I felt just a tad uneasy.

Flipping on the radio, I twirled the dial until I found a classical station to wrap me in a cocoon of Chopin. I managed to concentrate pretty well. After I'd read a bit, though, I got hot. I'd forgotten to turn down the thermostat out in the hall.

Jake and Glenna are more concerned with conserving energy than with being comfortable, so in the summer they keep their air conditioner far too high. When I'm there, I often creep out at night to turn it back a few degrees so I can sleep. I usually put it back before they wake up. And if you think that's dirty, you need to know that at my house, Jake lowers the thermostat in winter. He's even been known to go home without turning it back up, so Joe Riddley and I go around for several days shivering and thinking we are coming down with something before we figure out what's the matter.

I was halfway across my room headed for the hall when, above the music, I heard a small crash. I froze and listened intently. It wasn't followed by anything. "Must have been an unbalanced dish in the drain," I told myself firmly, opening the bedroom door.

"Scritch, scritch, scritch." The noise was so soft I could almost be imagining it.

I drew back. If it was mice, they could carry away the entire kitchen so long as they didn't come my way.

Then the noise changed to a soft "chunk, chunk, chunk."

That must be a whopping big mouse.

Nobody has ever given me a medal for bravery, and I loathe stories in which a supposedly intelligent heroine walks straight into danger. I was certain, however, that we were being visited by a rodent of some kind. It seemed too slight for a burglar. Besides, Glenna and Jake have an open chimney, and from time to time squirrels fall down. I expected to find one feasting on tomato peelings in the wastebasket.

"It can't be a person," I reassured myself aloud. "This house has dead bolts and burglar bars, and I've wedged a chair under each outside doorknob. Nobody could get in."

The den was so dark, though, that I decided to take the longer way through the living and dining rooms, where streetlights glimmered through the windows. I was so busy creeping that I failed to notice a dining room chair Glenna had pulled out earlier to set her purse on. I ran straight into the chair, toppling it with a crash.

The noise stopped.

The sunporch door slammed.

Feet pounded down the empty drive.

I ran to a front window and pulled back the blind. A shadow ran parallel to the drive in the darker shadow of Jake's tall redtips. All I got was a glimpse when it reached the street. I wouldn't have been willing to swear, but under a dark cap, I thought his hair was white.

I turned on the kitchen light. What I saw made me collapse onto the telephone chair in a breathless heap.

Before Jake glassed in the porch, the back door and one window opened onto it. Instead of moving the back door, he only put a glass storm door to the outside, leaving both the door with the dead bolt and the window still opening into the kitchen. When Glenna—who was helping him by painting trim—accidentally painted the kitchen window shut, Jake assured her, "That's fine. We won't need to open that window anymore, anyway." When he added burglar bars to the house, because that window was so securely stuck and its panes were so small, he'd not bothered to put bars on it.

My recent intruder had pried open the sunporch door, found the back door dead bolted, and tried the window. He'd broken a pane to unlock it—that was the small crash I'd heard—then, when he found it stuck, tried to chip it open with a pair of scissors Glenna had conveniently left out there in a mending basket. He must have been jabbing at the seal with the closed scissors when I disturbed him.

I shook like a pompom at the Georgia-Florida game. "Dear God!" I whispered over and over. "Oh, dear God!"

If Ricky Dodd was the intruder, I'd certainly brought it on myself. "Bragging about having Harriet's money, and flat out insisting he take Jake's name and phone number," I scolded myself. "Anybody could get the address from the phone book. MacLaren Yarbrough, you're about as dumb as they come." As early as it still was, with no cars in the drive and no lights showing, he may well have concluded nobody was home.

With trembling fingers I dialed 911. When the operator answered, though, I just couldn't face another police interrogation that day. If the would-be burglar left prints, they weren't going anywhere before morning. "Never mind," I said. "It can wait." I didn't care what she thought.

I knew I'd never get back to sleep. At first I couldn't even make myself lie down. I was shivering so hard I finally wrapped up in an old wool afghan I found on my closet shelf, but it did little to warm me. The chill seeped out of my bones.

Finally, still wrapped in the afghan, I lay down and tugged both the sheet and the bedspread over me. A second later I sat straight up, horrified.

That broken pane was too small to get through, but it was just what anybody with a key would need. If the boys who stole Jake's car came calling now, they could reach through the hole, take off the chain, shove away the chair, unlock the door, and walk right in.

I went to the kitchen and put every pot and pan I could find on the seat of that chair and around its legs. That wouldn't keep anybody from moving it, but they'd make a heck of a racket if they did. I went back for the afghan and stretched out on Glenna's Duncan Phyfe living room sofa. If I couldn't sleep, I could at least lie down.

Thoroughly frightened and miserable, I waited for dawn.

A cheerful look brings joy to the heart, and good news gives health to the bones. *Proverbs 15:30*

Thirteen

The brown-haired child looked up the long length of him. "How long will you be gone, Daddy?"

"A while." He spoke uneasily. "My new job is far away. But Granny will look after you. Be a good girl, now. You hear me?"

"Will you be back for my birthday?"

"I don't know, honey, but you listen to what your granny tells you. I don't want her calling to say you've been bad. Okay?"

"Can't I come, too?" Her big brown eyes pleaded. He looked away.

"Sorry, honey. You'll be better off with Granny. 'Bye." He bent and gave her one rough, quick hug, then ran lightly down the steps. "Thanks, Ma," he called over one shoulder, "I'll make it up to you." He jumped into the shiny blue car. A woman with yellow hair was waiting with the motor running.

The brown-haired child ran to the gate and climbed onto the board at the bottom. She swung and watched, watched and swung, until his car was out of sight.

"Clara? Clara! Open the door! I can't get in!"

Glenna rattled the front door and called again. "Clara!" As I struggled up through the cobwebs of my dreams to let her in, memories of the night before landed on my chest in one heavy pounce. I staggered to the door to let in Glenna and the dawn.

She gave the afghan and the dented pillow on the couch a puzzled frown. "Why were you sleeping out here?"

"I had a bit of trouble last night. But first, how's Jake?"

"He's going down at eight, they said. I came back now so we can get a bite to eat and get right back over there. What kind of trouble?"

"I'll show you." As I led her to the kitchen, I peered at my watch. Half-past six. I couldn't brag that I was getting much more sleep in Montgomery than I had in Albuquerque.

When Glenna saw the broken window and heard what happened, she went white. "Oh, Clara, what if you hadn't heard him? You could have been killed—or worse!"

"Oh, I don't think he came to kill anybody," I said more briskly than I felt. "I think it was that awful Ricky after Harriet's money. He probably thought there was nobody home. We'll need to call the police sometime today—I was just too tired last night."

"I'll call Carter Duggins, my cousin. He's a policeman."

I should have known Glenna would have a cousin who was a policeman. She has so many cousins in that neck of the woods that Mama told Jake on his wedding day, "You be nice to everybody you meet in Montgomery County, Jacob, until you find out how they're related to Glenna."

While she called, I rummaged in her closet looking for something else I could wear, but a skinny five-nine and a pleasingly plump five-three can't share much. I finally put on a bright figured Sunday dress of my own, with a pleated skirt I always hope makes me look slimmer. As long as I was wearing the dress, I went ahead and put on the big red earrings and necklace and the red pumps I usually wear with it. If I looked like I was waiting for church school to start as soon as surgery was over, so be it.

"What did Carter say?" I asked as we sat down to breakfast in the dining room. Neither of us could stand to eat on the sunporch that morning.

"He promised to come over right away to check for fingerprints."

"But we've got to get to the hospital!"

Glenna nodded and placidly buttered toast. "I told him that. I said I'd leave him a key under the back doormat." I wondered if Montgomery police had a policy about using doormat keys to enter the scene of a burglary.

We stayed with Jake until he went down, then spent a while in the hospital chapel. I hoped her prayers were more coherent than mine. Whenever I tried to frame a sentence, it invariably came out *Please, God, please, God, please!* Finally Glenna rose and touched my hand. "That's all we can do. Let's go get a cup of coffee."

If you have spent a morning waiting for someone you love to come through surgery, I don't have to tell you about it. If you haven't, I won't. That's one experience there is no need to rehearse.

I read my mystery novel and drank so much coffee I was considering going down to the hospital kitchen to teach them how to make it. The novel was good so long as I could keep my eyes on the page. As soon as I looked up and remembered where I was, I had a hard time breathing.

Sometime that morning I remembered to call the acting school in Atlanta again. They'd never heard of Harriet Lawson and didn't think they had a fifteen-year-old there under another name, but would check their records and call me back.

They couldn't call me back. Jake and Glenna not only don't have a cordless phone, they don't have an answering machine. If you want to figure out what to give somebody for Christmas, live in their house a few days. I told the acting school I'd call back later.

After an eternity or two, the surgeon came looking for us, beaming from ear to ear. "All done and done good."

Glenna's gray eyes shone and her hands trembled with joy. "He's going to be all right?" I hadn't seen her look like that since her wedding day.

"I think he's going to be fine. His color and signs are real good. But he's going to be in recovery most of the afternoon, sleeping it off. Why don't you all go home and get some rest, then come on back this evening when he's awake?"

We left feeling like two women who'd been run over by a Mack truck, slung in a pit, then suddenly and miraculously healed, and shown a sunlit open door.

"I think I could fly to the car if I tried," I told Glenna.

"I think I could just fly on home." She flung her arms around me and nearly cracked my ribs. "Oh, Clara, he's going to be all right! He's going to be all right."

At the house, we found a solemn little man in gray coveralls calmly reglazing the back window. "Officer Duggins called me," he told us. "Told me to fix this window and your back door and change all your locks."

Glenna thanked him, fixed all of us a glass of tea, and started making bread. "Sit down and rest," I urged her.

"I couldn't sit still right now, Clara. I feel like going dancing or something." She waltzed across her kitchen floor. Glenna? Waltzing? My baby brother must have more to him than I ever suspected.

After the man left, we had a bite to eat and stretched out for a while. I soon heard Glenna moving about in her room. "I can't rest," she protested. If it had been Joe Riddley, I would have felt the same.

"How about if we go to Western Union to get the money Joe Riddley is supposed to have sent me," I suggested, "then go to the mall and get me something to wear?"

"Oh, honey, let's do! I might buy a celebration dress of my own."

Joe Riddley had been more generous than I'd ever expected. I bought two skirts, three tops, a casual navy pantsuit, and a pair of navy flats with a pocketbook to match. Glenna splurged and bought not one but two very pretty dresses. "Even when you don't like shopping — and heaven knows I don't," I told her as we loaded our bags into the trunk, "it sure does occupy your mind."

But as soon as Glenna started the engine, she confessed, "I keep wanting to go on back over to the hospital, Clara. I know he's sleeping, but I'd like to be there."

"Why don't you go, then? If you'll give me a list, I'll stay home and call people to report on Jake. I can also answer the phone, do a load or two of wash, and maybe even hit your famous ironing basket. Come back to supper — I'll fix us a terrific Ain't-God-Wonderful dinner."

She'd barely left when the phone rang. The caller was male and sounded too young to be a police officer. He started out like the family member he is. "Cuddin' Glenna? It's Carter."

"Hello, Carter. This is MacLaren, Jake's sister. Glenna's at the hospital — "

"Hey, Miss MacLaren! Jake's told me a lot about you. How's he doing?"

I didn't waste time asking what Jake had told him. Jake's opinion of my occasional involvement in little problems around Hopemore has never been high, and he'd probably told Carter all about them. "He's doing real well, so far, but keep him in your prayers."

"Yessum, I sure will. Listen, give Glenna a message for me. Tell her we dusted the windowsill for prints, but whoever it was didn't leave any. I called a glazier—"

"He's come and gone. Thanks, Carter. You didn't find any shoe prints beside the drive, did you?"

"No, ma'am. Why do you ask?"

"Because I saw the man run down the driveway."

"You *saw* the perpetrator? Why the dickens didn't you call the police right then?"

I sighed. "It's a long story. For one thing, I was worn out, and I thought I recognized him. If so, I know where to find him if he left any prints."

"We didn't find any prints at all. Sorry. But we got some blood smears where he cut himself, so if you'll tell me where to find him, we can try for a match."

I gave him Ricky's name and where he lived, then added, "Carter, could you do me two big favors?"

"Why, yes, ma'am, if I can. What do you need?"

"First, I drove Jake's car yesterday without his permission, and it got stolen."

"Whooee! You are in big trouble."

"Not yet. Jake doesn't know. But I'm not sure the people down at the police station appreciate how much danger I'll be in if that car isn't back before he gets home. If you have any pull, could you stir them up a little?"

"It's not my department, and I don't have any pull at all, but I'll try. What else?"

"Could you look through the records for the past six weeks to see if an unidentified fifteen-year-old female has been found anywhere in the Montgomery area—either dead or injured? A woman I was talking to has a niece missing, but her husband is a stubborn old Bama grad who refuses to file a missing persons report. She's real worried." He sounded like the nice kind of young man who would not refuse a woman in distress.

"I can look, ma'am, but it may take awhile. We're pretty swamped right now. The family really needs to file a missing persons report, you know."

"You find somebody, and they will," I promised grimly.

By the end of that afternoon, I was prowling the house as restless as a cat in a carrier. I called the acting school in Atlanta and got the news I'd expected: Harriet was not and had never been there. I tried to call Dee to see if I could come out in a day or two to take her the money, but nobody answered. I couldn't read or find anything worth watching on TV, and it was too hot for a walk. I had just decided to call Lewis Henly to see if he'd learned anything from the girls at the center, when Josheba called me. "How's your brother doing?"

When I told her, she heaved a huge sigh of relief. "That's good. I tell you, Mac, all I've been able to think about all day was your brother's surgery and Harriet." She paused, then asked, "Did you call that place in Atlanta?"

"Yes. She isn't there. I've also asked the police to check for bodies or accident victims." That meant I had to tell her about the break-in, as well.

"Ricky!" Josheba exclaimed before I was halfway through.

"I think so, too. I just hope he won't try again."

"You need a gun, lady."

Her concern warmed me. I couldn't remember the last time I'd taken to someone as quickly as I had Josheba—which was odd, considering I'd never had a black friend (as opposed to acquaintance) before. However, I couldn't agree to her suggestion.

"Not on your life, Josheba. I'd rather face my Maker having been shot than having shot somebody else. Besides, I'd probably wind up shooting myself. The police have promised to request a patrol on the street for the next few days, though, and sent a man by to fix the damage and change our locks."

"Got any more ideas what we can do about Harriet?"

"I've decided to take the money out to her aunt's and let them worry about her. I don't have time to look for her right now. The only thing I thought I'd do first was call Lewis to see if the girls knew anything."

"I already called him," Josheba admitted a bit sheepishly. "He said Kateisha didn't show up today, and none of the other kids remember the last time they saw Harriet. One thought Harriet might have gone to see her mother."

"That's the third time we've heard that. I wonder if her other aunt—her mother's sister—would know?" I closed my eyes and tried to hear Nora saying the name the day before. "Eunice Crawley. She lives up in Chisholm. I think I'll give her a call."

We both searched our phone books, but neither of us could find her.

"Why don't I run by the library and get her address from the city directory?" Josheba offered. "Then, if you have time, we could drive up there."

I checked my watch. It was half past four. Glenna wasn't coming home until seven, and Eunice Crawley would probably be home from work by the time we got there.

"If you're working on a sainthood merit badge," I agreed.

A truthful witness gives honest testimony, but a false witness tells lies. *Proverbs 12:17*

Fourteen

This is Josheba again. Mac says I was so clever that afternoon, I get to tell about it.

I'd barely hung up from talking to her when the phone rang again. "Who you been yakkin' with, doll-baby?" Morse asked as soon as I'd answered. "I tried you three times."

"Just talking to Mac," I said without thinking.

"Who's he?" he demanded suspiciously.

"She. The woman I took home yesterday." Morse always wanted to know everything I did and everybody I talked with. When we first started dating, he just wrapped me up in concern and reminded me of Mama, always asking questions about my life. Today I felt a bit smothered. I didn't want to explain what Mac and I were up to, so I asked quickly, "How's the river?"

"Wet. It's dumped rain ever since we got here, and there's so much lightning, they won't let us out in the rafts. All day we've done nothing but sit around."

Of course, that's not exactly the way he really said it. I mentioned earlier, Morse grew up rough. His language still is. When he talked, I automatically deleted his obscenities. Having grown up in a preacher's house, I figured obscenity was something you got used to in other men.

Sit around drinking beer, I thought. I could tell that from his tone.

"I'm so sorry, honey," I told him. "Maybe it will clear up tonight."

"It better, or I'll — Josheba, why don't you cut classes these next couple of days and drive up here tonight?"

"It's tempting, Morse. but I've worked too hard this semester to throw it away. I've got an exam and a paper due Friday. If it keeps raining, why don't you come on back home?"

"Because this is my vacation. You work too hard, baby, and neglect old Morse. Can't iron my shirts. Can't come when I need you. What good's all that education going to do — "

There was no reasoning with him when he was drunk. I murmured a few sweet, soothing things and sent him back to his buddies. I needed to get on the road.

I picked Mac up and we drove to Chisholm in rush-hour traffic. "Harriet's other aunt," as Mac and I had started calling her, lived in a small frame house covered with green vinyl siding in a block that looked like some folks had lived there a long time. Several houses had the kind of additions people put on for themselves, and the yards were a hodgepodge — some carefully planted and some utterly neglected. Eunice Crawley's yard didn't have a single tree or bush except the kind with round blue flowers on each side of the bottom step. After I pulled up to the curb, Mac just sat. I wondered if she'd fallen asleep in the last block or two. "You ready to go, Mac?" I asked.

She gave a start, like she'd just remembered I was there. "Sure. I was just looking at Eunice Crawley's yard. She's got a bad case of chinch bug, and needs to prune those hydrangeas. They're getting leggy. We're in the nursery business, you know," she added.

"I didn't, but anybody seeing you go all googly-eyed over a bad case of chinch bug might have guessed." I reached for my door handle. "Welcome to Chisholm, where pickups and motorcycles outnumber people two to one." We climbed out into God's own blast furnace. "I sure hope Eunice Crawley has an air conditioner."

Mac paused to listen. "She does. I can hear it whirring around the corner."

This was a neighborhood of small houses with wide porches. Eunice's porch had two white rockers with faded yellow print cushions, and they looked like they'd had a heap of sitting in their day. Twenty years ago, every porch on the street would have been full at that time of the afternoon, but not a person was in sight. "Some people blame TV for the rise in crime in America," Mac told me as we climbed the steep porch steps, "but I lay a lot of blame on air conditioning. People on porches keep neighborhoods safe."

"Run for office on that platform," I suggested, "but not in July." I gave the bell a good solid push.

The woman who came to the door was probably forty-five years old and forty-five pounds overweight. She must have just come home from work and started to get comfortable, because her brown hair was still neatly tied at the nape of her neck with a smart navy bow and her eyes were still ringed with mascara, but she was barefoot, bare legged, and wearing a zip-front, sleeveless cotton shift in peach and peacock blue.

She waited for us to speak first. Mac obliged. "Ms. Crawley? I'm MacLaren Yarbrough and this is Josheba Davidson. We're trying to find Harriet Lawson."

The woman stepped back and started to shut the door. "You have the wrong address. Harriet lives with William and Dixie Sykes, out in McGehee Estates."

"I've spoken with them." Mac put one hand on the door to ask her nicely not to shut it in our faces. "They said she left home several weeks ago, and they aren't sure where she is."

Eunice Crawley looked at her blankly for a second, then shook her head. "I haven't seen Harriet for some time now."

"We're getting worried about her," I told her frankly.

Eunice hesitated a second, then seemed to come to some decision. "Well, why don't you all come in? It's too hot to stand out here, and I've just made a fresh pitcher of tea."

Some people have closets as big as Eunice's living room, but most closets don't have white walls, white woodwork, a white carpet, white blinds (pulled down), and white lace valances. Even the slipcovers on the love seat and fat armchair were white. A beveled glass coffee table sat like an iceberg on brass legs, and instead of pictures there were three mirrors in white frames. The woman didn't even have colored knickknacks on her mantle piece. She had glass candlesticks with white candles. Vanilla candles. I could smell them from the door.

The only color in the whole room was provided by a big blue and white needlepoint pillow showing a polar bear, propped in the middle of the love seat, and a soft gray Persian crouched on one end.

Eunice looked around her room with pride. "White makes everything seem bigger and cooler, don't it?" Her air conditioner was doing its fair share, too. I felt like I'd blundered into a refrigerator. "Sit down and let me get you some tea. You! Clear off that sofa!"

For one startled moment, I thought she was talking to us, but the cat stretched like he was bored to death, rose, and stalked out, tail a-plume. "Sit down, now. Sit down!" Our hostess patted the air with one plump hand to show that the last command was for us, then bustled into her kitchen without waiting to see if we obeyed.

Mac chose the love seat, disregarding the very good chance that her navy pantsuit would get covered with cat hair. I perched on the front of the armchair.

"Like I said before, I haven't seen Harriet in a coon's age," Eunice called breathlessly from the kitchen, "but she used to be in and out of this house all the time. She's just like my own, practically."

"Have you seen her since school was out?" Mac called back.

"No, not since her granny's funeral the end of April."

The cat came back, brushed against my leg, and stayed to lean, purring. I reached down and scratched him between the ears. Eunice returned with a tray. "Why don't you all come in to the dining room where we can be more comfortable?"

We obeyed, although four chairs, a table, a small corner hutch, and a life-sized picture of Hank Williams filled the room without us. Eunice spread a white cloth over the table, then went back for a tray with wavy green glasses of iced tea and a clear bowl of freshly cut lemon. "You like Hank?" she asked, handing out white paper napkins. "He's my love. I go up to the cemetery once in a while to talk to him. Now just let me get the cookies." She spoke in the breathless voice of an overweight woman who has hurried. I felt a catch in my throat. Mama used to sound like that sometimes.

I'd never eaten in a white person's house before, and wondered if she would have gone to all that trouble for just Mac or if she was showing off for me. From the sharp little looks she kept giving me, I suspected she was showing off. I gave her a big smile to show her I appreciated her thoughtfulness. Finally she set down a green flowered plate of Oreo cookies and squeezed herself into the chair nearest the kitchen door. "Now, what is it you're wanting with Harriet? And how do you know her?"

Mac nodded for me to begin. "I work at a library where Harriet used to come almost every week," I explained, "but she hasn't been in for quite a while. Then yesterday—"

Mac gave me a startled look. "Was it really only yesterday? It seems like a year."

I nodded. "I know. Anyway," I continued to Eunice, "Mac here was volunteering yesterday at a teen center where Harriet used to go, and the girls there said they haven't seen Harriet all summer."

"She left some things at the center," Mac picked up the story, "including a library book. That's how I met Josheba. When I took the other things out to her guardian—"

"Dixie Sykes—or Dee, I think she's calling herself now." Eunice nodded and reached for a handful of cookies. "I was just ahead of her and her brother Frank in school."

"Harriet's dad?" Mac asked.

"Yeah. He married my baby sister Myrna before she ever finished school. He was a lot older'n her, of course, and working. They had Harriet that next year." She shook her head like she was answering a silent question. "I haven't seen Dixie in years. Since she married money, I figured Harriet was sittin' pretty in that big fancy house." She looked around and sighed. "I'd have loved to have her here, of course, but I work all day."

My eyes met Mac's. Would a woman with a white living room really want a teenager? Eunice was antsy enough watching grown women drink tea and eat Oreos over her white tablecloth. Any crumbs that strayed from our napkins were immediately swept into her wide palm and brushed back onto the cookie plate.

"Harriet hasn't been at the Sykes's since early June," Mac said, taking another cookie. "They thought she was staying with a friend, but he hasn't seen Harriet since school was out."

"He? A boyfriend?" Eunice asked suspiciously.

"No, a foster child her grandmother kept. A brother, like."

I jumped in again. "The only other idea we have is that several people said they thought Harriet might have gone to stay with her mother."

When I was growing up, neighborhood children used to play a game called "Statues." Somebody would swing the others hard, then let go. You were supposed to freeze like you landed. Eunice Crawley froze just like a statue as soon as I said, "stay with her mother." Then she gave her head an emphatic shake. "Her mother? Why would they think that? Harriet hasn't seen her mother since she was a baby."

"Somebody thought Harriet had a letter from her," Mac explained.

A funny look crossed Eunice's face. "I doubt it. Myrna's not much of a writer." She pushed herself to her feet and began collecting the napkins and the cookie plate. "I haven't heard from Myrna lately myself."

I stuck out one toe and nudged Mac's leg, hoping she could read my mind: *Give me a minute or two.* "Could I use your bathroom?" I asked in what I hoped was an apologetic tone.

"Right through there." Eunice waved me toward a hall that led to bedrooms, as well.

Mac, bless her heart, picked up the three glasses and headed toward the kitchen.

"If you do hear from Harriet, would you tell her to please call Dee?" I heard her ask Eunice over the sound of running water. I appreciated her making all that noise.

I hurried with what I wanted to do, then gave the toilet a noisy flush and joined the others. It took all the willpower I had to give Eunice Crawley a grateful smile and say casually, "Thank you very much. Ready to go, Mac?"

Mac seemed in no hurry whatsoever to leave. When I headed to the car, she was giving Eunice her brother's phone number and asking her to call if she heard from Harriet.

As soon as she got in the car I pulled away and drove down a couple of blocks. Then I pulled over to the side of the road and stopped. "Mac, that woman reminded me so much of my cousin Stella that when she wouldn't look at us while she was saying she hadn't gotten a letter lately from Harriet's mom, I just knew she was lying. Stella always tucks letters into the frame of her mirror, so I thought I'd take a look. Sure enough—look!" I thrust an old charge receipt at her—the only thing I'd had to write on. "I scribbled down everything except her bad spelling. Read it, and tell me why that woman lied to us!"

> May 10
> Dear Eunice,
>
> Guess who I ran into? I can't tell, because I promised, but you'd be surprised. That's how I heard both Frank and Granny are dead. Good riddance to one, and the other was an old busy body, but sounds like she stood by Harriet. I think I should come see her. Maybe we could even move in together. But don't tell her anything. I'll write myself. I don't know when I can come, but sometime this summer. Don't be surprised when I give you a call and say Here I am! Love and kisses. Myrna.

"Harriet must be with her mother!" I told Mac as we headed downtown. "And from what I've seen of her at the library, if she had a letter saying to come to her mother's, she'd just go, and deal with hassles later. Harriet doesn't take anything off anybody, but she avoids conflict if she can."

"And the money?"

"Stashed in what she felt was a safe place until she got back. For the first time in several weeks, Mac, I feel okay—" An enormous peal of thunder cut me off.

Mac peered out her window and pointed. "Looks like we're going to get a terrific storm from the north. Jake's garden sure could use some rain."

I was making a tricky left turn, so I only gave the clouds a quick glance. "Morse called today and said they've had nothing *but* rain up in the mountains."

"That must have been unpleasant when he wanted to be on the river."

"Unpleasant is certainly the operative word." I carefully edged over a lane. "He's grumpier than Snow White's dwarf. How long've you been married, Mac?"

"Forty-four years this fall."

"Does marriage take a lot of adjusting?" As soon as I'd asked it, I half wished I hadn't. It felt real disloyal to Morse. But lately there were some things about him that made me feel—well, smaller. Like I was being swallowed up in Morse's opinions and Morse's preferences. Mac didn't act the least bit swallowed up in anybody. I wondered how her marriage worked.

She answered without looking at me, as if fascinated by those roiling clouds. "You have to learn to let the other person be who he is, but that takes a lot less adjusting if you like who he is in the first place. Then piddly annoyances stay small. Joe Riddley leaves dirty socks on the floor by our bed, for instance, and I can track him by his trail of dirty glasses, but he's so fine and honest and sweet—and he puts up with so much in me—that socks and glasses don't matter much. I'm real fond of the old coot."

"So you think it's important to admire and respect the person you marry," I translated carefully, thinking of some of the things I admired and respected in Morse. He was a good coach to the boys (*except when they lose*, a stupid little voice whispered), he paid me a lot of attention (*he eats up your life,* nagged that little voice), and he loved me.

Meanwhile, Mac was chuckling. "Admire and respect? Oh, I admire and respect Joe Riddley, but mostly I just downright *like* him."

"You're fortunate," I said softly, wistfully hoping I'd like Morse that much after forty-four years. I thought the conversation was over.

However—"I didn't get Joe Riddley in a lottery, Josheba, I *picked* him!" she said hotly. "Pick somebody you like, and you'll enjoy living with him." She flushed. "I'm sorry. I didn't mean to get so het up. But I need to confess something. Yesterday when I was going back to my room from washing up, I overheard Morse fussing at you about something. Your door was open a little, and he—"

"He was certainly yelling loud enough to be heard." I felt as embarrassed as she looked. "But the truth is, I'd let his very favorite shirt get wrinkled because I hadn't done what he told me to—take it straight from the dryer. It was all my fault. And Morse has been under a lot of pressure lately—"

"No matter what you had done or how much pressure he's been under, honey, he ought not yell at you like that—and you oughtn't to let him. Has he ever hit you?"

"Of course not!" I said indignantly.

She gave an embarrassed little laugh. "Good. And I can just hear Joe Riddley right now: 'Stick to your own business, MacLaren. The woman knows her own mind.'" She checked her watch. "I hope we can get me home fast. I promised Glenna a fantastic supper, and I haven't even decided what to have." We talked recipes the rest of the way home.

After leaving Mac at her brother's, I decided to swing by the teen center. Lewis Henly deserved a report on Mac's break-in and our visit to Eunice Crawley. Besides, maybe now that he knew one of the librarians personally, he might be open to a summer reading program for the kids.

He sat at his desk, munching peanut-butter crackers and swigging them down with grape cola. "Hot-shot executive meal?" I asked, raising one eyebrow. "Your roomful of secretaries said to come on in."

He raised one eyebrow right back. "And I told them not to let anybody in except potential donors."

"I could donate some time, if you'd let me start a reading program around here."

"Josheba, these kids don't want to read. They get reading at school. Next year I want to start a dynamite tutoring program, but I don't want to drive them away this first summer. They want to read, they can come to your library." He paused. "That what you came for?"

"No. I came to tell you I just spent the afternoon with Mac. Somebody tried to break in to her house last night."

"No kidding! Was she hurt?"

"No, she scared them away, but she thinks it was Ricky. She figures he was looking for Harriet's money."

"Good thing she put it in the bank, then. Want a cracker?"

"No thanks. I also wanted to tell you that Mac and I just visited Harriet's mother's sister. Harriet may have gone to visit her mother."

"Whoop-de-doo." He twirled one finger in the air. Seeing my face, he looked ashamed of himself—as he ought to. "I really do hope she's okay, Josheba, but Harriet was such a pain around here, and things are so much more peaceful without her riling people up, that I can't help being glad she's found somewhere else to spend her summer." He stood up. "Speaking about spending time, how about coming out to dinner? I thought all I was going to get was crackers, but if you feel like sharing a pizza, I sure would like to get away for an hour or so. Have to be back later for a basketball game."

I started to refuse, of course. Morse would throw a fit if he heard I'd had dinner with another man. "I don't really think—"

Lewis cut me off with one upraised hand. "Not a date. I dropped by the library this afternoon, and they informed me that their Ms. Davidson is engaged to be married to a handsome hunk—I quote—at Christmas. But since you didn't immediately say 'I have a date,' I assume you don't—at least for dinner. Does your engagement mean you can't even go to dinner with friends?"

Put that way, it sounded not only harmless, but like an excellent idea. Truth to tell, since I started dating Morse, I hadn't even been out with *girl*friends much. He liked me to stick close. I hated to admit how much I was enjoying some time to myself that week.

I'd have felt more virtuous, though, if Lewis Henly weren't so attractive. In a black turtleneck and slacks, he looked like a young priest.

"Hey," I asked, suddenly suspicious, "you aren't a preacher in disguise, are you? I don't even go to *dinner* with preachers."

He shook his head. "Used to be a lawyer, until last year. What you got against preachers?" He took my arm and led me toward the door.

"I drive," I informed him. "I've got a real liking for air conditioning. And how about if we go to Sinclair's instead of for pizza? I feel like a salmon salad."

"You don't look like a salmon salad, sister, but if you're driving, you drive where you want to go. Now, what is it you've got against preachers?"

I waited until we were on the road before I told him. "What I've got against preachers is, my daddy was one, before it got him killed."

He'd been fiddling with the radio, but he stopped and stared. "Henry Davidson? Used to go around with Martin Luther King?"

"Yeah, before I was born. Dr. King was shot before I made the scene. Daddy got shot when I was nine. Only difference is, Daddy didn't get statues and streets named after him."

"But he was a fine man." Lewis looked at me like he thought I was suddenly somebody, and said in this wondering voice, "I'm going out to eat with Henry Davidson's daughter. Think of that. You know what? You and I are old friends, Josheba. When I was a little boy, my granny used to go to your daddy's church. When we came to visit her, I used to see you sitting on the front seat in hair bows and frilly skirts. Your daddy was the first preacher I ever really listened to. Man, could he preach!"

"Yeah." I always hate it when people talk about Daddy, because mostly what I remember about him is how he died. "Look," I told Lewis, "if we're gonna talk about Daddy all night, I don't want to go. All right?"

"Sure. Whatever you say. No Daddy and no Harriet Lawson. I can handle that."

We had a terrific time. Sinclair's is a little restaurant somebody made out of an old Sinclair gas station. It's decorated in black and white, and has all these old photographs hanging on the walls. The food is delicious, too.

That night, though, I hardly noticed what I ate. Lewis talked about his days as what he called a "hotshot lawyer with more money than sense," and got me laughing so hard at some of his cases that I nearly wet my pants. I told him a little bit about working in the library and some of the funny things kids say, and he laughed so much he spilled his wine.

After dinner, we split a Bananas Sinclair — bananas, ice cream, brown sugar, butter, rum — oh, it was grand! By the time we'd scooped up all the runny parts from the bowl, I felt like I'd known that brother all my life.

It wasn't romantic or anything. He didn't touch me the entire meal, not even hold my elbow as we left the restaurant. But you know, it just felt good to walk beside him and know we were breathing the same air—together, yet our own selves.

When we got back to the center, he climbed out quickly. "The basketball team's gonna wonder where I am. Thanks!" He hurried inside.

I drove home slowly, savoring the whole evening. I wouldn't trade Morse in for Lewis, of course, but Lordy, how that man could talk!

I refused to think about the way my pulse reacted to his last smile.

As twisting the nose produces blood,
so stirring up anger produces strife.
Proverbs 30:33

Fifteen

While Josheba was having fun with Lewis, I—MacLaren—was fixing supper and calling Dee to report on our trip to Eunice's. When I told her there seemed to be a good chance Harriet was with her mother, Dee was bewildered. "Her mother? She hasn't seen her mother since she was two."

"Several people say Harriet's heard from her lately, though." I didn't add that I suspected Harriet's legacy might have had something to do with her mother's change of heart.

Instead, I asked when I could bring "a few things of Harriet's" over, and she suggested Friday morning. I couldn't bring myself to tell her that the things were hundred dollar bills.

I was feeling curiously deflated. Maybe it was a reaction to how over-the-moon I'd felt right after Jake's surgery.

I was certainly concerned about Josheba—that young man of hers worried me. But mostly I was feeling pretty low about not having found Harriet and having to give up the search in the middle. I've never liked leaving jobs half done, and it nearly killed me to realize it was entirely possible that I would never know if Myrna came, if Harriet was found, even if Harriet was still alive.

That evening I visited with Jake a few minutes, but he was too drowsy to care if I was there or not. I returned to the waiting room to find Glenna talking with a tall woman with iron gray hair swept back into a soft twist. Her skin was so thin, and her eyes so large and dark, that when I first saw her, all I saw was eyes. From the way she curved over an ebony cane, I suspected she was on the upper side of eighty.

Glenna welcomed me with a happy smile. "MacLaren, honey, I want you to meet my good friend, Lou Ella Sykes. Lou Ella, this is Jake's sister." The woman wore a soft blue cotton dress embroidered all up the front. It had probably cost about half as much as I'd spent on my entire shopping spree, and the pearl earrings she wore with it were the size of gumballs. I was so busy admiring her outfit that I scarcely heard Glenna tell her, "I think you're the only member of your family MacLaren hasn't met in the two days she's been here."

Her big dark eyes bored into mine. "Really? Why is that?" The woman's voice was musical, with a hint of somewhere other than Alabama.

"She's been looking for Dee's niece, Harriet," Glenna told her.

"Oh?" Lou Ella drew down her fine silver brows. "Why?"

"She's missing," I said.

"Missing?" She flapped one hand in dismissal. "Oh, pshaw. She's probably just gone off again. It's not the first time."

I shook my head. "No, but this time she's not with Ricky Dodd, like she was before."

Lou Ella was astonished. "How on earth do you know?"

"I went out there looking for her. She's not with her mother's sister Eunice, either."

"No, I don't suppose she would go there. Harriet's never had much to do with that side of her family." Remembering what Eunice had said about Harriet running in and out of her house all the time, and that Harriet might at this minute be with her mother, I figured Lou Ella didn't know as much as she thought she did about the girl.

Then Lou Ella surprised me. I'd have expected her to sympathize with Dee and William. Instead, she said, "Poor Harriet, she's had a hard time with William and Dee. She's been used to a lot of freedom, and they treat her the same way they do Julie, who has been much more delicately reared. I keep telling them that Harriet has to find her own way. Both her mother and her father had wanderlust in their blood. She's got it too. If I were them, I'd let her have her head a bit more. As for running away, I wouldn't give it another thought. Perhaps a few days on her own won't do her any harm."

"She's been gone six weeks," Glenna told her gently.

"Six weeks?" Clearly shocked, Lou Ella's long fingers seemed to wring the neck of the silver duck at the top on her cane. She turned back to me. "Are you sure?"

I nodded.

"I had no idea," she murmured. "And they haven't reported her missing?" Her voice dropped as if she were talking to herself. "Of course they haven't. I would have heard."

"William refuses to report her missing," I told William's grandmother frankly, "and unless he does, I don't think the police will do a thing."

Lou Ella's eyes grew even bigger and darker with worry. "I suppose — " she began, then shook her head. "No, it's unforgivable. Somebody ought to have looked for her."

"The thing I find the hardest to understand," Glenna told her, "is that nobody, absolutely nobody, seems to remember the last time they saw her. It's as if she has vanished from the face of the earth."

The old woman quivered with indignation. "Then we must find her." Her face wore a stricken look. "Not one of us ever gave that child a second thought. Now, I'm very much afraid we are going to have to answer for it."

Glenna decided to sleep in her own bed that night. On our way home, the storm broke over us like an egg. Long jagged lightning brightened the sky through a perfect deluge. We hadn't taken umbrellas, of course, so we were soaked between the car and the house. We dashed inside and dried off, then Glenna went straight to bed.

I was still reading when the telephone rang. I leaped from my bed and hurried through the dark house to answer it in the kitchen before it woke her. It was probably Joe Riddley again, or somebody from the church. Hopefully it wasn't another volunteer opportunity Jake had kindly left me.

"Crane residence," I said softly. "This is MacLaren, Jake's sister."

Lightning flashed. Thunder rolled. A loud whisper hissed through the receiver to fill my ear: *You'll never find Harriet Lawson. Harriet Lawson is dead!*

> I applied my heart to what I observed
> and learned a lesson from what I saw.
> *Proverbs 24:32*

Sixteen

The brown-haired child looked up from a smeared, torn paper. "Granny, I can't do this math! Come help me."

The voice from the kitchen was weary and short. "I don't know nothin' about math, girl, and I got things to do. Ask your teacher to help you. That's what they're there for."

The teacher towered over her desk. "No homework again? And you've failed another test. If this keeps up, I will have to call your parents. Put away that book and pay attention." She moved on down the row of desks, stopping to rest one hand on a boy's shoulder. "Good work. Another perfect paper."

He turned his head and gave the brown-haired child a satisfied smirk. She glowered and returned to her novel. Nobody saw the tear she wiped off her cheek.

"No!" I moaned. "No! Help her! Help her!" I woke to find my lips still mouthing the words. When I looked at the clock, it was only half past two. A heck of a lot of night still to get through.

I got up and padded into the bathroom for a drink of water. In the lavatory mirror I saw the big dark eyes of the child in my dream. Now I recognized her face. It belonged to my older granddaughter.

I sank onto the toilet with a groan. What if it *were* my granddaughter who was missing? We'd have turned over heaven and earth by now. Would nobody turn over even one clod of dirt for poor Harriet?

Clod of dirt.

Grave.

I remembered the phone call. Had that been a dream, too?

No. I could still hear that loud, hissing whisper, then a click.

I hadn't been really frightened. The thunder and lightning effects outside the window made it seem more theatrical than scary. But who would make such a call? Why?

"Maybe Ricky?" Josheba suggested when I called her early Thursday morning. I felt like I'd burst if I didn't tell somebody, and I didn't like to tell Glenna. I think I woke Josheba up, but I didn't even apologize.

"I thought of Julie, myself," I told her. "She's down at Gulf Shores all week with a friend, but kids these days think nothing of using long distance. And my favorite suspect is William. Especially if his grandmother called him after I met her in the hospital last night. She was appalled that he hasn't reported that child missing before now."

"Then he could well be trying to scare you off," Josheba agreed. "Or maybe Eunice was more upset by our visit than she seemed."

We weren't saying anything I hadn't already thought. In the dark kitchen after the call, I'd come up with good reasons why the caller could have been anybody I'd talked to so far.

"Why would anyone bother? That's the big question, Mac."

"It's not the biggest one, Josheba. Do you think Harriet is truly dead?"

"The only question I have," Lewis Henly said later that morning, "is why you and Josheba can't leave poor Harriet alone."

I called the teen center from the hospital while they were moving Jake from intensive care to a real room. I wanted to tell Lewis about the call to see what he'd say.

What he said was, "I don't for a minute believe she's dead. In fact, if she heard you were looking for her, she could well have made that call herself."

"Looks to me like if she heard somebody was looking for her, she'd have showed up at the center to get her money back," I argued.

"Don't get too hung up on the money thing, Mac. Kids around here shed belongings like a snake sheds skin. I've known a kid to leave every stitch of clothing he owned, including a brand-new leather jacket, lying in the bathroom at an interstate rest stop because somebody offered him a ride he didn't want to lose. With these kids, it's easy come, easy go. Harriet will come back for the money if she needs it. Meanwhile, she's just gone."

"You don't sound very sorry." As soon as the words were out, I regretted them.

He didn't sound offended, though. "I'm not very sorry, Mac. Harriet can be a royal pain in the *be*-hind. She loves finding out things about people, and if she finds out anything about you that isn't perfectly up-and-up, heaven help you after that."

I wasn't sure I understood. "You mean she tries to blackmail people?"

Lewis barked a short laugh. "Not tries to, does. Look, you may as well have the whole picture. One of the guys at the club got into trouble some years back. He's clean now, but Harriet found out about it. She sidled up to him one day and asked for Coke money. When he refused, she asked, 'Do they know about you around here?' and told him enough to convince him she could blow his cover real good. He went numb and handed her money without thinking. Next thing he knew, she was coming after him for money on a regular basis."

"What did you do?"

"What did I *do*? What *could* I do?"

"You could tell her to stop bothering him, couldn't you?"

"Sure—and I did, once I found out about it. I even paid her a little bit to answer the phone after school. I felt sorry for her. Heck, I know what it's like to be short of cash. But don't go painting a picture of Saint Harriet in your mind. Saintly she isn't."

This opened all sorts of possibilities, though. "If she operated like that around the club, she may have tried the same thing with other people. Ricky Dodd, for instance."

"He'd have wrung her neck before giving her a penny."

"Okay, not Ricky, and not Dee, probably, but maybe William? Or Julie? Maybe somebody got tired of it, or—"

Lewis interrupted in exasperation. "Look, Mac, the girl hasn't turned up dead. Even if a dozen people wanted to murder her, nobody has. Can't you get that through your head?"

"No, because something's wrong, Lewis. Penniless fifteen-year-olds don't disappear leaving three thousand dollars behind. I hear what you're saying about kids being careless about possessions, but not money, Lewis—surely not money."

"This one was. And if you want the honest truth, my center is a pleasanter place this summer without her. I suspect the Sykes house is, too. So if she ever does come back, the only two people singing the 'Hallelujah Chorus' will be you and Josheba." He must have realized he'd climbed up on his high horse, because he added in a gentler tone, "You've got plenty of other things to do with your time in Montgomery, Mac. The only question I have is, why can't you and Josheba just leave poor Harriet alone?"

"I can't, Lewis. I started all this because it was a puzzle, but it's not a puzzle any longer. It's a child. I never saw her, but I dream about her. She has my granddaughter's face. This week has showed me how much I care for Jake. I keep thinking somebody ought to care about Harriet like that. Until we find her, I can't forget her—and neither should you."

He gave another short laugh. "What you really mean is, 'I can't forget her, so neither *will* you,' isn't it, Mac? You and Josheba are gonna make sure of that, aren't you?"

"Probably so," I admitted cheerfully. "I keep thinking *Just one more person and we'll find her*. Well, I have another person I want to talk to. The other day Kateisha mentioned somebody named Ms. Scott who might know something. If Kateisha comes in today, will you ask her how to find Ms. Scott?"

He laughed, and finally he sounded amused. "You and Josheba are two hearts that beat as one. She's already bugged me this morning about Ms. Scott. I'll talk to Kateisha. Call me back after lunch, and I'll tell you what she says."

I called back while Jake took his afternoon nap. "All Kateisha would say is that Ms. Scott was a friend of Harriet's grandmother," he told me.

I was already looking up Scotts in the telephone book—which I kicked myself for not doing earlier. There was a C. Scott on the Lawson's old street in Cottage Hill.

~

The voice on the phone, cracked with age, brought to mind immediately black-eyed Susans and wisps of white hair escaping from a straw hat. "You the same woman come by here t'other day lookin' for Harriet?"

"I sure am," I told her, "and I'm still looking."

"You haven't found her?" The old woman was obviously surprised. "Did you ask Dixie? Didn't she tell you Harriet's gone away for the summer?"

"Not exactly. She said Harriet and her uncle quarreled about some summer plans, and Harriet ran away. They haven't seen her since June."

"June? Do tell! You better come talk to my daughter Claire, then. She gets home about five. I'll tell her to look out for you."

Just before five, I pulled Glenna's Ford up near the little blue house with cream shutters. Not long after, a silver Lexus parked in front of the house. A woman with platinum hair got out, reached for a smart black briefcase, and started toward the house. If I was forty-five and that long and skinny, I'd have permed my hair instead of wearing it so short and severe. She must be good at whatever she did, though, because her car, her light gray suit, and that particular briefcase don't come cheap.

I got out in a hurry. "Claire Scott? I am MacLaren Yarbrough, and I'm trying to find Harriet Lawson. Your mother said you'd be getting home about now and I should talk to you. Have you seen Harriet recently?" I couldn't imagine any reason why she should have. This lady wouldn't bother herself with teenagers. I doubted if she bothered herself much with anybody. She was looking *me* over in a way that made me wish I'd worn my navy linen, pearls, and heels instead of my new blue pantsuit and flats.

I repeated the explanation I'd given so often I could spout it in my sleep. "I found some of Harriet's things at a teen center where I was volunteering earlier this week, and I've been trying to return them to her. Your mother first suggested I try her aunt, but she's not been there since early June."

Claire didn't look at all bothered by that. "Of course not," she said impatiently. "Didn't they tell you she's in Atlanta?"

"No," I replied, annoyance making me feel more like my own capable self. "They told me she and her uncle had a row about her *going* to Atlanta, and she ran away from home. They haven't heard from her since."

Claire looked more disgusted than puzzled. "I can't believe this. Just as I thought she was finally growing up a bit. I *told* her to tell them gently, but she probably blurted it out as soon as she got home."

"Tell them about the summer acting school, you mean?"

"Yes. It wasn't the smartest idea in the world, but at least she was showing interest in something that meant work. I thought it might be good for her—with her aunt and uncle's permission, of course. I guess she went without it. Heaven help her when she comes back."

"A brochure from the acting school was among the things I found," I said gravely. "I talked to them yesterday. Harriet's not there. In fact, I can't find a single person who has seen or heard from that child since early June. I am getting seriously worried."

Claire stared at me for a long minute, then stepped back and motioned with a long skinny hand. "Won't you come in?"

The room within was spacious, bright, and expensive, in a bare bones kind of way. Not much furniture, but what there was was very good. Wooden blinds instead of drapes. Wood floors dotted with Chinese rugs.

"I'm home, Mama," Claire called as we entered. The old woman did not reply.

Claire didn't bother to offer me anything to drink, but kicked off her shoes and flopped onto an oatmeal linen sofa, waving me to a matching chair. Following her lead, I slid my feet out of my shoes, too. "I love your house," I said frankly, admiring a sleek crystal sculpture on a bare oak coffee table.

She didn't exactly sparkle when she was pleased, but at least the ice thawed a little. "I hated this house growing up. Couldn't wait to leave. But after my divorce, when Mama invited me to come back, I discovered Cottage Hill is some of the nicest real estate in Montgomery. The houses are solid, the rooms are big, there's not much yard to keep up, and I'm five minutes from work. As soon as I discovered heart pine floors under the shag carpet, I offered to buy Mama out. I had some restoration done, and it turned out quite nicely." She looked around in content. "Now Mama keeps the yard, I do the house, and we bumble along real well together." She tucked her feet beneath her and got right down to business. "Tell me who all you've talked to about Harriet."

"Her aunts in McGehee Estates and Chisholm, and Ricky, a boy who used to live with her grandmother—"

"Ricky? Now there's a real prize. I wish Harriet would forget him."

"She isn't out there right now, at any rate. One of the girls at the center said Harriet talked about you a lot, so I thought perhaps you'd seen her. Are you friends?"

Claire's eyes widened in surprise. "Heavens no! I thought you knew—I'm her trustee. I'm an investment broker, so Bertha Lawson, Harriet's grandmother, asked me to manage the money until Harriet's twenty-one. Bertha and Mama were friends, so I hated to say no."

"Pardon me for asking, and don't answer if you don't want to, but it doesn't look like there would have been very much to manage. The house couldn't have brought much, did it?"

"About twenty thousand. But Harriet's dad died last winter and left a life insurance policy for his mother, and

Bertha had one little vice." Her face thawed again slightly into what passed for a smile. "When the riverboat casinos opened a few years ago, Bertha and Mama started going down a couple of times a month. 'I've got a system,' Bertha used to tell me. She never told me what her system was, but it must have worked. Real often she'd bring back money to invest. When she died, she was worth nearly a hundred thousand dollars."

"Merciful heavens! And it all went to Harriet? That hardly seems fair to Dee."

This time Claire's smile was broad, and not very pleasant. "Apparently it was Dixie's idea, years ago. Pardon my calling her Dixie. I know she changed it to Dee in college, but I still think of her as the bratty little princess across the street. Anyway, Bertha said Dixie told her several years ago that William could take care of her and their little girl, so Harriet ought to get whatever Bertha had. That was before Dixie thought she had anything, of course, and back when she assumed Harriet would go on out to her dad when her grandmother died."

"Felt guilty for not coming to see her pore old mama," Claire's own mama called from a back room. I was startled, for I hadn't realized she'd been listening, but given the way she'd cocked her ears the first day I was on the street, I should have expected it.

Claire permitted herself a small, embarrassed frown, then admitted, "After she married William Trevor Sykes the Third, Dixie wasn't seen much around these parts. But after her mama died, she was real put out she'd lost all that money and I was Harriet's trustee. There wasn't a thing she could do, of course. Bertha had put it all in her will, and explained to the lawyer who drew up the will that since I'd been managing her money all along, she wanted me to keep managing it."

"So you have to approve things like the acting school."

"Right. Harriet brought me a brochure around the middle of May, and said her grandmother had a cousin up there she could stay with. At first I thought it was a dumb idea, but when I checked it out, I began to think that even if she didn't learn to act, she could learn how to hold her body and build a bit of self-esteem. I even thought she might get leads on modeling jobs using her eyes."

"Her eyes?" That completely lost me.

"Harriet's got gorgeous eyes. A sort of amber color, and they fill her face. I thought the acting school might put her in touch with places that want models for eye makeup. After I checked out the school, I called her grandmother's relatives in Atlanta to be sure they'd let her stay there, and they agreed. That's when I told Harriet she could go if she got permission. She assured me she had. I'd never have gotten her money from the bank, otherwise."

As soon as she said "money from the bank," I felt like I did one time when I swam out too far and went down twice before Daddy got there. "Do you remember when you went to the bank?"

She reached into her briefcase for a worn Daytimer and thumbed through. "Tuesday, June fourth. School was out, so Harriet was free. She met me at the bank at nine thirty, grumbling royally about the hour, but I had appointments the entire rest of the day."

I couldn't keep my voice from trembling. "Was Harriet carrying anything?"

She thought a minute. "A book, I think. Yes, a library book, because she put the money in the envelope with her brochure and stuck them both in her book. I said that that was an expensive bookmark, and warned her not to turn it in at the library by mistake."

"Did you just leave her at the bank?" I didn't mean to accuse, but it sounded that way.

"No, I drove her over to a teen center just off Rosa L. Parks. I wanted to take her straight to the post office, but she said she'd go after twelve. She had to answer phones or something, because whoever was supposed to be there had to come in late. I dropped her off right in front, just a little past ten."

"Pardon me if I seem to pry, Ms. Scott, but could you tell me how much money you took out? I found some, you see, among her things. I wonder if it was the same amount."

Finally Claire laughed aloud, a sound like crystal breaking. "I certainly hope not. We took out three thousand dollars, in one hundred dollars bills."

"That's exactly what I found." I felt as chilled as she looked.

I wondered how to ask tactfully why the dickens she'd let a fifteen-year-old walk around town with three thousand dollars in cash. The question must have shown in my face, because she said defensively, "I wanted to get a cashier's check, but Harriet wasn't used to checks, and insisted on getting a post office money order. She also insisted on hundred dollar bills, because she'd never seen one. I offered to drive her straight to the post office, but she was worried about being late to answer the phones. I drove her over there and dropped her off—with all that money. Hassling Harriet when she sets her mind isn't worth the trouble."

I didn't really feel like offering her one speck of comfort, but honesty compelled me to remind her, "She wasn't robbed, Ms. Scott. I have the money. It's Harriet I can't find."

After that, there wasn't anything constructive to say. Claire's knowledge of Harriet was limited to money, and she was so upset about what she herself might have done or not done, she very soon lost sight of the child. "I shouldn't have left her with all that money. How could I do that?" she said over and over.

I reassured her as best I could, but I'm afraid I wasn't very convincing. By that time I was ready to blame every blooming person who ever knew the girl.

I finally took my ornery self home, fixed a glass of tea, and headed outside to see if smelling a few roses would help. Carter's call caught me at the door.

After we'd got through the standard greetings and a report on Jake, he finally got down to business. "Was this female you wanted white? You forgot to say."

My stomach took a plunge off a three-story building. "Yes. Why?"

"Somebody answering the description you gave me was found dead out near the airport July second. Carried no identification, and apparent cause of death was a heart attack."

"Heart attack? Did you say heart attack?" I was having enough trouble believing Harriet was dead. A heart attack was too unexpected to take in.

"Yeah. Probably her first, but a big one. She looked like she'd been tramping a while, so she could have been in a weakened condition. Nobody's identified her so far."

"Do you have a description, Carter?"

"Five-six, brown hair, no identifying marks."

"It could be the right person," I said slowly, feeling around blindly behind me for a chair. "What was done with the body?" Dear God, please not an unmarked grave.

Carter surprised me. "She's still down at the morgue. We keep them for a month or so, hoping for an identification. Did you say you knew her aunt?"

"Call her uncle instead. He's the one who wouldn't report her missing, so it's simple justice if he has to identify her." I told you I was feeling ornery.

I hung up feeling like a new jigsaw had turned out to be all black pieces.

It also had a big hole in the middle. If Harriet disappeared around June fourth, where had she been—and what the heck had she been doing—until July second?

Carter called back late that evening. I clutched the receiver so hard I nearly mashed it, and I wasn't in the mood for chitchat. "Was it her?"

"No. Mr. Sykes came down to see her, and he said it's not her at all."

I was so thankful I completely missed the beginning of Carter's next sentence. ". . . so then he asked for a second look and said no, he was mistaken."

I felt as puzzled as he sounded. "He first said it was Harriet, then changed his mind?"

"Yeah. Looked at her, nodded, and said right off, 'Yeah, it's her all right.' Then, when we got halfway back down the hall, he said, 'Could I look at her one more time?' When he'd taken another look, he said, 'No, I was wrong. It's not her after all. I guess I was so upset I didn't take a real good look.' Freaky, isn't it?"

The next question was real hard to ask. "Was she—you know, hard to identify?"

"Not really. And he's absolutely certain this isn't her."

"He ought to know, I suppose. Keep looking for her, Carter, will you?"

"I'm real sorry, Miss MacLaren, but without a missing persons report, I don't have authority to do that."

"Didn't he fill out a report while he was there?"

"I asked him about it, but he insists his niece isn't missing. Said his wife thinks she's gone down to her mother's or something."

I went to bed with a lot of unanswered questions.

A gift opens the way for the giver and ushers [her] into the presence of the great. *Proverbs 18:16*

Seventeen

I dropped Glenna off at the hospital Friday morning and headed straight to Dee's. It sure would feel good to get rid of that money. Every time we entered the house nowadays, Glenna and I went straight to the laundry basket to be sure it hadn't been disturbed. Anybody peeking in the window would have thought we worshiped at the Shrine of Clean Clothes.

Dee wore black slacks with a black eyelet top. Mourning? Or because she looked so wonderful in black? In my new khaki skirt and crisp green cotton sweater, I didn't look bad until I saw Dee. Immediately I felt my hair wilt and my nails split.

She welcomed me like we were old friends. "Come in! I just made coffee."

She gave a careless wave toward the sunroom table, strewn with cookbooks. "I was planning menus so I can go to the grocery store. You know." I didn't dare tell her I didn't know at all—most of the time I just go to the store and grab whatever looks good or easy.

She waved me to the love seat and fetched coffee in charming mugs decorated with berries. "The police seem to be looking for Harriet," she said, settling on the chaise. "They dragged poor William off the golf course to go down and look at a body, but it wasn't her. I just don't understand where she could be."

"I don't either," I told her, "but I've brought you three things. This is a list of compact disks Harriet borrowed from a girl at the center. If you find them, would you call Mr. Henly, the center director? He can figure out a way to get them to the right people." Joe Riddley would be proud of me. For once, I wasn't volunteering.

Dee looked at the list briefly then set it aside. "Julie will know more about this than I do. What were the other things?"

"The brochure from the acting school, and this." I handed her the envelope. "I didn't give it to you the first time I came, because I felt like I ought to give it straight to Harriet. Since she's . . . not around, I think you ought to keep it for her."

When Dee opened the envelope she was merely curious. When she drew out the money, she could have caught whole hummingbirds in her mouth. "This belonged to Harriet? Where on earth did she get it?"

"I talked to Harriet's trustee yesterday. She said she and Harriet withdrew it on June fourth, for the acting class. I don't know why Harriet left it at the center, but—"

Dee started shaking so hard I was afraid she'd fall off the chaise. She flung down the money, then she flung a fit. "Claire Scott was going to let Harriet spend three thousand dollars on a summer acting class? *Three thousand dollars?*" Her voice was shrill, her face flushed like an angry child's. "I *told* that lawyer Claire doesn't know the first thing about teenagers. And she spends money like water. She can't *possibly* make that much. How could Mama leave her in charge of all that money?" She nearly screamed the last three words, then came to an abrupt halt and gave an embarrassed little laugh. "I'm sorry, Laura. This isn't your problem, and you've been real sweet to go to so much trouble for us. It's just that whenever I think about Claire Scott having her greedy hands on Mama's money, I could spit! I think Mama was getting a bit senile right before she died, but I couldn't convince the lawyer." She picked up the envelope and slapped it against her palm. "But I really appreciate everything you've done, and maybe the police will keep looking for Harriet."

"Not unless you file a missing person's report. You really need to do that, Dee."

She bit her lip and thought about it, but then she shook her head. "Not yet. William won't." Her blue eyes were anxious, like the first time I saw them.

I opened my mouth to ask how much later it needed to get, but the phone rang. When Dee heard the voice on the other end, her face brightened. "Why, honey, how sweet of you to call. Are you having fun?" She paused. "Well, maybe a day or two, but not much longer than that. You've got to get ready for your trip with Gram." Another pause. "I know, honey, I wish you didn't either, but she's gone to all this trouble—"

I touched her on the shoulder and motioned that I could find my own way out. I knew from experience that that conversation could take a while.

I sat with Jake that afternoon while Glenna went home to lie down a while. In the mid-afternoon he opened his eyes. "Isn't it about time for me to be out chasing women?"

I lightly rattled his IV tube. "With Glenna on the other end of your leash? How're you feeling?"

"Fine. Doc says I can go home in a few days if I'm good."

"How soon does he expect you to be back to normal?"

He was already slipping back into sleep. "When's the first Auburn game?"

"I'm glad you've got your priorities straight, Bubba." He was already snoring.

I opened a book. He moaned in his sleep, and I gently touched his arm. Suddenly I remembered the first time I ever touched him. He was all red and wrinkly, wrapped in a soft white blanket. Daddy laid him in my lap, and I felt like I was holding the universe. Gracious! Was that really fifty-five years ago?

I blinked back tears. "I sure do love you, Bubba," I murmured.

"Hmmm," he said drowsily.

Did he hear? It didn't matter. Everybody ought to say it now and then.

About four-thirty, Lou Ella and Nora Sykes tiptoed in. Lou Ella wore a simple gray linen dress. Nora wore camel slacks with a thick and silky cream top and heavy gold jewelry. She also carried a lovely basket of fruit with a big red bow. "We didn't know if Jake was on oxygen, so Lella got something you all can nibble on, instead of flowers. How's he doing?"

Jake opened one eye. "Well enough to hear every word you're saying, so you'd better be careful."

Nora bent over to kiss his cheek. "If you're getting sassy, you must be almost well. Glad to see it, Jake."

"Me, too," he agreed weakly.

They stayed just a few minutes, then started to leave.

"If you're taking Lou Ella, could you run MacLaren home, too?" Jake asked Nora.

"Glenna will be back right after supper," I objected.

He glared. "I really don't need you both riding herd on me day and night. I'd like a few minutes to moan and groan all by myself."

If I were him, that's what I'd be wanting, too, and Nora assured me that Glenna's was "Just a hop, skip, and jump from Lella's."

"I've had Irmalene make a chicken casserole for you folks," Lou Ella added as further incentive. "If you take me home first, Nora, Jake's sister could take it with her. And drive through downtown so she can see it."

I didn't have the heart to tell her I'd been coming to Montgomery for forty years. As if it were my first time in town, she pointed out the state Capitol, the White House of the Confederacy, the church where Martin Luther King preached, and the new high rises built with state pension funds.

"I'm sure she knows all that," Nora told her impatiently.

"She might not know about the pension funds," Lou Ella insisted. "Man came down from the North—the North, mind you!—and got the bright idea of investing all the state pension funds in office buildings downtown. Prettied up the downtown and made a good investment at the same time. Pretty smart for a Yankee, don't you think?"

"Very smart," I agreed. "You really love Montgomery, don't you?"

"I do! It's a city, but retains the flavor of a little Southern country town. Not real sophisticated, but very charming. It's also a political town—always has been—and I love politics. My husband was a state legislator, you know, and so was my son. And oh, we used to be so active! Football games, mystic society balls—in the season we went to a ball almost every weekend. We all loved to dance in those days. Today nobody knows how to dance, and the balls have become just huge cocktail parties." She stopped again, then said wistfully, "I live very quietly now, of course, but sometimes I miss it all."

Nora passed the governor's mansion. A few doors down, she turned into the drive of a big white house sheltered by deep porches, wide old oaks, and magnolias. When I admired it, Lou Ella sighed. "I probably ought to sell and move into something smaller, but I just hate to give up my flowers and trees. This house was built in the eighteen nineties, and those oaks were here before the War Between the States. I planted that castor"—she pointed to a plant towering at the corner of the house near the drive—"the year we moved in." She stopped and flapped one hand. "Oh, you don't want to know all that. I'm just an old woman who lives alone and has to talk to anybody about everything. Come in while Nora gets the casserole."

We went in the back door. Her kitchen was big and comfortable, with avocado green appliances. She probably hadn't modernized since the sixties. I felt right at home and said so.

"It's a lot of house to keep," Nora pointed out while Lou Ella took a casserole from the refrigerator and tied it into a quilted carrier.

"But I'm fortunate to have good help," Lou Ella replied. She explained to me, "Irmalene has been with me for nearly fifty years. I don't know what I'd do without her."

"I don't either," Nora said, "and when Irmalene is gone, I don't know what you're *going* to do. You know it's almost impossible to get servants these days."

I could tell they'd had this conversation before, especially when Lou Ella replied shortly, "I'll do what I have to do."

Nora picked up the carrier. "Well, let's be off. The only thing I ask, MacLaren, is that you don't mention that wretched Harriet. She brought William and Dee more than enough grief to last a lifetime. I hate to say it, but they are better off without her."

Lou Ella gave a little grunt of disapproval, but said nothing.

Death and Destruction are never satisfied. *Proverbs 27:20*

Eighteen

On Saturday, Jake hit the traditional third-day-after-surgery low.

Sunday he got what Glenna called "the male grumpies."

In addition, his recovery was being celebrated by half of Montgomery. Between answering all the calls from well-wishers, accepting food and flower gifts, and spelling Glenna at the hospital, I didn't have a minute to even think about Harriet the entire weekend.

Monday I was sitting with Jake when Glenna called about half past one. "You just had a phone call from a woman named Myrna Lawson. Do you know who she is?"

"Myrna Lawson? Harriet's mother? Where is she? Is Harriet with her?"

"I don't know all that. She just said to call her, and left a number." I guessed Glenna had been woken from a nap, poor dear. She sounded a bit cross.

Myrna sounded like a Kewpie doll who'd had too many drinks and too few grammar lessons. "Hey! I'm glad you called back. I'm up at Eunice's. She said you might have a clue where Harriet could be. I been lookin' for her. Called down to that teen center Eunice said she used to go to, but they ain't seen her. Listen, I got somebody coming, and I think they're at the door, but I sure do want to talk to you."

"How about if I come up? It'll take me about an hour to get there." I'd have to see how fast Glenna could get to the hospital.

It was more like forty-five minutes after the call when I pulled up in front of Eunice's house and climbed out into the still, dead heat of early afternoon. The street was bright and deserted. The day was so still I could hear the buzz of bees and the thrum of the air conditioner, but Eunice's front door stood open behind the screen.

My heels sounded loud on the cracked walk. Inside, I heard a slight sound of alarm. Then I heard running feet, and a door slam at the back of the house.

Startled, I watched someone dash across the side yard, hurl himself over a neighbor's fence, and disappear behind that house. Ricky Dodd.

Had he been the visitor Myrna mentioned? If so, what was his hurry now?

I walked thoughtfully up the steps and across the porch toward the open door. It was hotter than blazes. Why should Myrna leave the front door open?

I rang the bell. Nobody answered. I knocked. Still nobody. Finally I leaned toward the screened door and called, "Hello? Myrna? It's MacLaren Yarbrough."

Still no answer. Only the buzzing of bees and flies.

I pulled the screen open and took one hesitant step into the living room. "Myrna? Myrna Lawson? Are you here?"

Myrna didn't—couldn't—answer. She lay on the couch like Sleeping Beauty. Except this Sleeping Beauty had a small bullet hole in the center of her forehead.

Her house leads down to death and her paths to the spirits of the dead.
Proverbs 2:18

Nineteen

It was hard to tell what the woman really looked like, because her hair was bottle blonde, her eyelashes fake, her mouth a pout of dark red lipstick, and her cheeks a brighter purply-pink than any God ever made. Her eyes were amber, like her daughter's, and they stared like she was thinking about something very serious. Maybe she was, but not in Alabama.

On the floor beside her, the Polar Bear pillow lay shredded.

Do you know what finally got me moving again? Flies. Great big bluebottles that gorged themselves on her forehead, then circled the room. Getting their exercise, I guess, but they made me sick. I couldn't bear the thought of one of them touching me.

"Get away! Get away!" I shooed them and headed for the kitchen phone to call 911. When I told them there'd been a shooting, I also asked them to tell Carter Duggins that MacLaren Yarbrough was on the scene. I had no idea if the dispatcher got all that, but by then, I needed to hang up and go hang over the toilet.

I waited in a porch rocker. The old gray Persian leaped onto the porch and settled on my lap, as welcome as a hot water bottle in that heat. I let him stay. I had no energy to push him off. I also kept my feet firmly planted on the floor and didn't rock. Between the heat, my memory of Myrna, and the sound of the flies, my stomach was awfully queasy.

It seemed like hours, but was probably less than five minutes before a squad car screamed to a stop at the curb. Two officers dashed to the house, a man and a woman. I couldn't tell if the man was Carter or not. He didn't look the least bit like Glenna.

They looked at me curiously. "Are you the one who called?" the woman asked.

"Yes. She's in there." The man hurried inside. The woman stayed with me. She had tightly permed blonde hair, a dusting of freckles, and light but very bushy eyebrows.

"You live here?" she asked.

"No, Eunice Crawley does. That's Myrna Lawson inside, her sister. I just found her. Was that Carter Duggins?"

"No. You know him?"

"I've talked to him on the phone a couple of times. I asked for him to come."

"We didn't get that. Just got word of a shooting. You actually heard the shot?"

"No, I found the body. She was dead when I arrived."

She looked puzzled. "And you are?" She poised a pen over her report pad.

I gave her my name, Jake's address and phone number, and said I had come by the house on business. That seemed simplest. "You might want to call her sister," I suggested. "Eunice Crawley, the one who lives here. A neighbor might have her work phone number."

"We'll find her." She wiped sweat from her brow with one forearm and went inside.

Another squad car pulled to the curb, and a man got out. He was as tall and lean as Glenna, less than thirty, and had a lopsided grin that probably broke hearts on a regular basis. I greeted him from my rocker. "Carter? I'm MacLaren, Jake's sister."

He gave me a little wave and loped up the steps. "Hey, Miss MacLaren. What's happenin'?" When I told him briefly, he headed for the door. "I'll get right back to you."

He didn't, but I didn't mind waiting. I figured after a while I'd get popular. Meanwhile, I watched the comings and goings of a slew of people whose business it is to investigate a homicide. I thought about going to ask one of the neighbors how to call Eunice, but as hot as that old Persian felt across my legs, I hated to move him. I hated to move, period. If I weren't there, the police would get Eunice's number. They didn't need me to do it for them. I stroked the cat and waited for Carter.

I found I didn't have the least bit of curiosity about what was going on inside. I had no interest in butting in, either. Do you know what I kept thinking? I kept looking at those daisies across the street and thinking it wasn't fair that Myrna wouldn't see them again.

Finally Carter came out on the porch, slumped into the other rocker, and stretched out his long legs. "Please tell me what happened and what you're doing here, Miss MacLaren."

I told him about the call from Myrna, and about coming to the house.

"You didn't know her at all?"

"No. She called and said she was Harriet's mother—"

He stared at me like I'd gone stark raving crazy. "*Harriet's* mother? You mean the one you asked me to look for, Miss MacLaren?"

"I think so. I know it sounds like a coincidence, but—"

His voice was full of disbelief and more than a little peeved. "That makes no sense at *all!* Did you see that woman in there?" He jerked his thumb toward the door.

"More of her than I'll ever be able to forget."

"How old would you say she is?"

I tried to work it out. "Her sister said she got married before she finished high school, so by now I'd guess she'd be—what? Thirty-one or -two?"

"How can a woman in her early thirties be the mother of somebody who's fifty?"

Our trains were traveling down two different tracks. "Fifty?"

"You said a fifty-year-old female."

Silently I tried out the two words. "I guess over the phone fifteen could sound like fifty, Carter, but Harriet's fifteen. A child. How old was the woman you showed William?"

"Fifty-four. We've identified her, by the way. She was from Huntsville."

"Why on earth would William have identified her, then? You said he did, didn't you?"

"Positively, at first. He changed his mind later, but there's no way he could have mistaken her for fifteen, no matter how upset he was. I'll want to talk to Mr. Sykes again."

In the next few minutes, I told him about coming up the steps, hearing a noise inside, and seeing Ricky Dodd run away—and that Ricky was the person I thought had tried to break into Glenna's. "Did you ever compare his blood with that on the glass?"

He looked embarrassed. "No ma'am, not yet. Since you all were okay and nothing was taken, I put that on a back burner, I'm afraid. We're pretty busy. But you know him?"

"I've met him, looking for Harriet. He lived as a foster child with Harriet and her grandmother for a while, and a couple of times she ran away and went to his place. He hadn't seen her this time, though."

"Did you see if he carried a weapon today?"

"No, and I saw him pretty clearly. Besides, if he'd had a gun and had already killed one person, why would he have run away instead of coming after me?" Until I said that, I hadn't given a second's thought to the fact that I could have been in danger myself. It was a good thing I was already sitting down.

"You never know what people will do in a panic." Carter hadn't lived long enough to know as much about that as he sounded like he had.

The woman officer came out. "Thought I'd look around outside for a possible weapon." Given that Eunice only had two bushes, her search was as complicated as a two-year-olds' egg hunt. She reached into the hydrangea just to the left of the steps and pulled out a pistol. "The murder weapon," she crowed to Carter. "I'll bet you a steak dinner on it."

That rooster wouldn't fly. "No wager, no dinner," Carter told her.

She looked disappointed, but brightened when he added, "But we've got a suspect." He gave her everything I'd told him, then turned back to me. "We'll bring him in. He'll swear he didn't do it, of course, but since you found him standing over her . . ."

I've been a magistrate's wife long enough to know the importance of precise evidence. "I didn't even see him in the house. I heard a slamming door and saw him running away."

"That's close enough to start. Let me send somebody out to pick him up." He went to his car without suggesting that I leave. I didn't think I could summon the energy, anyway.

After a while he came back and went inside. I heard him tell the others, "We've got an ID on the gun. Belongs to a Beverly White."

"Carter," I called through the open door, "I think she's the girl Ricky lives with."

Carter slapped his thigh. "Hot diggety! One we can solve in time for supper!"

He wasn't so cocky when he arrived at Jake's room a little past five. After hugging Glenna and teasing Jake about getting a vacation the hard way, he asked, "Hey, Jake, can I borrow your sister for a cup of coffee?"

"She's a little old for you, isn't she, son?" Jake inquired mildly.

"No pretty woman ever gets old, Jake. You know that."

"Well, watch your step. She's got a lean, mean husband."

"This is a weird case, Miss MacLaren," Carter said a few minutes later, stirring enough sugar into his coffee to ice a cake and giving a girl at the next table a smile that would keep her happy for days. "You know you called 911 and asked for me?" I nodded. "Well, I wasn't far away, but the reason that other car arrived first was, there'd already been a 911 for the same address, a few minutes before."

"Who on earth—?"

"It gets weirder. The caller spoke in a loud whisper and claimed to have heard a shot. And, like yours, that call came from inside the house. What do you think of that?"

"Ricky?"

Carter shrugged. "He swears he wasn't there but a second when he heard a noise and ran. But it's his gun, all right—or his girlfriend's. He's on probation and not allowed to have a gun. But given that the gun was there and he was there—"

"Why would Ricky go out front to throw the gun away, then go back into the room?"

Carter shrugged again. "Your guess is as good as mine. Maybe he was planning to rob the place, but you disturbed him. All he says is, he was there, heard the noise, and, with his record, was scared he'd be blamed, so he ran."

I'd heard Ricky talk. I appreciated how much editing Carter was doing for my benefit. I offered him a gift in return. "Ricky said he didn't know Myrna. I have witnesses to that."

"He *still* says he didn't know her. That's all he *will* say, though, until he gets a lawyer. He's been through the system a few times already. He knows the ropes."

"But he took a gun to her house, Carter? Why?"

"That's the weirdest part of all. He says he hadn't had that gun for weeks. He swears Harriet's had it."

"*Harriet?*"

"Yeah. I told you it was weird. Beverly corroborates that, by the way. She says she bought the gun for protection before she met Ricky, and forgot all about it. Harriet found it and got real mad they had it, with Ricky being on probation and all, so she took it and said she'd put it in a safe place where it couldn't hurt anybody. Looks like she didn't."

I was cold all over. "Oh, Carter, I do hope she hasn't killed her own mother!"

> Give beer to those who are perishing,
> wine to those who are in anguish;
> let them drink and forget their poverty
> and remember their misery no more.
> *Proverbs 31:6–7*

Twenty

When Josheba called Jake's room to ask how he was doing, I couldn't very well tell her about Myrna's murder with old Big Ears right there. "I'd like to see you," I said formally. "How about if we go out for supper? Glenna's ordered a tray to eat with Jake."

Josheba plumb flabbergasted me. "Lewis is coming over to my place for lasagna and a glass of wine, Mac. Why don't you join us?" *Lewis?* I'd thought Morse was coming home the day before. Before I could ask, Josheba urged, "Come on over. I've got plenty."

I accepted. The way those two bickered the first—and, so far as I knew, *only*—time they'd been together, I might be needed as a referee.

I am ashamed to admit I'd never been a guest in an African American home before. I felt a bit dashing driving up to Josheba's, and wasn't sure what to expect. I discovered she lived just a few blocks from Glenna and Jake in a modest six-room brick house very like theirs. The main difference was, Josheba's furniture was newer and better. She had a collection of African art and sculptures I could have appreciated more if I hadn't been keeping one eye on Lewis and Josheba. The way they carried on in the kitchen, they could have known one another for years. I had never heard her laugh so much.

The food was delicious, but while we ate I obeyed Josheba's command to "fill us in on the latest developments." My news got far more attention than the lasagna. They were as shocked as I that Harriet's mother had been shot with a gun last seen in Harriet's possession.

"Tell me truthfully," I finished, looking from one pair of concerned dark brown eyes to the other, "do you all think Harriet is the kind of child who would shoot somebody?"

Josheba looked shocked. "No way!"

Lewis looked grave. "I hope not, but she has a temper. If pushed far enough — "

Josheba covered her ears with her hands. "I won't listen to this! What are you going to do next, Mac?"

"I'd like to go talk with Eunice again." I was surprised to hear myself say it. I thought I was going to leave everything to Carter, but if Carter was looking for Harriet because he thought she'd shot Myrna, I wanted to find her first. "I think I'll go offer condolences tonight and ask who else might have known Myrna was here. Do you all want to come?"

Josheba nodded. "I'll come. You, too, Mr. Henly?"

We turned toward him and found him sitting slumped over with his eyes closed. "You praying?" Josheba demanded bluntly.

"No," he murmured, "I was just wondering if I'd brought out jigsaws the first day Mac came to the center, whether she'd have given this Harriet thing a miss."

"Think how dull your life would be," Josheba scolded, but her eyes danced.

"My life isn't going to be dull for a long time, woman." He pushed back from the table. "I've got a meeting. Call me, Josheba, and keep me posted." He tried to sound casual, but he didn't fool me one bit. I wondered if he knew about Morse—and where Morse was.

When he was gone, I sighed. "I'd have felt a lot safer driving up there at night with Lewis along—even if he does rank as a suspect."

Josheba stared. "What do you mean a suspect, Mac?"

I started gathering up dishes to take them to the sink. "Only so many people could have known she was in town, and Lewis was one. When Myrna called me, she said she'd already called the teen center."

Josheba followed me with the serving platters. "Well, you know good and well Lewis didn't shoot her. He wouldn't kill anybody!" She started rinsing dishes for the dishwasher.

"Do!" I said, running some hot soapy water for the pots. "Sounds like you know Mr. Henly better than I supposed."

Her face grew slightly rosy and she turned away. "We've had dinner a couple of times, that's all. As friends." She moved to put things in the refrigerator.

"A couple of times? When? And where's Morse? I thought he'd be home by now." My boys and I used to carry on that way. I hoped Josheba knew I was teasing.

Her voice was muffled from having her head in the fridge. "Morse isn't studying coming home. He called Friday to say the weather had cleared up, the river was fantastic, and he was staying an extra week." She stood up straight and added, a bit defiantly, "And Lewis and me—well, it isn't what you think, Mac. We had dinner twice, that's all. After you and I went up to Eunice's I dropped by to tell him about that visit and your break-in. He was about to get some supper before a basketball game, so he asked me to go along. Not having anything better to do, I accepted."

"That's once," I counted.

"Well," she looked a little embarrassed, "on Friday, when Morse called, I could hear a party going on in the background. Men *and* women. Morse likes to party. So when Lewis called right afterwards and asked if I'd like to get some dinner again, I was just mad enough with Morse to accept. I figured if he was having fun, why shouldn't I?" She lifted her chin, then her eyes sparkled with mischief. "I must have been madder than I realized, though. I put on my prettiest turquoise pantsuit and my best perfume. But it doesn't really mean a thing, Mac. Lewis doesn't mean any more to me than those women up at the river mean to Morse, and I refuse to build a marriage on suspicion and jealousy."

"Next thing I know, you'll be running for Miss Virtue," I told her, scrubbing the baking dish. "But don't you break Lewis's heart, now."

From the happiness in Josheba's laugh when I said that, I suspected if she wasn't careful, she might break her own. It's so easy, once we have put on the armor of resolve, to think we're invulnerable to temptation.

Josheba couldn't stop talking about Lewis. When she went back in the dining room for the last few dishes, she called back, "I can't break Lewis's heart, Mac. He's already given it to that filthy teen center. He just likes to have somebody to eat with before his evening basketball game. But he sure is fun to be with. That man can *talk!*"

"Did he tell you anything about himself?" I asked as she returned. I wouldn't mind knowing a bit more about Mr. Henly myself.

"Sure. He told me about being a lawyer, and trips he used to take back when he was making money—Aspen to ski, the Bahamas and Jamaica for Christmas . . ."

"Looks like he wouldn't have wanted to give all that up for dirt and teenagers," I commented, wiping the last counter. "Did you ask him about that?"

"Yeah. He just shrugged and said, 'Some things you gotta do. Sometimes you owe a debt you have to pay.' Now come on, Mac, let's get up to Eunice's before it gets dark."

As I led the way to Glenna's car, I couldn't help wondering what kind of debt a man could pay off better as the director of an inner-city teen center than as a wealthy lawyer. Maybe I'd been the wife of a magistrate too long, but it sounded suspiciously like community service to me.

Eunice's house was dark and circled with crime tape, but on the porch of the house next door several women were gathered in a huddle. When I asked if they knew where Eunice might be, the crowd parted like the Red Sea. A stocky woman turned toward the open screened door. "Eunice," she bellowed, "you got comp'ny."

Eunice appeared behind the screen. "Hello, folks. Thank you for coming." She was neatly dressed in a gray skirt and white blouse—probably what she'd worn to work—but her hair was shoved about and her face was red and blotched from crying. "Come on in."

This house was different from its neighbor. Maybe it was people coming in and out, but it was scarcely cool. The living room was a small, dim cube filled with shabby overstuffed furniture all facing a huge color television. A collection of dusty china bells filled the sill of the picture window, a collection of dusty Avon bottles the top of the television.

"My neighbor Raye Hunter's lettin' me stay here with her until the police are finished with my house. This here's her granddaughter Jennifer." Eunice flapped one hand toward a pretty girl with long black curls and bright pink lipstick watching a television program. Eunice's eyes were rimmed with red. "So far I can't seem to do anything but cry," she apologized unnecessarily.

She led us to the dining room, an arch away from the living room. It was far too small and brightly lit for the warm crowd it held. Instead of a maple table and hutch, Mrs. Hunter had an old red Formica table and an assortment of mismatched chairs that had probably been dragged in from the rest of the house. A couple of women stood and insisted we take their patched plastic seats. Eunice spoke to a skinny woman with carrot-orange hair hovering by the kitchen door. "Raye, these here are friends of my niece Harriet."

"Let me get you a beer." Raye darted into her kitchen and reappeared almost at once with icy bottles, brimming with foam. I hate beer, but sipped mine to be polite.

I was wondering how to start a conversation when Eunice did it for us. "It don't seem right, Myrna coming so far just to die." She sniffed.

"When did she get here?" I asked.

"This very morning. Took the all-night bus." She sniffed again. Somebody pressed a blue tissue into her hand. "Me'n her wasn't what you'd call close, but I can tell you, it upsets me to think of her coming home to see her baby, then getting herself killed." The last word was a wail. Reaching for another tissue, she blew her nose like a trumpet. "Harriet and Myrna was all I had left in the world. Now Myrna's gone and Harriet's disappeared."

The girl in the living room decided the live show in the dining room was better than the one on the screen. She came in and held up part of the wall. "I read in the paper about a girl who disappeared several years ago." I figured she was trying to show sympathy by making the only connection she could with Eunice's grief. "She and her stepdaddy had a fight and she ran away with her boyfriend. Maybe that's where your niece went."

"Maybe so." Raye Hunter moved over to give her granddaughter's shoulders a squeeze of praise. "Anyway, Eunice, I'm sure Harriet's okay. Kids sometimes just need some space."

Eunice was momentarily diverted. "Did that girl ever come back?" she asked, dabbing her eyes with a sodden tissue.

The girl shifted uneasily. "Uh, well . . . not exactly. But her mother saw her picture in the paper and recognized her." Her voice dropped.

"Why was her picture in the paper?" Raye wanted to know.

The girl looked utterly miserable. She turned and muttered something we couldn't hear. Raye shook her roughly and shoved her toward the arch. "Don't you let her hear you say that!" she hissed.

"It was in the *paper,*" the girl said sullenly, gliding back to the television show.

Trying to distract Eunice again, I asked loudly, "Who might your sister have called in Montgomery besides me, Lewis Henly, and Ricky Dodd?"

"Who?" Eunice seemed at a loss.

"He's a boy I saw running away," I prompted her. "The police are holding him."

"I didn't know his name. The police just said they had a suspect. And I don't know why she'd have called him—or anybody else, for that matter, except maybe William Sykes. Dixie's husband? He's got a big store out on the Eastern Bypass, so I told Myrna to call and ask if he could give her a job, or steer her toward one. She wanted to stay home and . . . and make a fresh start." She put her head down and bawled.

Mrs. Hunter obliged with more tissues. Another woman came back from the kitchen with a fresh set of bottles, potato chips, and homemade onion dip. She set them down and announced, "I called the station. It'll be on the ten o'clock news."

Eunice nodded without raising her head.

I was horrified. "Don't you watch it! You don't need . . ."

Josheba ground her heel into my toe as Raye asked, "Didja ask 'em for a video tape? On account of it being in her house and all?"

"Yeah. They said we'll have to tape it ourselves. Do you have a blank tape?"

"Yeah." Raye went toward the living room.

I sat there feeling sick. Nothing could make me look at any part of that gruesome afternoon again. My own memory was likely to keep me up half the night.

Eunice, however, said with satisfaction, "The cameraman got good shots of me getting out of the police car and coming up the walk, and just when I first seen her, but he didn't know how much they'll be able to use." She turned to me. "Did he get you, too?"

I shuddered. "No, thank heavens. I left before the press arrived."

Raye Hunter looked up from where she was fixing a blank tape into the video. "Ain't that always the way? And there you was, the one who found her. Looks like they'd have told you to stick around."

Eunice was ready to rehash her tragedy once more. "I went off to work and left her sitting right there in the living room, drinking her coffee and looking pretty as a picture. It don't seem right that she's gone."

I raised my voice and spoke to Raye. "The police said somebody called about hearing a shot. Was that you?"

Raye shook her carrot head. "Lordy, no, I don't hear a thing in the afternoon. I'm on disability, you know, so I have to rest. I lay right there on my couch with my TV stories, and the air conditioner runs so loud outside that window, I have to turn the sound up. I probably wouldn't hear a fire truck less'n it come through the door."

"I don't know who else it'd be, either," Eunice said with a sniff. "All my other neighbors work."

I couldn't think of another thing to ask, and I was feeling more than a bit queasy. Maybe it was the way Eunice was piling up sodden tissues right beside the potato chips and dip. I shoved away from the table. "We just wanted to tell you how sorry we both are. Don't come with us to the door. We'll find our way out."

"Thank you for coming." Eunice extended a plump, damp hand.

As we went through the screened door, we heard her confide to her neighbors, "That woman's just like a sister to me. In and out of my house all the time. I don't know what I'd do without her."

> They cannot sleep till they do evil;
> they are robbed of slumber till they
> make someone fall. *Proverbs 4:16*

Twenty-One

Monday night I didn't dream about the brown-haired child. It's hard to dream when you aren't sleeping. Whenever I dozed, I saw a pale white face with a hole in its forehead.

When I finally fell asleep, it seemed only a minute later that Glenna was shaking me. "William Sykes wants you, honey. He won't come in, says it will just take a minute."

I dragged on my robe and stumbled to the front door. He stood at the bottom of Glenna's three front steps, holding a plastic grocery bag.

The morning was hot and still. Boxwoods beside the stoop sent up the delicious musty smell that always reminds me of the house I grew up in, which made me greet William more pleasantly than I might have. "Good morning!"

William looked very smart in a gray suit and red tie. He thrust the bag up at me. "Dee found these CDs in Harriet's room. Can you get them to the kid they belong to?"

He wasn't dumb to come early. Before my first cup of coffee, I'll agree to almost anything. "Sure." I smothered a yawn. Sunlight slanted through the tall pines into my eyes. As he turned to go, I added sleepily, "Did you all hear about Myrna Lawson?"

He turned back slowly. "What about her?"

"She was shot yesterday in her sister's living room."

His mouth fell open. "Dead?"

I nodded.

He came back to the bottom of the steps and stared up at me in disbelief. "Yesterday? Here in Montgomery?"

I nodded again.

"Are you sure?"

"Very. I found her." I had to take a deep breath at the sudden picture in my head.

If I expected sympathy, I was wasting my time. "How'd it happen? Do they know?" He seemed awfully eager to know.

"Not yet. Eunice said she'd told Myrna to call you about a job. Did she?"

His head shot up like an animal scenting danger. "No way! And if she had, I wouldn't have hired her. Can't you just picture what people would think if I kept a peroxide blonde ex-hooker around the store? Havin' her kid around was bad enough."

"You need to report Harriet missing," I told him straight out.

"We will, if she doesn't come back by the time school starts. Until then, we don't consider her missing. Now, please excuse me. I've got to get to work."

"But William!" I protested. "She's just a child. You can't—"

"In some ways, she's older than you and me put together." He stomped down the walk, then turned back.

"And you tell your cop buddy I'm not going down to look at every corpse he finds, either. It's not like lookin' at photographs, you know, and I've got enough to deal with at home trying to keep Mama and Dee from killing each other before Julie goes to college. Women!" With that flattering pronouncement, he drove away.

I stood there watching two sparrows flutter around after something in the pine straw. I wasn't really noticing them, I was thinking. Something William said reminded me of something else. Church chimes startled me back into this world. Eight o'clock. Not too early to call Carter. I wanted to talk to him as soon as possible.

Before I could even get to the phone, the police called Glenna. "Mrs. Crane? We found your husband's Buick. You'll need to come identify it and have it towed."

"I'll go," I offered.

Glenna shook her head. "I may have to sign papers or something. Just let me call Jake to tell him why we'll be late."

"At least let me do that." I hurried to the phone before she could object. I've had fifty-five years' experience in telling Jake just what I want him to know. "Hey, Jake. We're going to be a little late this morning. We need to get the car checked first."

"What's wrong with it?" he demanded.

"We're not sure. Seems to be missing a bit. We'll be there as soon as we can." I hung up with the comfortable conscience of one who has told the exact truth.

The Buick sat forlornly in the police lot. It was scratched up and missing four wheels, a radio, and a tape deck. I was devastated.

Glenna was more philosophical. "It's just a car, Clara. After nearly losing Jake, it scarcely matters. We'll have our mechanic just put tires on it for now. Jake can worry about the radio and the paint when he's up and about."

Not if I had anything to say about that.

I made Glenna leave me at the Buick dealer to wait for wheels to be put on, and I spent most of the morning there. While waiting for them to balance the tires, I finally reached Carter to explain the idea I'd had when William left.

"It's worth a check, I guess," he agreed dubiously, "but we're very thorough about things like that."

"Just check it out," I pleaded.

It felt good to be driving the Buick again. I do like a powerful car.

I headed straight to the teen center, hoping to find Kateisha.

In the lounge, I called her to a private corner and held up the disks. "Harriet's aunt found these and sent them back to you."

Kateisha grabbed them eagerly. "All *right!* I sure thought I could kiss these good-bye. Dré was gonna kill me."

"Now you can kiss them hello. I don't guess you've heard from Harriet, have you?"

She pressed her full lips together. "I tol' you before. I ain't studyin' Harriet. It ain't no skin off me if she wants to split. Now I gotta go. Dré's gonna wanna see these CDs." Before I could blink twice, she was gone.

In the hall, Lewis saw me leaving. "Hey, Mac! I've gotten permission to visit Ricky Dodd in jail. Want to go with me?"

"Why on earth would you want to do that?" I was dying to go myself, but couldn't see one earthly reason why Lewis Henly should.

He shrugged. "It's my job, remember? I help teens with problems. Ricky certainly qualifies. Want to come?"

I hesitated only an instant. "Sure. Shall I drive? Jake's car is back in circulation."

"Is his air conditioner also circulating? If so, I accept with pleasure."

On the way over, being what Joe Riddley calls nosy and what I call interested in other people, I tried to sound

Lewis out about Josheba. All he'd say was that she seemed to have a good mind. It hadn't been her mind he'd been moony-eyed over the night before, but I dropped the subject. Interest in other people can only take you so far before you do get nosy.

I'll edit our visit with Ricky a bit, in case you find cussing as boring as I do.

To see that Ricky was furious was not hard. To see that he was also scared wasn't too hard, either, although he was trying hard to hide it. "What you want?" he growled suspiciously as Lewis and I met him at the barrier.

Lewis spoke softly. "Just checking up on you, Rick. How're they treatin' you?"

"It ain't the Ritz, but I been here before." Ricky flicked back his hair.

"I wondered if there's anything I could do to help."

Ricky sneered. "Can you get me out? Harriet said you're a lawyer."

"Not in Alabama. Sorry. Didn't the court give you somebody?"

"Yeah, but I don't know if he's any good."

Lewis looked at him intently. "Makes it hard on a lawyer if the client is guilty. Did you kill that woman?"

"No!" Ricky slammed the table with one fist.

"Calm down," a guard warned.

"What were you doing there, then?" Lewis asked. Ricky looked at me. "She's okay," Lewis told him. "What were you doing up there, man?"

Sullen but goaded, Ricky talked in short bursts. "Some dame called yesterday. Said she was Harriet's old lady. I told her I ain't seen Harriet for months. She said that's okay. She knew where Harriet was."

"She knew where Harriet was?" I echoed. "Did she say where?"

"Nanh. Just said she wanted to talk to me about something." His eyes darted like a lizard's toward the guard and back.

"What . . ." I began, but Lewis's fingers dug into the small of my back. I was so startled, I shut up.

Ricky was still talking. ". . . told me to come up to her place about two. I said I'd have to get a bus. She said okay. That was all." Ricky became very interested in picking at a scab on the back of his hand.

Lewis prodded him. "What happened then?"

Ricky's muscular shoulders rose in a shrug. "Nothin'. I went to the house and knocked. Nobody answered. The front door was open, just a little, so I went in. Then," he swallowed hard, his shell cracking just a little, "I saw her. She was lying on the couch, staring at the ceiling with . . . I saw . . . a hole in her head." He swiped his forearm across his mouth and stopped, as if reliving the moment. His eyes swung wildly from side to side as they must have at the time. "Then I heard somebody outside, coming up the walk. Man, I just split, out the back. I don't know how the fuzz found out, but they come later, looking for me. They think I killed her. I didn't. I swear it!"

"They found your gun," I reminded him.

He glared at me. "I ain't seen it for a couple of months. Harriet took it."

"Harriet could back you up, man," Lewis pointed out. "If you know where she is—"

"I told you, I ain't seen her in weeks."

While they were talking, I finally realized what the "something" Ricky went to talk about might be: drugs. I also had a dreadful thought about what might have happened to Harriet. "Ricky, did Harriet ever sell or buy drugs?"

"Nanh. Harriet hates drugs. She don't even like cigarettes. And if you so much as mention drugs—ooee!"

"Harriet *hates* drugs," Lewis agreed emphatically. "Now, Rick, I'm making you an offer. You're in serious trouble here, man, and it's not the first time. I can't represent you in court, but when you get out, if you decide you want to go straight and get some help, give me a call. I'm in the book. You know my last name?"

Ricky's lip curled derisively. "Lew-is Hen-ly," he said in a singsong. "Harriet says it five times an hour. She may be sweet on you, man, but I ain't no nigger lover. I may need help, but I don't need *yours*."

He stomped past the guard back into his temporary home.

On the way back to the club, I was so embarrassed I didn't know what to say. Lewis, too, seemed to be glad to ride in silence. I dropped him off and drove to the hospital beneath huge gray thunderheads that exactly matched my mood. Occasional green lightning cracked the sky as I would have liked to crack Ricky Dodd's head.

Tuesday evening, I stayed with Jake while Glenna went to a women's circle meeting. As I was fixing to leave, a tremendous jag of lightning split the sky. Less than a minute later, a sheet of rain lashed the window. "Will you be all right?" Jake asked, his eyes anxious.

"I don't melt," I assured him, "and I got a parking space near the door."

"Parking space?" He raised one eyebrow. "I thought Glenna dropped you off."

"Gotta run," I told him, giving him a swift kiss.

I was halfway through the door when he roared, "Clara, if you're driving my car — "

"Don't have another attack, Jake. I can't spend all summer over here."

Long before I reached the car, I was soaked to the skin. The rain was unexpectedly cold, and my teeth chattered as I unlocked the Buick and dropped soggily into the seat. My hair wilted down one side of my face. "You look a mess," I informed my reflection.

I drove home slowly, steaming in the hot car but too wet to want the air conditioner on. The rain bucketed down. I had to concentrate so hard on driving that at first I didn't notice the lights behind me. Then, although they followed me as far as Fairview Avenue, I wasn't worried. I figured somebody else from South Hull District or Old Cloverdale had been at the hospital until visiting hours were over, too. The lights were awfully bright, though, and in a flicker of lightning I saw the hood of a pickup.

"Get off my bumper, buster." I muttered as I turned left onto Glenna's street. When the truck followed, I slowed a little and pulled over, hoping it would pass. Instead, it pulled in behind me coming so fast I put on the gas and spurted ahead, afraid I'd get hit. The truck hugged my bumper, its lights bright in my mirrors.

I put on as much speed as I dared, but it stuck like a burr. I passed Glenna's house and kept going, turning at the next block. It did, too. At the corner was a stop sign I dared not ignore. The other driver pulled into the left lane beside me, swerved to slam my left fender, reversed, and roared away. I got one quick glimpse of a red door and hair that gleamed almost white in the night.

I was trembling so hard I knew I shouldn't drive quite yet. I was wondering whether I should switch off the engine for a minute, when I heard a roar, raised startled eyes to my rearview mirror, and saw the same brilliant lights bearing down on me again. The truck banged my back bumper with a jarring impact that skidded me into the intersection and buried my nose in Jake's airbag as the engine died.

Would I suffocate first, or be hit by another car? To my relief, the airbag suddenly went limp. I could see that I was still the only vehicle on the wet, shiny road.

Thank God! Also thank God, the engine started at once. Driving with the airbag was awkward. My left headlight was out. When the car moved, it made a strange grinding noise. I, however, was past being particular. I headed home.

Glenna must have brought some women home from her circle. A Honda like Josheba's sat in front of the house, behind a gray car I did not recognize. I thought about not going in as awful as I looked, but that attack had been deliberate. What if whoever it was knew who I was — and where I was staying? What if he came looking for me again?

I squished toward the house, tears of rage mingling with rain. As I sloshed into the living room, three pairs of startled eyes met mine.

"What on earth, Mac?" Josheba gasped.

Glenna headed for the kitchen. "Get out of those wet clothes. I'll get hot coffee."

It was the third person I was happiest to see. "Oh, Carter, I'm so glad you're here. I think somebody just tried to kill me!"

Speak up for those who cannot speak for themselves, for the rights of all who are destitute. *Proverbs 31:8*

Twenty-Two

Carter was immediately official. "Could you identify the perpetrator, Miss MacLaren?"

I shook my head. "A red pickup, blonde driver." I described what had happened.

"Man or woman?"

For the life of me, I didn't know. "I just saw hair. That looked light and long."

"Did you get a license number?"

"Heavens no! It all happened too fast."

He looked at me gloomily. "Had you heard that Ricky Dodd was released tonight? Somebody came down and paid his bail."

I was both astonished and suddenly chilled. "You reckon Ricky tried to kill me?"

"I don't know, but I'd watch my step for a few days. He found out you're the one put the finger on him for being up at Myrna Dawson's murder site, and he's not a happy camper."

Josheba had another question. "Who does Ricky know with enough money for bail? He doesn't look like he has a penny, and I wouldn't credit him with a friend in the world."

Carter shook his head. "Somebody who wished to remain anonymous. It was arranged through a bondsman who doesn't reveal his sources. Whoever it was, though, must think they can keep Ricky under surveillance until his case comes up. They put up a hefty amount."

"Either wanted to keep him under surveillance or had a use for him," Josheba pointed out. "Mac, you be extra careful. You hear me?"

"It's too late to worry about that. Jake's going to kill me anyway. His car is wrecked."

Glenna came back with coffee in time to hear my last words. "Don't fuss, honey. He doesn't need to know a thing about it. We'll take the Buick to a body shop first thing in the morning and leave it until it's as good as new. Now drink this. It's got lots of sugar in it for shock. Then go change your clothes."

Suddenly I realized how wet and chilled I was. "How about if I take it with me while I change?" As I stood up, I thought to ask Josheba, "What are you doing here?"

"I came to bring some leftover lasagna. I thought you all could nibble on it between hospital visits."

"That was real sweet of you." My teeth chattered so hard I couldn't say another thing.

I stripped down to my birthday suit, rubbed myself with a towel, and put on my pajamas and robe. This was twice in one day I'd be entertaining a man in my pajamas, but I was too worn out to care. Besides, I had something important to ask Carter as soon as I got back to the living room. "Did you have any luck with what I asked you to check on?"

"Yes, ma'am. That's one reason I came by tonight—besides wanting to check on Jake, of course. I found the one you meant." He pulled a sheet of paper out of his shirt pocket and consulted it. From the look of it, it was a copy of a police report. "She was positively identified as Inez Foster, seventeen, by her mother and stepfather, Ada and Paul Baker. She had been missing three years."

I explained to the others, "This morning, William informed me that identifying a dead body isn't like looking at a photograph. That made me think about something a teenager said last night, about a missing girl whose mother recognized her picture in the paper. I just wondered if it could have been Harriet, instead."

"No, ma'am," Carter shook his head. "I'm sorry."

"When was she found?" I pestered him.

He put his finger on something on the sheet. "At five P.M. on Monday, June tenth."

"This past June?" I felt a big hand clutch my stomach and give it a squeeze. From Josheba's expression, she felt the same. What happened to me less than an hour ago went plumb out of my head.

"Do you have her description?" Josheba asked, her voice unsteady.

Carter nodded, and used one finger to mark the place. "Adolescent female. Five-one. Brown hair. One hundred and fifteen pounds. Wearing black jeans, black sandals, and black T-shirt. No sign of sexual violation. Found under bush by woman walking her dog."

Josheba's gaze flew to mine. "That could have been Harriet. She always wore black."

"When do they think she got killed?" I asked, nearly breaking my neck trying to read that sheet for myself.

Maddeningly, Carter pulled it closer to his nose, scanning for the answer. I couldn't see a thing. "She didn't get killed, Miss MacLaren," he said, in that insufferable tone polite young men use when correcting older women. "There were no signs of foul play, but there *were* signs of vomiting and diarrhea on her clothes, like she'd had flu or eaten something that didn't agree with her. No poison, though."

"Well, when do they think she died, then?"

He shrugged and read verbatim. "Indications for time of death uncertain. Estimated lying there since Friday. Mowers covered the area Thursday, June sixth, and saw nothing."

Nobody said a word for a few minutes. Whoever the child was, she deserved better than to wind up under a bush. I felt like an empty bucket somebody had just filled with sorrow. "Carter, if that child was Harriet Lawson instead of that Inez whatever, how could we prove or disprove it?"

"Her mother came down to the morgue and identified her, ma'am. You can't get clearer than that."

That was a whammy. A mother ought to know. Still, Raye's granddaughter said she'd been gone for several years. And if she'd been under the bush for several days—

"Where did you get the picture you put in the paper?" I asked.

He paused. "Well?" I pressed him.

"She'd laid there too long to take a picture, so they had an artist make a drawing. It was a picture of the drawing we put in the paper." He wriggled uncomfortably. I knew what he was thinking. It was one thing to discuss bodies down at the station, quite another to describe grisly details with three ladies. I'd been around police officers too long to be squeamish, however.

"And her mother just identified her from the picture?"

"No, ma'am. She came down and identified the actual remains."

"But how much could she see, really? Was there enough to make a true identification? And did you do dental records, things like that?"

"She hadn't had any dental work, but her mother was sure." His face wore what my mother called a balky look.

"Didn't she carry any other identification?" Glenna leaned forward to ask.

He read his notes, relieved to be free of me for a minute. "No, Cuddin' Glenna. Nothing found with her."

"Not even a pocketbook?" I demanded.

"A bookbag, more likely," Josheba added.

"Nothing. Just a couple of dollars in one pocket." I couldn't blame him for sounding impatient, but I was convinced they had made a mistake.

Josheba spoke before I could. "That doesn't make any sense. No teenager would be traveling around without a pocketbook or backpack."

I put in my own two cents' worth. "Could we at least get yearbook photos of both girls, Carter, to see if the artist thinks it could have been Harriet instead of Inez?"

"I hate to keep harping on this, Miss MacLaren, but her mother identified her. And unless Harriet's folks report her missing, we don't have any reason to be looking for *her*."

"I could get Harriet's yearbook picture," Josheba offered, as though he hadn't spoken. "I have a friend who teaches at Lanier, where she went through the end of the year."

Glenna reached out and touched him gently on the knee. "Can you get Clara a copy of the photograph from the paper, Carter? It would save her going to the library to look for it."

"I can, sure, but the big boss isn't going to like this."

"What if you all made a mistake?" Glenna's gray eyes were darker with worry.

"If we made a mistake, it won't look good for the force."

"But when you come up with the right solution, think how impressed they'll all be," I pointed out. "Carter, please bring me the picture. If it's not Harriet, I'll give up. I promise."

"I'll bring it, Miss MacLaren, but if anybody finds out, my name is mud."

Let the wise listen and add to their learning, and let the discerning get guidance. *Proverbs 1:5*

Twenty-Three

Jake developed a slight fever overnight, and Glenna went to the hospital early Thursday, forgetting all about taking the Buick to a body shop. That was all right with me. I'd had an idea about that.

About mid-morning, Carter dropped by the artist's picture and a photo of Inez from three years before. I could see a superficial resemblance between those two, and was amazed that the artist could do so well. When Josheba arrived a little later and looked at the drawing, though, she said flatly, "It's Harriet. The artist did an incredible job. Look!"

As soon as I compared the drawing with Harriet's picture in the Lanier High School yearbook, I felt like I did the Christmas I learned there was no Santa Claus. Even last night I hadn't quite believed Harriet was dead. Now, I was sure.

We sat in silence, thinking of the child nobody loved.

I studied her face again, trying to put her features on the spirit child I'd carried with me all those days. It was no good. She was a perfect stranger. "Well," I said finally, setting the picture aside, "we know when we lost Harriet. We just don't know how and why."

"That's Carter's problem." Josheba looked at her watch. "And if I don't get over to the library, I'm gonna have a problem, too."

I knew what I wanted to do next. I wanted to find out why Dee hadn't identified the artist's picture herself.

The Sykes's driveway was empty. I almost drove away without ringing the bell, but Julie opened the front door to see who was in the drive, then waved and ran to the car, cheerful in sunny red shorts. Her fingernails were painted to match, and from her ears swung delicate silver spiderwebs with silver feathers dangling from them.

I rolled down my window. "I thought nobody was home. Where's your car?" I peered up at her, trying to decide if those dream-catcher earrings were like the ones Kateisha had.

"Daddy's truck got banged up, so he's borrowing the Miata while it gets fixed. I followed him to the shop, then he dropped me by here a few minutes ago. I wish he'd waited. I found a note saying Mom's out at Gram's—probably fighting about college."

"How do you feel about that?" I asked, genuinely curious.

She shrugged. "I don't really care. A lot of my friends are going to Bama, so that would be fun, but I haven't traveled much, so it might be fun to go somewhere else, too. I don't really have to decide until next year, anyway. I just wish Mama and Gram would stop fighting about it."

I was so busy wondering whether Julie had any idea of what college was for besides having fun, I nearly didn't notice when she looked down the drive, frowned, and repeated, "I wish Daddy had waited."

"Why?"

"When he called Gram this morning—he calls her every morning, you know, just to be sure she's okay—well, today she asked him to come over on his lunch hour to look at a new tree she's gotten. He could have taken me, too."

"I'll take you," I offered, feeling like a low-down sneak, but absolutely delighted that Julie was making this so easy.

"Would you? That's great!" She went back to grab her pocketbook. As she rounded my car, she stopped to touch the front fender. "Boy, what happened to your car?"

"I had a little accident last night. Say, which garage does your daddy use? I'd like to get this fixed before my brother sees it—it's his car."

She climbed in and slammed the door, then scrabbled through her pocketbook and handed me a card. "I picked this up while I was waiting this morning. He must be good. Daddy uses him all the time."

"Thank you," I murmured triumphantly as I started my engine. That card almost made up for having to drive all the way out to Wynlakes—which seemed like halfway to Georgia.

"I like your earrings," I broke into her chatter a little later. "Where did you get them?"

"I—uh—" She gave me a sharp look. "They were Gram's. They're called dream catchers. Aren't they pretty?" She shook her head so they'd dance.

I just knew she was lying, but this wasn't the time to press her. We were at the entrance gate to Wynlakes, and I needed her to get us past the security guard.

As it turned out, I didn't. The guard cheerfully waved us through without a question. So much for security. Montgomery isn't a very dangerous place anyway. Except for Harriet.

"Wynlakes is named for Winton Blount, the man who gave the land and money for the Shakespeare Festival," Julie told me, taking her great-grandmother's place as tour guide. "Isn't it simply gorgeous?"

It was far newer and more lavish than I would feel at home in, but the homes and grounds would be beautiful when the trees grew a bit. Nora's house was what I think they call French something or other, a large gray stucco house with a soft green lawn. Like William's, her yard had lots of healthy flower beds. She also had several Bradford pears, a couple of dogwoods, and an unplanted oak, roots balled in burlap. I wondered why anybody as savvy about plants as Nora was planting a tree in midsummer.

Nora herself welcomed us wearing a stunning mist green linen shirt and matching pants, but her cheeks were red and her eyes snapped with anger. She gave us a strained smile.

"Miss Laura brought me out," Julie said, stepping into the cool elegant hall like a princess.

"I needed to see Dee," I explained.

Nora hesitated, then stepped back. "Come on in. Julie, ask your mother to come. She's in the kitchen." From her tone, I suspected they had been arguing again, but Nora couldn't have been more gracious as she led me into her ivory and gold living room. In the morning sunlight her gold jewelry glittered and her red hair gleamed.

"I love your necklace," I gushed as I took my seat. "I used to have a silver one something like it. Do you ever wear silver?"

Nora lightly touched her flaming hair. "With this coloring? Never."

I tried not to let my elation show. "I also couldn't help noticing your tree. We're in the nursery business — "

" — and you're wondering why I'm planting just now. A friend was digging that tree up to put in a new carport, and I couldn't bear to just let it die without giving it a chance. Of course, even if it lives, it won't be much to look at until Julie has grandchildren."

I gave her an approving smile. "You have to care about the future to plant an oak."

Dee joined us right then, worried eyes seeming out of place with her casual khaki skirt, scarlet top, and sandals. Her nails also matched her shirt.

She looked puzzled to see me, but perched on the edge of an ivory brocade chair. "Were you able to get those CDs to Harriet's friend?"

"If not," Julie spoke from behind her chair, "I hope you kept them for me."

"Kateisha was overjoyed to get them," I told them.

"Not as overjoyed as I was to get rid of them," Dee replied.

"Oh *Moth*-er!" Julie moved to a chair between us.

"I came to show you this." I held out the sketch to Dee, and scarcely breathed.

Julie reached ahead of her mother and took the picture. "Hey, that's good! But I'm surprised Harriet didn't make them put in that little mole just under her eye. Her beauty mark." She drawled the last sentence out sarcastically.

Dee took the picture from her and Nora moved over to join her.

"Who did this?" Dee demanded. "And when? Have you found her?"

Now that I'd come right down to it, I wished I'd left it up to Carter to tell them. "A police artist drew it. It's a picture of someone they found in a cemetery June tenth. It was in the paper. I'm surprised you didn't see it."

Julie gave a little squeal and her earrings danced. "Harriet's dead?" She took the picture back, looked at it quickly, then thrust it at her mother as if she couldn't get rid of it quick enough. Dee pressed one hand to her mouth and looked positively sick.

"June tenth, you said?" Nora said thoughtfully. "We left for the mountains Friday afternoon the seventh—William, Dee, Julie, and me—and stopped our newspapers for the next week. This is dreadful, MacLaren, but I am glad they've finally found the child. It was time."

"It was past time," I said angrily.

Dee narrowed her eyes and poked one cheek with a cerise-tipped finger. "I can't be positive it's her, though. It looks very much like her, but—they didn't take a picture?"

I was past being nice. "It was too late for that."

"Oh!" Her eyes flew to Julie. "Honey, would you get us something to drink? Real Cokes, with lots of ice?"

"You just want to get rid of me," Julie protested angrily.

"Julie!"

"Okay, but you'll have to tell me everything later." She flounced out.

"I'll come with you," Nora offered. We heard them talking softly in the kitchen.

"Where did they find her—this person?" Dee asked in a low voice as soon as Julie was out of earshot.

"Under a bush in Oakwood Cemetery."

"What was she wearing?" It sounded like one last desperate bid for hope.

"Black jeans, black sandals, and a black T-shirt."

Dee covered her mouth with her hand and moaned. "Oh, Laura, Harriet *always* wore black. Even her fingernails. Part of the fight she and William had was over whether she could dye her hair." Her eyes were stricken. She leaned back against the chair and closed them, and tears seeped from beneath her lashes. "I should have tried to find her."

Maybe I ought to have patted her hand and told her everything was going to be all right. The thought did cross my mind. But then my eyes lit on Harriet's picture again, and all my sympathy dried up. "How long was she gone, again?"

Dee opened her eyes and numbered the days on her fingertips. In a sudden shaft of sunlight they seemed dipped in blood. "She was there Sunday while we were at church – that must have been the second. She took her bathing suit and some shorts. She came back Tuesday while I was shopping and getting my nails done, because I'd left some clean clothes on her bed and they were gone."

Julie came in and haughtily deposited a tray with two tall glasses of iced Coca Cola on the mahogany coffee table. She handed me a drink and a green paper napkin, then sat down with the look of somebody who has paid her dues and plans to stay.

"Were you home that Tuesday, Julie?" Dee asked. "The one right after school was out? I can't remember."

Julie jumped and flushed. "Tuesday? No, I told you. I was with Rachel." She threw her grandmother an anxious look, but Nora didn't notice. She was considerately rising to adjust the blind so the sun wouldn't be in my eyes. Julie started to babble. "Rachel and I were at our house on Wednesday, though. Remember? You went strawberry picking. Harriet didn't come by that day at all."

"And I was up at the lake all week," Nora added, lifting a glass of something clear to her lips.

Julie gave her another anxious look, but said nothing. Instead, she leaned toward her mother. "Weren't there some things gone on Friday, too? While you were at that women's luncheon and we were at the movies? I think you said so."

Dee buried her face in her hands. "I can't remember. It seems so long ago! But I hate to think that any child who's been left in my care . . ." Her voice trailed off. I noticed she did *not* say "any child I've loved."

"What happened to her?" Julie asked. Nora threw me a silent plea not to supply sordid details.

"I don't know," I told her honestly. I didn't add that the police didn't, either.

The Miata purred up and parked on the crowded drive. Through the living room window I saw William climb out of the driver's seat, look angrily at Dee's Mercedes, and run toward the door. He stopped in the living room archway and gave Dee a worried look. "What are you doing here?"

"I've got Julie's and my itinerary planned for our little trip," Nora told him with dignity, "and I wanted to discuss it with Dee."

"Can't you leave that alone until we can all sit down and talk about it?" he demanded.

Nora silenced him with a wave and continued, "But before we finished talking, MacLaren arrived to tell us something dreadful about Harriet."

He noticed me for the first time. I regret to say, he swore.

"William," Dee protested. "Look!" She held out the picture and burst into tears.

"Get some tissues, Julie," Nora commanded. The girl hurried from the room.

William took the picture and studied it. Nora stood beside him, just touching his arm. "So?" William demanded. "It's a good likeness, but what does it prove?"

"That's a picture of a young girl killed last month up in Oakwood Cemetery," Nora told him softly.

"An artist drew that from the—remains," Julie added, bringing a whole box of tissues as if she couldn't be bothered to pull out one or two. She tried to sound real concerned, but the avid look in her eyes betrayed her. *Miss Pris got her nose out of joint when her cousin moved in,* I thought, *and isn't too sorry she was permanently removed.* Which, coupled with the earrings, raised a disturbing possibility.

Dee dabbed her eyes and blew her nose. "She was dead, William. Too long for anybody to even identify her. I just *knew* we should have looked for her. I knew it!"

"You don't know anything, Kitten," he said gruffly. "Those police artists just draw what they like—somebody they've seen recently, maybe—and nobody can tell them it's wrong. This could be any number of girls. It doesn't have to be Harriet."

"But, honey, she was wearing clothes like Harriet's, and she was found the week after you and Harriet had that big fight."

"You hush!" William's ruddy face grew suddenly mottled.

Dee's eyes widened in bafflement and she appealed to Julie. "What did I say?"

Julie gave her a look of scorn. "Figure it out for yourself."

Nora bent over me. "Perhaps you'd better go now, dear. We're all so upset—"

I stood. "It's time to get upset," I told them all angrily, "and it's time to call and report Harriet missing. That way the police can make a proper identification."

"And we can all get on with our lives," Nora agreed. "It's certainly past time."

Armed with the name of William's favorite body shop and the knowledge that his truck was at that very minute being repaired, I took Jake's car by on my way home.

The garage was a small concrete building, badly in need of paint, but restful. Its walls reflected the morning sun. Wildflowers bloomed in tall clumps of grass that miraculously poked their way through cracks in the pavement. I parked close to a stall where a blue backside was bent over the front fender of a red pickup truck, approached the truck, and checked out the fender. "Looks like they hit somebody," I said pleasantly.

"A tree, he told me." That stringy old man had probably been around the garage almost as long as it had stood. "Something I can do for you?"

I checked the card Julie had given me. "Are you Mr. McGuire?"

"Yessum, that's me." He wore his grease-stained chino shirt and pants with dignity.

"Is that William Sykes's truck? His daughter gave me your name."

He nodded. "Yep. Skidded in the storm last night. Needs a coupla dents removed." He spoke in fragments rather than sentences, as if more accustomed to silence.

I pointed toward the Buick. "I've got a similar problem. Something skidded in the rain and hit me. Any chance you could make that good as new?"

The practiced hand he ran over my dents was oil-black in the seams and gnarled, as if it had worked with cars too long to ever be clean again. "Can't get to it till tomorrow, and I'll probably have to get a new fender and back bumper. Don't make cars like they used to. And it sounds like you've got a problem with your rear end alignment, too. That'll need fixing."

"Whatever," I told him. "Just work as fast as you can. The car belongs to my brother, and he's getting out of the hospital in a day or two. He won't be able to drive for a few days, but I don't want him fretting over his car."

His dark eyes glinted with amusement. "He know you banged it up?"

"No, and let's keep it that way. That's why I asked the Sykes's for the name of somebody good and quick." I went over and stroked the pickup fender. Against the vivid red was a darker streak of a different red—the same color as Jake's Buick. I felt myself tremble with excitement, but I called as innocently as I knew how, "Look! It looks like this truck could have hit my car."

The mechanic compared the smear on William's right front fender and the dent in the Buick's left front fender. "Sure does." His experienced fingertips stroked my dent again. "How'd you say yours got banged up, again?"

"Somebody hit me in the rain. I didn't see who it was."

He shook his head. "It was a bad storm. You mighta got in Mr. Sykes's way and he didn't even know it. That'd be something, wouldn't it? You knowing each other an' all."

"It sure would be something," I agreed.

I left him Jake's keys and telephone number and called a cab from his crowded little office. If necessary, I would have a witness that William Sykes's truck hit me last night. But who was driving the truck?

Many a man claims to have unfailing love, but a faithful man who can find? *Proverbs 20:6*

Twenty-Four

Mac was going to spend Wednesday afternoon with her brother. I—Josheba—was planning to put my feet up and do nothing. About two, Lewis called. "You free for a while? I'm taking this afternoon off, and there's a place I want to go."

My stomach did a queer flip-flop that was odd for somebody expecting Morse back by Saturday. "I guess so. I've got some studying to do, but it can wait. I've got some things to tell you anyway. Let's take my car, though. I'm partial to air conditioning."

"Me, too. Why do you think I asked you along?"

He came out to the car wearing a light blue shirt and white jeans and looking so fine I couldn't help exclaiming, "You look *good* today!"

He checked out my white pants, batik shirt, and sandals. "You don't look so bad yourself." I'd better not. I'd spent the past half hour deciding what to wear.

Before I started the car again, I said, "I hate to start out the afternoon with bad news, but you need to know two things. First, somebody tried to run Mac down last night. Ricky's out of jail, and it could well have been him."

"Is Mac okay?" He looked so worried, I could have hugged him.

"Shaken up a bit, but okay otherwise."

"Who bailed him out?"

"I don't know. The police said it was somebody who wishes to remain anonymous."

Lewis grunted. "That's one anonymous donor we could all have done without." He was silent a minute, then asked, "You said two things?"

That one was harder to say. "Mac and I think Harriet is dead. They found a body up in Oakwood Cemetery last month not long after she disappeared, and the artist's picture looks exactly like her." My voice wobbled a little.

He was silent a moment, then he laid one hand over mine. "I'm sorry, Josheba, if she is. I really did think old Harriet would come stomping back in one day to keep us all in line. You said they found her last month. Why are they just getting around to identifying her?"

"They aren't identifying her, Mac and I are." When I had explained, I finished up, "So the police aren't sure yet, but we are. I can't believe how sad this has made me, Lewis. I didn't even know her well—just at the library—but I've been thinking about her all day."

"Sounds like you could use some distraction. Start the motor, sister, and drive on." He wouldn't tell me where we were going, just said things like "Turn right at the second corner" or "Now go straight a while." Finally we turned onto North Hull, and I knew.

"I haven't been here since grammar school! I used to love to prowl around this place." We were heading to Old Alabama Town, a few blocks where they've brought together a lot of old buildings to represent Alabama a hundred years ago. There's a farm, a church, an old grange hall, an apothecary, a little school—a whole little village right near downtown.

"I come here whenever I need to get perspective," Lewis told me. "It reminds me that people in the past had problems, too, and things did change. Our problems won't mean much in a hundred years, and maybe some more things will have changed, too."

"We'll be dead by then," I reminded him.

"There is that," he admitted.

The front office was crisp and cool, but when we went back out, the heat swelled back toward us like a wave. Lewis looked around, surprised. "I guess nobody else is around today."

"Everybody else is smart," I informed him.

He shifted his shoulders in his blue shirt. "It is a little hot and muggy today. Do you mind?"

"Sure I mind, but is Montgomery in July ever anything else?" It wasn't very funny, but he laughed, then I laughed, then we both laughed just because we were laughing. In spite of all the worry over Harriet, I'd laughed more that week than I had since Mama died.

Then I felt a twinge of disloyalty to Morse. "I shouldn't be here," I told him.

He shrugged. "Well, so long as you are, you might as well have a good time. This is a day the Lord has made, Josheba. Let's rejoice and be glad in it."

I shook my head. "I told you, Lewis, I don't believe in God anymore."

He turned and gently tilted my chin. "Daddy got killed, so God gets the chill?"

"You got that right," I said fiercely. "I won't believe in a God who lets good people die. I want a God who keeps people from dying!"

He gently stroked my cheek with a finger as light as the kiss of a rose. "Honey, your daddy died because he believed in a God who would die *himself* for somebody he loved. Think where you and I would be today if people like Dr. King and your daddy hadn't lived and died. Their very lives were a prayer. And you know what else? Everything you've done this week to find Harriet is following right in your daddy's footsteps. Don't tell me you don't believe in God. You pray and don't know it."

I broke away and walked angrily toward a house made of two separate rooms connected by a breezeway. As long as we were here, we might as well get our money's worth, but I didn't plan to speak to him again the entire afternoon.

Lewis caught up with me as I was climbing the steps. "They call this a dogtrot house. Actually it looks like a woman trot house to me. Can you imagine running back and forth every time your pot boiled over or your baby cried?"

I knew he was trying to make me smile, but I wouldn't give him the satisfaction. Stalking away, I headed toward the old grange hall. It was infernally hot. Lewis found a switch to turn on ceiling fans, but they merely stirred the heat into a muggy stew. While he wandered about looking at faded pictures of once elegant houses—white folks' houses, now destroyed by time—I strolled over to an old loom and stroked it gently. He came up behind me and covered my hand with his. I trembled, turned, and pulled away.

He drew me back and turned me to him. Before I knew it was coming, he bent his head and gently kissed me full on the lips.

I would have pushed him away, but the world was swinging around so fast I needed to hold on for dear life. I don't know whether we stood there a minute or an hour. Probably somewhere in between. Finally I found the fortitude to jerk away. "No, Lewis!"

I hurried over to examine an old carriage as carefully as if I planned to buy it to ride my children in. He spoke softly behind me. "You can't just pretend this hasn't happened."

I took a step away and spoke over one shoulder. "I can try. And I can make sure it doesn't happen again." Oppressed by the heat and the weight of my own feelings, I stepped past him and into the bright sunlight.

In the shotgun house, I averted my eyes from the sagging rope bed and looked carefully at an insipid doll with a white china face. Lewis wandered into another room. I was glad he was away from me, but as I caught a glimpse of him through an open doorway, his back and trim dark head seemed dearer than any I had ever known.

Determined I could beat this thing, I wandered into the room where he was and looked over the furniture. Then, just as I turned to read a plaque on one wall, he turned to look at an old dresser on another, and suddenly I was in his arms again. Once more we seemed to fuse together.

He broke away this time, and gestured to the door. "Let's go down on the farm, where it's cooler."

He led the way to a corner set up like an old farmyard, complete with log cabin. There he sank to the silver porch boards at the top of the steps and motioned me to sit down beside him. I made sure to leave enough space between us.

"This looks a lot like the house my granddaddy used to have," he said when I was settled. "Feels like a good place to talk. How attached are you to this man you're thinking about marrying?"

I was so startled that I replied in one word: "Very."

"Then why are you spending so much time with me?"

I started to answer, but he held up one slim brown hand. "I know, you wanted my help in finding Harriet, right? But now you've found her. So why are you here?"

"Well," I said slowly, "I guess because I enjoy your company. And as you yourself pointed out not long ago, surely a man and a woman can be friends without . . ."

He shook his head in quick denial. "I'm not as sure of that as I was."

"Neither am I," I admitted in a small voice.

We didn't say a word for several minutes, watching a bright Monarch butterfly gently fan its wings on a head of Queen Anne's lace. When Lewis did speak, he talked to the butterfly instead of me. "I want to tell you some things about myself, things I'm not proud of. After that, you may never want to see me again, but if you do, I won't always be worrying you'll find out." He reached into his pocket, brought out a toothpick wrapped in plastic, opened it, and stuck it into a corner of his mouth.

"You look like a hayseed," I muttered, hoping to distract him from getting serious.

"I am a hayseed," he told me. "My granddaddy was a sharecropper. Now listen! When I got out of law school, I was plumb broke. I'd borrowed so much money I thought I'd never be able to pay it back, and everything was so expensive! Books, the right clothes for interviews, a car to drive—I had my eye on a Jag in those days."

"Something's happened to your eyes," I told him, thinking of his broken-down Ford.

He laughed, but it wasn't humorous. "Yeah. I started seeing more clearly. Back then, though, not too long after I found a job at the bottom of a firm in Nashville—the very bottom, sort of a glorified clerk—some men approached me. Told me they would lend me a condo in the Bahamas several times a year if I'd do a little job for them. I thought they wanted me to represent them, but that wasn't it. They wanted me to pretend to represent them so I could travel back and forth and carry drugs."

"You could have been arrested. Or killed!" I added, horrified.

He shook his head. "They had it fixed up so there wasn't as much risk as you'd think. These guys knew what they were doing. And they offered me a lot of money—like they knew exactly how much debt I had. I told myself I wasn't using drugs or selling drugs, and if I didn't bring them in, somebody else would. Why shouldn't I get all that money? When I told you about how much money I used to make as a lawyer? It wasn't as a lawyer." He gave a bitter little grunt. "My granddaddy used to plow with a mule. I bet he never thought one of his grandsons would be one." He fell silent.

"What made you quit?" Then I had a terrifying thought. "You did, didn't you?"

He nodded soberly and threw away his toothpick as if it had suddenly gone sour. "One day I got a call to come get my little brother Tony out of jail. He'd been picked up selling drugs on his college campus. You know why he was selling? To support his habit. My baby brother! He was in college, with the whole world in front of him, and—" He shook his head and his eyes filled with sudden tears. "You can't imagine how awful it's been, Josheba. I've spent almost every penny I made carrying drugs trying to get Tony off them. He's been in and out of rehab so many times I've stopped counting, and he never stays clean more than a month. Almost as bad as what's happened to him is what it's done to our mama. She wouldn't believe it in the beginning. Now she's given up hope.

"I found myself furious with whoever started him on the stuff. Then I found out it was somebody Tony met at my place one afternoon, one of my own contacts. When I pointed a finger at him, I pointed three at me. I couldn't keep doing what I was doing and look myself in the mirror. I decided it was time to spend some time helping other kids stay clean. Call it penance, call it a memorial to Tony, call it whatever you want, but I quit the firm and called a law-school buddy down here who's always worked with kids. He found me this job."

He sighed. "Harriet found out about my past, by the way. Tony came by one day looking for money and when I turned him down, he yelled something about my being high and mighty now, but pushing drugs before. I hadn't, of course, not technically, but Harriet heard. She got on my case after he left, said she'd spread the word if I didn't give her Coke money." He laughed. "Like I told you once or twice before, it was a bit of a relief when she decided to up and go." He sobered. "I wouldn't have wanted her dead, though."

I didn't know what to say, so I blurted out what came first to my mind. "Will you ever be a lawyer again?"

"I may go back to practicing someday. I don't know. But I do know I had to tell you all this before I ask you to marry me instead of old what's-his-name."

I lifted my head, startled. He was serious!

He held up one hand to keep me from speaking. "Don't answer yet. I don't even want to know what you're thinking right now. Just promise to think about it, okay?"

I dropped my eyes and studied a robin hopping around on the walk. "I don't need to think," I said stubbornly. "I like you, Lewis, but I can't marry you." I slid a few inches farther away and began to trace circles on a silvery old board between us. "You — this may sound trite, but you are very special to me. Very special," I repeated with emphasis, "and I have never felt so cared for, so" — I raised my eyes to meet his — "so in tune with somebody."

His eyebrows rose. "Never?"

I shook my head and answered honestly. "Never. But a few months ago I made a promise I intend to keep. Morse hasn't done anything to deserve this." I thought about Morse raging about that silly shirt, whining about the bad weather, or partying up there with any women who came along. "Morse doesn't deserve this," I amended it swiftly. "You matter to me a whole lot, but my word means something, too."

"Even if the person you gave it to doesn't."

"Don't say that!" I cried hotly. "Morse does matter, in many ways. He hurts me sometimes, sure. Deep inside I keep wondering if what I feel for you isn't just a reaction …"

He reached out and gripped my wrist hard. "Don't say that!" he repeated my own words. "What we feel is real and special and ours. Say it!"

"What we feel is real and special and . . ." I faltered, then looked him straight in the eyes. ". . . ours. You're right, it is. But it's got to stop."

"You could change your promise," he suggested, taking my hand and tracing a circle over and over in my palm. "Make it to me, instead. If you have regrets — "

I pulled my hand away and massaged the scalp under my braids to stimulate my brain. "Who knows why I have regrets, Lewis? Maybe it's just because Morse's away. Or because we had a fight right before he left. I don't even know you, not really. We've spent most of our time talking about Harriet — "

"Spare me Harriet," he said sourly.

"Okay. But what I mean is, I can't promise to love you while I'm still promised to Morse. If I did, you ought to worry whether I'd change my mind again sometime. My mama taught me that every time we break our word or hurt somebody, it gets easier, until some people get to the place where they can abuse others, even kill them, without a twinge. The men who killed Daddy were like that. I saw them, you know. Don't look at me like that. I did. I was at the window when he went out on the porch. I saw them shoot him and saw their faces when he fell. They laughed! I hated them. Mama spent the rest of her life teaching me it was possible to become just like them if I let myself hate, or if I valued other people, my own self, and my honor lightly. Maybe that's why I can't let this Harriet thing go."

"Amen to that," Lewis murmured. He leaned back and crossed his ankles. "But continue. I haven't been to church this week."

I jumped to my feet. "Never mind."

He caught my wrist again. "Hey, I'm sorry. But you do remind me of your daddy, honey, did you know that? He used to talk about not valuing yourself and others lightly, too. I remember a sermon he preached once—I couldn't have been more than nine, but the image was so clear. He said that if even a butterfly gets hurt"—he pointed toward the Monarch, still waving its wings gently in the heat—"ripples go out until the very core of the universe gets bruised. While he was talking, I could just see it happening. Now that I've lived a while, I see how true it is. I've bruised more people in my lifetime than I like to remember."

I nodded. "We live in a bruised and hurting world, Lewis. I don't want to add any more than I have to."

"You don't mind leaving me hurt and broken." He spoke lightly, but his eyes were full of pain.

I bit my lip. "I'll tell you what I'll do. The only thing I can do. Morse is out of town, but he ought to get home tomorrow or the next day. After that, I'll rethink my promise to him and see what seems most honest. But I can't even think about it while he's gone. Fair enough?"

"I don't know what fair's got to do with it," he said glumly, "but if it's what I've got, it's what I've got. Come on!" He pulled himself to his feet and reached for my hand. "We've got to plant rosebuds while we may."

"Surely it's 'gather' rosebuds?"

He shook his head firmly. "Nope. I want them to multiply. Come on!" He tugged my hand, and together we ran, laughing, through the heat.

Does not wisdom call out? Does not understanding raise her voice?
Proverbs 8:1

Twenty-Five

While Josheba and Lewis were gallivanting all over Old Alabama Town, I, MacLaren, was trying to talk some sense into Carter. When he came by to see Jake, I walked him to the elevator. "Dee Sykes identified that picture as Harriet, Carter."

He said a word he would never say in front of Glenna, then turned bright red. "I've heard worse in my life, honey," I told him, "and you've got a lot on your plate right now."

"You don't know the half of it, Miss MacLaren. A lot of people are on vacation this week, another batch is down with a virus, and we've had a series of burglaries that have us all hopping. And now you tell me we may have messed up a case back in June. That's going to mean an incredible amount of paperwork, and the Sykes family is important enough that it could hit all the papers. That isn't going to make *anybody* happy."

He'd left out one thing. "You haven't even mentioned the trouble of finding out when and how Harriet died."

He cleared his throat and looked miserable. "I doubt we ever will, ma'am. Not after all this time. Forensics could tell us how long she lay there, by looking at the . . . uh . . . well, maggots. But after that long lying out, nobody could tell when she died."

I heaved a deep sigh. "I hate to think of that child being just one more unsolved murder, Carter."

"She wasn't murdered, Miss MacLaren!" *Can't you get that through your thick head?* He didn't say those words, but they rang in the silence, and his face was flushed from holding them in. "There was absolutely no sign of foul play. That girl just got sick and died. Look, it's really great what you've already done, but it's also enough. With Jake going home tomorrow—"

He didn't have to finish the sentence. We both knew what he meant. His mama just hadn't taught him any polite way to say it: *Old woman, bug off!*

He jabbed the elevator button. "I guess you'll be heading back up the road pretty soon, won't you?" He didn't need to sound so relieved.

"Pretty soon, I guess. By the way, Carter, I took Jake's car to William Sykes's mechanic this morning, and found him fixing William's truck. It has a streak of darker red paint on it that the mechanic and I both think came off Jake's fender."

Carter looked at me with what I hoped was admiration and not exasperation. "You sure do beat all. Just happened to use William's mechanic, huh? Will he testify?"

"Since I was pretending to be a friend of William's, I couldn't ask. Besides, I doubt we'd ever bring charges. But at least the mechanic will remember, if it comes up again."

"I'll go see him tomorrow. I owe it to Jake." Carter took down the address. "You said the person who ran you off the road had long blonde hair. Mr. Sykes is nearly bald."

"Maybe he had on a wig. I don't know. I didn't get that good a look. Or maybe it was Ricky. Did you ask him?"

He frowned and scratched the back of his neck. "We can't find him. Somebody went by the trailer where he used to live, but his girlfriend said while he was in jail, she threw out all his stuff and moved her brother in. She didn't know where Ricky is."

"Good for her, at least. Now, Carter, I sure do wish you'd try to find *somebody* who saw Harriet after June fourth. That's the day her trustee took her to the bank."

"Bank?"

I realized I hadn't told him everything, but from the way he was eyeing that open elevator door, this wasn't the place or the time.

"Tuesday morning is the last definite time anybody remembers seeing her," I said hurriedly. "I wish you'd see if you could find somebody who saw her later."

He left without promising a thing.

On the way back to Jake, I remembered something: June fourth was a Tuesday.

I puttered around Jake's room for a minute or two, watering his flowers and straightening his blind, then I asked, real casual, "Did you work the desk down at the teen center on the first Tuesday in June?"

Jake glowered. I was interrupting a rerun of *Perry Mason*. Jake prefers his mysteries in one-hour segments with somebody else doing the detecting and doing it fast. "How do you know anything about a teen center, Miss Nosy?"

"Because some woman from your church made me cover for you last week. You owe me one, brother, and don't forget it. But don't worry about that right now. Just stir your brain cells a minute and tell me if you volunteered down there the first Tuesday in June."

He thought a minute, then nodded. "Sure. It was my first day, because school had just let out." He turned back to Perry Mason, who was doing his usual fancy stuff in the courtroom. Then Jake's brain finally kicked in. "Are you poking your nose into something that doesn't concern you, Sis?"

"No, Bubba. It concerns me. It concerns me a lot. So let Perry Mason handle his own case for a minute and help me with mine."

"I swan," he said, disgusted. "Leave you alone in a town for one blooming week, and you dig up a mystery."

"I didn't exactly dig it up—more like pulled it up. So would you tell me what you remember about that morning?"

He was silent. I could almost hear him turning mental pages. "I had to go to the dentist first, I remember. Hated to be late my first day, but a crown came off the day before, so I called the director and told him I'd get there as soon as the dentist could glue it back. He said one of the kids would answer the phone until I got there. Little white girl. Only one I ever saw down there, in fact, and she was just there the one day."

"Harriet?"

"Yeah, Harriet. Not a name you hear much anymore."

Speak for yourself, I thought. "Did Harriet stick around after you got there?"

"Yeah, all morning. In fact, she was fixing to leave when I did, so I gave her a ride downtown to catch a bus."

I couldn't believe this! "Did she say where she was going?"

"I don't remember—wait, she said something about miracles. No, I know! She asked if I believed in miracles, and I said, 'Sure I do.' Then she said, 'Well, maybe I'm gonna start believing in them too.' Her eyes were right pretty—yellow and shining. I don't think I've seen her around the center since that day, though. What's this about, Clara? Why do you want to know about Harriet?"

"You'll need to ask Glenna—and here she is." I turned him over gladly to the next shift. I figured Glenna would tell him enough to satisfy him but not enough to upset him. Glenna didn't know yet that Harriet was dead. I hoped she'd have enough sense to leave the Buick out of the story, too.

When we got home that night, I had one of those moments of deep sadness that always come after somebody dies. I stepped out of the car and took a deep breath of thick, hot air sweet with honeysuckle, roses, boxwood, and Russian tea olive. Then it hit me that Myrna and Harriet couldn't enjoy that splendid evening. I found myself brushing away angry tears for two women I never actually knew.

Propped on my pillow a little later, I reached for my Bible and hunted through the gospels for the parable of the lost sheep. When I located it in Matthew's eighteenth chapter, I found, to my surprise, that it was framed as a question: *What do you think? If a man owns a hundred sheep, and one of them wanders away, will he not leave the ninety-nine on the hills and go to look for the one that wandered off?*

"Not anymore," I muttered bitterly. "We let them wander off and don't even notice they're gone."

What do you think? The words leapt from the page as if newly written.

That was the question, wasn't it? Not what did anybody else think, but what did I—MacLaren Crane Yarbrough—think? I answered aloud. "I think somebody ought to find out what happened to that poor child, but nobody else but Josheba seems to care." My eye fell on a later verse: *Your Father in heaven is not willing that any of these little ones be lost.*

Okay, so it was me, Josheba, and God, but two of us were fresh out of ideas.

~

As I lay in the dim room waiting for sleep to come, I got to thinking about how often circumstances and people get woven together into a pattern none of us can see at the time. Some people would say it was just coincidence that Jake signed up for the center on Tuesdays, that he had his heart attack on a Monday so I went in his place, that I am the kind of person who can't sit in a filthy room without cleaning it up, that I pulled out the sofa bed and found Harriet's money, that Josheba—who was already concerned for Harriet—was at the library desk that particular morning, that Glenna has a cousin in the homicide division. I pity those people. They see the pattern, but miss the Weaver. As an archbishop of Canterbury once said, "Coincidence? Sure I believe in coincidence. When I pray, coincidences happen."

And in case you're about to stand up and stump for free will, think about this: I had free will as to whether I sat in that filthy room without cleaning it. God just knew I wasn't likely to do so. I guess it's a matter of knowing the kind of threads you have to work with, and choosing the right ones.

Which, considering the kinds of assignments I sometimes get, is a most unflattering thought.

~

We trudged side by side, the brown-haired child and I. We passed through gates as large and hollow as the doorway to hell. Inside, I could see leaning white tombstones and tall obelisks crammed together against a dark gray sky. As we walked down a crooked dirt path between the tombstones, she reached out and clutched my arm. I looked at her. She had a new face. Harriet's face. And she was terrified.

Poverty is the ruin of the poor.
Proverbs 10:15

Twenty-Six

Thursday morning, I lay in the dim dawn light listening to birds waking up, trying to think through everything I knew. I didn't get any flashes of inspiration, but I did get a few more questions. What made Harriet suddenly believe in miracles? Who took her back to Dee's for clothes? Why did she go to the cemetery? When? How? Where did she stay that weekend after she left Dee's?

It was possible I would never know all the answers, but I might be able to find some. Where she had stayed that weekend, for instance. If anybody knew, Kateisha would. And surely Harriet hadn't walked to the cemetery. Was that where she was going when Jake took her to the bus? Would a bus driver remember her?

Also, I wanted to visit the cemetery where her body was found.

But first, this was the day we were bringing Jake home. I was both delighted and, as you can well imagine, full of dread.

Sure enough, as soon as we pulled in their driveway, he growled right off,"Where's my car?"

Bless Glenna's heart, she said, "It needed to be moved, honey, so I could get you close to the walk. Come on in, now, and let's get you settled, so I can start fixing you some lunch."

Joe Riddley called not long after we got there. "Well, Little Bit, did you get the old deadbeat home? Let me yell at him." As soon as they'd exchanged insults, Jake handed me back the phone. "I think he wants to talk to you again. I can't imagine why."

"When you comin' home?" Joe Riddley demanded. "Sunday suit you?"

I couldn't think of a single reason for staying later that wouldn't bring him to Montgomery by tomorrow morning. "I'll try to get a plane on Sunday afternoon."

He hooted. "You've been in Montgomery so long you just said *after*-noon, like they do over there. I need to get you back home so you can learn to talk *right* again. See what reservations you can get and call me back. I'll be at the airport with bells on."

"Forget the bells, honey," I told him. "Just be there on time."

Jake and Glenna both needed to rest after lunch, but I didn't dare lie down. I feared my dreams. This might be a good time to see Kateisha, and maybe Josheba would like to go with me. "Want to meet me at the center and see what she has to say?" I asked.

"I'll do better than that," Josheba offered. "I'll come get you."

"Is Morse home yet?" I asked as I climbed in the car.

"Not yet, but he's promised to get back by Saturday. My club is having a big dance, and I don't want to miss it."

Two blocks from the center we stopped for a light and saw Twaniba standing listlessly on the corner. Josheba rolled down her window. "Do you want a ride to the center? We're going over to see if Kateisha is there."

"Kateisha's home with toothache," Twaniba murmured, scarcely moving her mouth.

"Do you know where she lives?"

"Yessum." Twaniba gave lifeless but accurate instructions.

Kateisha lived in one of the most dilapidated houses I'd ever visited, a dingy white bungalow with a sagging porch, faded brown trim, chipped cement steps, and a bare dirt yard. Not one flower bloomed around the spindly, untrimmed spirea that cowered in front.

Kateisha herself was sitting on the edge of the splintery porch, picking her hair. She hadn't made the spout yet today, so it all stood straight off her head like she'd stuck her finger in a socket. One cheek was plumper than usual.

"I hear you've got a toothache," I greeted her, concerned. "Have you seen a dentist?"

"Don't need no dentist. It'll get better. Always does. What you all doing here?" She tried to sound casual, but I could tell she was both pleased and embarrassed.

"Looking for you." Josheba sat on the rough porch boards with her feet on a cracked concrete step. In honor of my new skirt, I decided to stand.

"How'd you know how to find me? Did Screwy Lewey give out my address?"

"No, it was Twaniba." I swatted away a curious fly.

"Good old Cowface." Kateisha pulled a weed that grew up beside the porch and used it to tickle her plump, bare knee. She looked at Josheba from the corner of her eyes. "You still seeing Mr. Henly?" she asked suspiciously.

Josheba laughed, but seemed nervous. "I'm not *seeing* him, girl. I'm engaged to a man named Morse."

Kateisha glowered. "You like him, though. I can tell." She threw the weed into the dirt. "Could be dangerous. Harriet used to like him. Now she's missing."

I looked at her sharply. "Do you think that's why she's missing?"

Her big shoulders heaved in a shrug. "Don't ast me. All I know is, Harriet got somethin' on Screwy Lewey, and two weeks later she up 'n' disappeared."

"We think we've found her," Josheba said flatly.

Kateisha's eyes widened. "Where? What she been doing all this time?"

"If it's really her, she's dead, honey." I gave her as many details as I thought wise.

Kateisha sucked in her breath and winced as the air hit her sore tooth, but she didn't mention the pain. She sat silent for some time, then demanded, "*When,* you say?"

"June tenth, in Oakwood Cemetery."

"What'd I tell you?" Kateisha muttered in a low voice. "She got something on Mr. Henly, and somebody offed her."

"What do you mean she 'got something on him'?" I asked. "What was it?"

Josheba clasped her hands so tightly in her lap, the skin was almost splitting.

"I don't know," Kateisha shook her head. "But 'bout two weeks before school let out, Harriet say she found out somethin' about Mr. Henly he didn't never want nobody to know. She say she could get offed for knowin', but he was payin' her—"

Josheba yanked a weed that was growing right in the step, and twisted it like she'd like to wring Kateisha's neck. "That's not the way it was, Kateisha. I know what Harriet knew about Mr. Henly. It wasn't anything to get killed for knowing."

"I know she hit on him for money not to tell," Kateisha insisted, rolling her eyes.

Josheba rolled her eyes right back. "So she couldn't have been afraid of him, then, could she?"

"Maybe not." Kateisha picked her hair like she had nothing better to do. In a minute she muttered, "Harriet had something on her uncle, too, but I don't know what. Bragged all the time he pay her ten dollars a week not to tell her auntie." She wiggled around and stuck the pick in her back pocket. "Could be he offed her 'stead of paying up one week." She thought it over and rejected her own suggestion. "Nanh—he wasn't payin' that much."

I shared her doubts. "How about Ricky Dodd—do you know him?" I asked.

"Sure. He ain't much, but he was sorta like a brother to Harriet, you know? 'Cept'n more so. I don't worry over Dré like Harriet did Ricky. Dré can take care of himself—and if he don't, it's no skin off me. Harriet worried all the time over Ricky—but she didn't take nothin' off him. Said if he gave her trouble, she'd see he got busted."

"For what?" I wondered if Kateisha knew about Ricky's recent jail stint.

"Oh," Kateisha waved casually, "you know. Drugs, that sort of stuff. He's been in twict already." She sounded like that was a normal part of life. Maybe in hers, it was.

"Did you know that Harriet took a gun away from him?"

"Course I knew. She stashed it in a drawer, but I told her she better put it in a safer place. Anybody coulda found it there—that cousin of hers, her auntie, her uncle, anybody. Even her auntie's maid. Folks don't look too kindly on kids with guns." You'd have thought she was the world's foremost authority on that subject.

"So what did Harriet do with the gun?"

"I dunno. Said she'd get rid of it, but I forgot to ast if she did." Kateisha found a scab on her knee and started to pick at it.

"Did Harriet ever talk about money?"

Kateisha hesitated, then nodded. "Her granny lef' her some. I don't know how much, but Harriet was allus talking about what she was going to do when she turned twenty-one." Her voice grew mournful. "Now she won't get to do it."

"I want to try and find out who did this to Harriet, Kateisha," I told her, "but I need your help. Harriet's aunt said she left their house on Saturday, June first, but she wasn't found dead until the tenth. Do you have any idea where she was staying?"

"I know where she was staying up to Tuesday," she boasted—adding, "but I can't tell."

"Why not?"

"I promised Harriet."

"Harriet's dead, Kateisha," Josheba reminded her.

"She might still be listening," Kateisha said mulishly. "I don't want her hanging around my bed at night."

She's hanging around mine instead, I thought. Instead of saying it, I played a hunch. "Let me guess, and you just nod or shake your head. Was she staying here?"

Kateisha hesitated, then nodded.

"Did somebody—your brother, maybe—take her back to her house for clothes a few times?"

She nodded, stopped, shook her head, stopped, started to nod again, then sighed. "I didn't make no promises about that. Dré and Z-dog, his homie, borrored my uncle's car 'n took her back onct, Sunday mornin'."

"How long did she stay here?"

Kateisha started to balk, then relented. "Saturday 'til Tuesday. Mama didn't like it much—she don't trust white people—but she say I can sleep on the floor and give Harriet my bed if I want to. When Harriet left without saying thank-you, Mama's so mad she say she never take in a white chile again. We didn't know she was . . . passed on."

"She left on Tuesday?" I wanted to hear her version of that day. "Tell me about Tuesday. What did Harriet do?"

Kateisha's tongue darted out of her mouth and moved back and forth while she thought. "She met Miz

Scott . . . that's her trusty . . . and then she went down to the center to keep the telephone some. I had to go to clinic, so she say she see me down to the club."

"Did you see her?"

Kateisha nodded. "Sitting at the desk like God A'mighty, taking down messages and actin' like she own the place."

"Where was Mr. Henly?" Josheba asked.

"Runnin' things and givin' Biscuit instructions about what to do all day."

"Then what happened?"

The girl would not be hurried. "Nothing. She got a few calls and wrote down messages, then Mr. Crane—hey, that's your bro!"

I nodded.

"Well, he come, but she still hung out in the lounge, readin'. I was mad, 'cause I was wantin' her to come back to the gym. Mr. Henly was formin' a volleyball team that afternoon, and we needed practice *bad*. Nex' thing I know, Harriet's lef' 'thout so much as a word. Just walked out, and never come back." She sounded as glum as she had the day we met.

"And you had no idea why?" I pressed her.

Kateisha grunted. "Know what Twaniba say, if you can believe *her*. She say Harriet bragged she was goin' to meet her mama."

"Her mama?" I echoed. "Are you sure?"

Kateisha shrugged. "That's what Twaniba say. Say her mama call and say, 'Come meet me.' I thought that's funny, 'cause Harriet didn't *have* no mother. 'You mean her auntie,' I told Twaniba. But old Twaniba got stubborn and say Harriet say she goin' meet her mama." Kateisha's lip trembled. "Looks like she met her Maker, instead."

That kept us all quiet for a minute.

Finally, I had to ask, "Did Twaniba say anything else Harriet did?"

Kateisha thought, then her eyes sparkled with mischief. "Harriet made Twaniba take your bro on a tour of the center when his time was almost up, whiles she kept the phones. Twaniba was real put out, 'cause she don't like to stir if she don't have to."

"Who else was in the room at the time?"

"Nobody. Soon's they got back, Harriet left." Kateisha heaved a huge sigh. "Here I been thinkin' she 's with her mama or somethin', and I been put out with her for leavin' without sayin' good-bye, 'n' . . ." Her lip quivered, and huge tears rolled down her cheeks. "If I'da known, I'da gone with her." No friend could say more than that.

I bent down and laid one hand lightly on her broad heaving shoulder. Josheba patted her knee. While she sobbed, I considered what she had told us.

This was the first we had heard of a call. After the call, Harriet borrowed bus fare to go "meet my mother." Did Myrna Lawson indeed call, then lie in wait to kill her? Did someone know Myrna had called, and kill Harriet before she got to her mother? Or did someone else call and pretend to be Myrna?

Whoever called, Harriet had not trusted her completely. Before she left, she got everyone else out of the room and carefully hid a book containing three thousand dollars.

At last Kateisha raised a tear-stained face. "I tole you all I know. What *you* know?"

"Not much more than you do," I confessed. "We know her aunt found clothes missing two or three times, like Harriet had come by for them, but nobody remembers seeing her after Tuesday. We know Harriet planned to go to an acting school in Atlanta—"

"For real?" Kateisha sniffed and wiped her nose on one bare forearm.

"For real. She and Mrs. Scott took the money out of the bank that morning to pay the tuition. But she never left Montgomery."

Kateisha didn't want to dwell on that. "What else you all know?"

"We know Harriet's mother did come to town, but not until this week, and she was shot the day after she arrived."

"Her, too?" Kateisha was dumbfounded. "Who offed *her?*"

"I . . . Ricky was seen running away from the house, and they found his girlfriend's gun nearby. It had killed her, so they arrested him — "

"Harriet took that gun," Kateisha reminded me. "She'd never of given it back. Never! She wouldn't shoot her mama, either. Not if she knew it was her."

"Well, Ricky was arrested for the shooting, but somebody bailed him out. Now he's disappeared. The police don't know where he is."

Kateisha tossed her head proudly. "I know where he is. Leastways, I know where he's gonna be Sunday mornin'."

Josheba clearly didn't believe her. "How do you know that?"

Kateisha stuck her nose in the air. "'Cause he and Dré do some business together."

"What kind of business?" I asked before I thought.

She waved one hand. "You don't want to know. But Ricky was over to our house last night, 'n' I heard him and Dré makin' plans." She cast a furtive look around. When she spoke, her voice was low. "They havin' a meetin' down to the teen center six-thirty Sunday mornin'."

"I thought it was closed until one on Sundays," Josheba objected.

"It is. That's why they meetin' then."

"How will they get in?" I asked.

"Biscuit's made a key. Said it was the safest place in town at that hour. Mr. Henly's not an early riser. What's the matter with you?" she suddenly asked someone behind me.

I turned and saw a young man racing up the cracked walk. "Gotta meet somebody, and I forgot somethin.'" He hurried breathlessly inside, slamming the torn screened door behind him.

"That's my brother Dré," Kateisha said with offhand pride.

I had seen him clearly. A little older than Kateisha and far thinner, he wore running shoes and a gold watch that both looked far too expensive to belong to this house. But that wasn't what made me take a couple of steps after him. It was his face. He was the boy who spoke to me in the library, the day Jake's car was stolen.

Josheba stood and started purposefully down the walk. "We got to be goin', Kateisha. See you later."

Good manners left me no choice but to say a quick good-bye and follow, but as I slammed the car door, I protested, "That boy was one of the ones in the library last week. His friend stole my pocketbook, and probably Jake's car! I should at least speak to him."

"I recognized him," Josheba answered grimly. "Let the police talk to him, Mac. I just want to get the heck out of here."

I left messages for Carter all afternoon, but he didn't call back until we were eating. "Sorry, but we've been real busy," he apologized. "I saw that mechanic, though, and he told me what he told you—looks like those two vehicles hit one another. If you want to take Mr. Sykes to court to recover repair costs, I think he'd swear to it."

Trying to speak softly enough that Jake couldn't hear, I murmured, "That's great, but I was calling about something else."

"Speak up. I can't hear you. What did you say?"

"I've found the friend of the boy who stole Jake's car and snatched my purse. At least, they were reading magazines in the library together."

"Are you sure?"

"Positive. His name is André, Dré for short. I don't know his last name. But here's the address."

"Wahoo!" A crow of delight floated over the line. I could hear the scratch of Carter's pen writing it down.

"He may not be there right now," I cautioned. "He came dashing in saying he'd forgotten something and had to meet somebody somewhere. Kateisha, his sister, may know where he is, but Carter, please—don't let Kateisha know it was me who turned him in."

Not until we'd hung up did I remember I hadn't told him about the Sunday morning meeting. By the time I looked up the number and called back, Carter had already left.

> Remove the dross from the silver,
> and out comes material for the
> silversmith. *Proverbs 25:4*

Twenty-Seven

Glenna and Jake slept late Friday morning. I could hear two sets of gentle snores, and pictured them cozily nested—enjoying the comfort of being reunited with a dear and familiar weight on the other side of the bed. I was getting ready for some of that myself.

I tiptoed to the kitchen and made coffee. In the backyard, sunlight again played through the hackberries. They make Jake's backyard a shady delight on sunny days, but a treacherous place to be in a storm. Glenna once told me that hackberries have no staying power. Just like some people.

I was standing admiring the hackberries and inhaling coffee fumes from my mug when the phone rang. I grabbed it before it could waken the happy sleepers.

"It looks like you were right, Miss MacLaren." I knew it was Carter, even if he didn't say so. "That girl was Harriet, all right. Dee Sykes identified her from the picture, and when we asked about any identifying marks, said she'd broken her arm when she was six. That showed up in the autopsy, but we hadn't asked about it the first time, since the other family was so sure. We checked with them again, and their daughter never broke hers. As you can well imagine, that's got things pretty stirred up down here. I knew you'd want to know."

"I'm glad to know, Carter, even if I'm not *glad*. Know what I mean?"

"Yes, ma'am. Sure do. Also, we picked up the boy you mentioned, and got more than we expected. Remember I told you we've had a series of petty break-ins? When we printed him, he's one of the perpetrators. They've been stealing—"

"Old coins!" I finished for him. "I should have known. They were reading up on the subject in the library. Did you get the other one?"

"No, Dré won't tell us who or where he is. And there's something else. Something you aren't going to like. A witness to one of the break-ins got a good look at the getaway car. They'd muddied the tag, but—"

"Oh, no!" I sat down, suddenly weighing a ton. "Jake's?"

"Afraid so. We'll need to bring it downtown and go over it. Tell him, will you?"

"You're asking the condemned woman to sharpen her own guillotine, you know."

Glenna got to the kitchen before Jake. When I told her what Carter had said, she said, "I think you're making more of this than you have to. You were doing Jake a favor—"

"Who was doing Jake a favor?" Jake himself stood in the doorway, pink and rumpled from sleep. He tied the belt of his robe a bit tighter and sat down.

Southern women are experts at diversion. "It's nothing, honey." Glenna patted his hand. "What kind of cereal do you want? I bought several new ones I think you'll like."

Grumpily he looked over the selection she set out. "Grass and hay," he muttered, pouring himself out a bowlful and digging in. Before he was half done, though, he gave me a sharp look. "Okay. Tell me what this favor is you were doing me."

"I told you. I took your place at the center." I poured myself another cup of coffee.

"And?" His face was getting pink.

"Don't worry about it, honey," Glenna told him sharply.

I sighed. "He's going to find out sometime. It might as well be now. Okay, Jake, it was like this. And if you have another heart attack over it, I'll never forgive either one of us. Keep that in mind."

I started backwards: "Your car—

"My car!" He yelped. He turned to Glenna. "Did you let her . . . I *never* let her drive my car. You know that!"

"Well, I did," I told him shortly, "and you might as well get used to that fact, because that's the least of it. Sit there and keep your shirt on until I finish."

"Where *is* my car?" he demanded. "I want the dad-burned truth."

I propped my chin with two fists and leaned over so my face was close to his. "You want the truth, brother? Here it is. Your car is at the mechanic's getting the dents out from when somebody rammed me. That was right after we'd gotten it back and put on new tires from when it got stolen. I'll get you a new radio and a paint job later. But while it was stolen, it got used in some robberies, so now the police need it a while. They'll bring it back once they've gone over it. Is that enough to put you back in the hospital?"

He glowered at me. I glowered right back. My face felt as red as his looked. Maybe we'd both have heart attacks. They could give us a double room.

"Don't forget, honey," Glenna said, laying a hand on his shoulder, "MacLaren got into this mess trying to help *you,* taking your place at the center."

Jake hitched up his bathrobe and scowled ferociously. "She didn't have to use my car."

I'd had about all I was willing to stand. "If that car is more valuable to you than your life, go ahead and have another heart attack and get it over with!"

Jake glared at me, breathing hard, but after a minute he nodded. "Hate to admit it, Clara, but you're right for once. One of the orderlies told me I could stay calm if I'd just remember two things: don't sweat the small stuff, and it's mostly all small stuff." He swallowed hard. "I'm glad you're okay. And the car? Well, it's just a car." We all knew how hard that was for him to say.

To give him a minute to regain himself, Glenna said quietly to me, "I forgot to tell you, Clara. I spoke with Wylie Fergusson from the bank when he came to see Jake yesterday. He told me privately that William's store is barely making it. The bank gave William a loan on June fourth, but if things don't change, William could lose everything."

In case you're wondering why a banker would confide that sort of thing to my sister-in-law, you may not know that when Glenna's daddy died, he left her half that bank.

Glenna took a sip of coffee and sighed. "Poor Lou Ella."

"Poor William," I added. "And poor Dee and Julie. Their nail-polish bills alone would put a lesser man in the poor house."

Carter came over on his lunch hour. When I had a minute alone with him, I asked, "Carter, could you show me where they found Harriet?"

"Sure, Miss MacLaren, but why on earth do you want to go poking around up there? There won't be anything there after all this time."

"I know," I admitted, "but I don't think I'll ever sleep easy until I've at least seen it. What I imagine has got to be worse, and if that sounds odd—"

"My daddy says an abnormal reaction to an abnormal situation is normal behavior."

"Is your daddy a psychologist?"

"No, ma'am. He works at the zoo."

That afternoon I drove Glenna's Ford past a white gazebo, pulled over the crest of a hill dotted with tombstones, and drove around behind. I parked and got out. It was a beautiful spot, but the mosquitoes had it to themselves. I fanned several away as I looked around.

This, the oldest part of Oakwood Cemetery, covered a large gentle hill with towering cedars dripping moss—which was surprising in itself. Montgomery is generally north of the Spanish moss line. Back in 1817, the cemetery would have been on the outskirts of town. Today it is surrounded by city, yet retains the same sense of separateness and peace. A little one-lane, the only road, winds over the top, is cut into the hill about halfway down at the back, and curves back around the crest toward the gate. Where it had been cut out, the hillside is reinforced with stone walls.

On the back lower side of the hill, my car and I were both hidden from view unless somebody happened to be in the newer cemetery on an adjoining hill. Today, nobody was.

Tombstones only marched halfway downhill on the lower side of the road. Beyond them, grassy lawn rolled toward what looked like a stream with a small bridge across it.

"Hank Williams is buried on top of a hill in the new part of the cemetery," Carter had told me, "and the police station is sort of between the two, just beyond the gully. Call me when you leave home. I'll look out for you and come up when you get there."

I walked along the road a short way, swatting mosquitoes. Only when I turned to retrace my steps could I see the police station and a smattering of cars, hidden by ivy and kudzu from where I had parked. Carter waved and loped toward me.

"Sure aren't any living people around," I commented as he arrived, waving away his own mosquito escort.

"Too hot. Nobody up here at this time of day but us bugs." Carter pointed down the hill. "She was found in that patch of kudzu."

Involuntarily, I shivered. The mound of pesky, rapid-growing vine with its large dull leaves was a perfect hiding place. Even if people came to wander among graves, they wouldn't poke around in kudzu. I once heard James Dickey read a poem about the stuff. Only James Dickey could find meaning in kudzu. He said snakes thrive underneath it, and if I were a snake, I'd crawl under there, too, out of the sun and away from mowers. Somebody must keep this kudzu cut back, though. Unchecked it would have covered the entire cemetery in a month, the city of Montgomery in three, and the state of Alabama in six.

I meandered downhill, feeling soft grass brush the tops of my feet and the sun beat down on my head. At the edge of the gully, I peered in. At the moment the bottom was only a trickle of water and a bed of beautiful sculpted sand. Imagine taking that much trouble with a stream bottom! Then I looked at the gully walls. The watermark was ten feet above the bottom. Beyond the gully was a single railroad track.

"That's where she lay," Carter repeated from behind me. He went right up to the kudzu and knelt in the grass. I looked around for a stick in case I needed to defend him from copperheads. "The police and medical examiner checked everything at the time, of course, in case it was a homicide, but by now there's nothing left. Not with all the insects and the rain we've had this summer."

"And she had no pocketbook or anything?"

He shook his head. "I checked again. They found a couple of packs of cigarettes underneath her and one in her pocket, but that's all she had except a couple of dollars."

"Cigarettes?" I was puzzled. "She didn't smoke, Carter. Ricky and Lewis said Harriet had a fit if anybody smoked around her."

He swatted a mosquito. "I'm just telling you what they found. Maybe the cigarettes were there when she lay down, and she felt too bad to move them."

I felt faintly sick as I looked at Harriet's last bed. Why wasn't that child alive to enjoy this wonderful day? "She must have been utterly exhausted to lie down there. Could she have been bitten by a copperhead?"

He smacked a persistent mosquito. "Nope. Copperhead bites are seldom fatal – she'd have been in pain, but she could have gotten to help. And if she hadn't, she'd have had enough swelling so that forensics would have spotted it right away."

He stood and brushed grass off his knees. "You've been reading too many mystery novels, Miss MacLaren. These days they look for everything. She wasn't bitten by a snake, poisoned, shot, strangled, or beaten to death. She just got sick and died."

I stood looking at that mound of kudzu, trying to picture the brown-haired girl with golden eyes feeling weak, staggering downhill, and lying under the vine where it was cool. "She'd have gone across the bridge," I objected, pointing. "The police station is right over there. If she'd gotten sick she'd have gone there, Carter. She wouldn't have lain down in a patch of kudzu, for heaven's sake. You know that as well as I do."

I turned and laboriously climbed toward my car up a short spur of unpaved road – no more than wheel ruts and big gravel, really – that humped up from the lawn toward the pavement and made walking easier. That was good, because I couldn't see very well. Tears blurred my vision.

Carter took my elbow the last few steps. "You had enough?"

"More than enough. I'll let you solve the murder. All I wanted to do was find the child." I felt a hundred years old.

He spoke slowly like he was feeling for the right words. "Miss MacLaren, I know how you feel, but you just have to accept something: there wasn't any murder. There was no evidence whatsoever of foul play. None. We had the wrong girl, sure, so we'll let the other family know, but after that, the case is closed. I really appreciate your nosing around and finding out who she was, though." He chuckled. "Jake's always said you have the instincts of a first-rate bird dog."

I had to turn away so he couldn't see my face. "You won't be talking to people who knew her or anything?"

"It's a mystery, ma'am, not a homicide. Well, I'd better get back to work. You know, from the station, I couldn't even see your car. It's a good thing you went for a little walk."

I drove home slower than usual. Once again I'd forgotten to tell Carter about Sunday's early meeting, but I scarcely cared. I didn't really think Ricky Dodd had killed Myrna, so I didn't care if Carter found him again or not. What mattered to me was Harriet. I knew in my bones she didn't just up and die on that hillside. Somebody helped her. And I wouldn't sleep well until I found out who.

I felt like I ought to go see Eunice again. If I didn't tell her about Harriet, who would? She might be back at work, of course, but from the way she'd carried on, I didn't think she'd return until after Myrna was buried.

The crime tape had been removed, and the little green house dozed in the sun. As I approached, Eunice's old Persian leaped onto the steps from beneath the porch and sashayed up ahead of me.

Eunice came to the door in saggy blue Bermuda shorts and a white T-shirt from the Atlanta Olympics. She seemed delighted to have company. “Hello! Come on in.”

Wisps of hair had escaped from a careless ponytail, which she swiped at as she led the way into the living room. Once again it was as cold as an Arctic afternoon. “Stay a while,” she invited. “Can I get you some tea?”

Today the room was not all white. I sat gingerly on a dark blue chair that had been set where the sofa used to be. Had the sofa been sent out to be recovered, or sent to a dump? I tried not to picture it as I had last seen it, covered with Myrna.

On the coffee table was another spot of color—a bowl of pink and yellow daisies in front of a framed photograph of a mother and child with the same dark hair and tawny eyes. I picked up the picture and looked at it. The child’s chubby features were vaguely familiar. “Myrna, with Harriet?”

Eunice nodded. “That’s the only picture I have of her. Seemed fittin’ to put it out.”

I took a deep breath. “I came by to tell you something about Harriet.” There was no way to soften it. “She was found dead last month in Oakwood Cemetery. They have just identified her.”

Eunice leaned forward and scratched an itch behind one ear. “Dead? Harriet’s dead? Who killed her?” She seemed far more interested in that than in the fact itself. I couldn’t help wondering if she was already imagining herself back on the ten o’clock news.

“They don’t think anybody killed her. They think she died of natural causes.”

“Natural causes? You mean like drugs?”

“More like a heart attack or something. Do you know if she had a bad heart?”

"Could have. It runs in our family." She heaved a heavy sigh. "Last month the doctor told me I'm heading for a stroke if I don't get my pressure down. But with Myrna getting shot, it's probably sky-high. And now, Harriet." She stopped and shook her head gloomily. "The Good Book says God won't give you more than you can bear, but seems lately like he's overestimating my abilities."

"God didn't shoot Myrna nor kill Harriet," I told her sharply. I managed to refrain from adding that overeating probably had something to do with her blood pressure. "There's one thing I don't understand, though. An artist's drawing was in the papers for several days after she was found. Didn't you see the picture? Didn't it occur to you then that it looked an awful lot like Harriet?"

"I might have seen it, but I hadn't seen Harriet since not long after that picture there was taken." She pointed to the coffee table. "Harriet wasn't hardly walking good. After Myrna left, there wasn't no reason for me to bother with her baby. Frank was taking care of it, and his mother."

"I thought you told me you saw her at her granny's funeral."

"I told you I hadn't seen her since the funeral, which was the honest-to-God truth." Eunice said that without a trace of a blush, although she and I both knew she'd also told me Harriet was in and out of her house all the time. Of course, that's what she'd said about me, too . . .

"What family did Harriet have besides the Sykeses?" I asked.

"Nobody but Myrna 'n' me. Dixie and I are the onliest ones left, now." She seemed struck by a sudden thought. "If Harriet died before Myrna, then wouldn't Myrna have inherited anything she had to leave? You reckon it comes to me now? Dixie won't like that."

Eunice didn't act like that bothered her one little bit.

It was nearly suppertime, but instead of heading home I drove on west out Fairview, toward the bus company headquarters I'd found listed in the telephone book. I had only a faint hope that I'd be able to get the name of the driver on the route near Oakwood Cemetery the week Harriet disappeared, and it was getting so late, he or she might have ended the day's schedule. I had no idea what hours bus drivers worked. "Carter ought to be doing this," I fumed aloud.

I sat in the parking lot and watched several buses pull into the lot. I was right, it was about time for the day schedules to get over. Hesitantly I climbed from my car and looked uncertainly toward the office.

"May I help you, ma'am?" A gentle giant of a man towered over me, the setting sun behind him obliterating the features of his dark face.

"I . . . I don't know quite what I'm looking for," I admitted. "I am wanting to find out who was driving a bus up near Oakwood Cemetery the first week of June. I'm trying to find out if they remember taking a child—" I fumbled in my purse for the copy of Harriet's picture I'd begun to carry.

He studied the picture, then looked at me inquiringly. "I remember this girl very well, ma'am. I'm Jerry Banks, and I carried her to a stop about two blocks from the cemetery. Is something the matter?" His face was bony, the eyes deep-set and kind.

It must have been the sun in my eyes. Suddenly I felt too dizzy to stand. "Come with me," Jerry Banks told me. "Here. This way. Lean on my arm."

He led me to what I assumed was a driver's lounge—vending machines and scattered tables. "Drink this," he urged, handing me a cold canned Coke and showing me to a table. He sat down across from me and waited.

I sipped the drink gratefully and tried to laugh, but it came out more of a splutter. "I'm sorry. I just couldn't believe I'd found you right away."

"It was odd, wasn't it?" he agreed genially. "I'm not normally around at this time, but I forgot my lunchbox. Halfway home I suddenly remembered. Now what is it you want to know about that girl?" He clasped huge hands in front of him on the table.

"For one thing, do you remember when exactly you took her to the cemetery?"

He started to shake his head, considered, then nodded. "In fact, I do. It was a Tuesday. I don't know the exact date—"

"The fourth. I know that much. But you're sure it was Tuesday?"

"Absolutely. The reason is, the next day I woke up with a stomach virus and was out the rest of the week. Oo-ee, I was sick! I wasn't on that route again until the next Monday."

"Do you remember what time you dropped her off?"

"Round 'bout noontime. She complained that it was a far piece to walk in that heat, and she was right. After I drove off, I wondered if she was going up to Hank Williams's grave, on account of, it would have been nearer for her to ride a little farther to another stop." He looked at me curiously. "Do you mind telling me what this is all about?"

"The girl was found a week later, dead under a bush in the cemetery."

"Dear God a'mercy!" He rubbed one hand up and down one side of his face.

"Her picture was in the papers," I pointed out. "You didn't see it?"

He shook his head. "I don't read papers. Ought to, but never seem to have the time. But you say this girl died up there that day?"

"They don't know when she died. Not many people even remember when they saw her last."

He sighed. "I knew I ought to take her home to my Netty. Netty knows what to do with strays. She feeds 'em, loves 'em, and tells them about the blessed love of Jesus. That girl should have gone home to my Netty."

I felt as sad as he looked. "She sure should have gone home to someone. Could we find out if anybody picked her up on the way back?"

He shook his head. "I'll ask around, but most times we don't remember people. I just happen to remember her in particular because she was as feisty as a tiger kitten, and seemed bound and determined to get up to that cemetery no matter how hot or far it was."

Going to meet her mother, I thought sadly. "Mr. Banks, if you think of anything more about that day—anything at all—or find somebody who picked her up on the way back, would you call me?" I handed him Jake's number and opened my purse. "I owe you for a Coke."

"Don't mention it, ma'am. I'm just glad I forgot my lunchbox and came back for it. Looks like the good Lord wanted us to have this conversation, don't it?"

My eyes were so full of tears that all I could do was smile, nod, and reach out to clasp his big hand tightly.

By that time, I was convinced that whoever Harriet met on that hilltop on Tuesday afternoon was the last person to see her alive. Where she was from Tuesday until she died I did not know, but I wanted to know where everybody who knew Harriet was around noon on June fourth. Kateisha had said Lewis was forming a volleyball team that afternoon. She would have noticed if he'd left, I was sure. Claire, Harriet's trustee, had said she'd had meetings all day. That left Eunice, Ricky, and the Sykes family. Glenna suggested she could talk to the Sykeses easier than I could. I could read between the lines. She wanted to prove to me that nobody *she* knew had murdered a child in cold blood and left her under a bush.

Saturday morning, she sat right down and made the calls. First she thanked them for all they had done while

Jake was in the hospital, and reported he was almost back to his old ornery self. (Actually, she said it nicer than that.) Then she told them how sorry she was to learn that Harriet was dead, and asked if there was anything she could do. In the middle of all that she managed to find out the following:

- Lou Ella and William had lunch together that day, after he got his loan.
- Dee bought a dress and had her nails done (which I already knew).
- Nora was at her lake house all week. (I already knew that, too.)
- Julie and Rachel "hung out" all day, whatever that meant.

"So none of them could have done it," she said, utterly satisfied. But the truth was, there wasn't one soul, including Lewis and Claire, who couldn't have slipped up to the cemetery and met Harriet. If I'd been heading up a police investigation, I'd have sent people out checking with William's sales clerks and Dee's manicurist, Julie's friend and Nora's lake neighbors, probably even interviewing Lou Ella's maid. All I knew to do was call Eunice.

"Why, that was the day I went to the doctor," she said when she checked her calendar. "Remember? I told you, he said my blood pressure is mortal high. Like to worried me sick. It's come down some now—although I don't understand how it can, with all that's been going on." I didn't, either. My own was probably sky-high, too.

Especially since there wasn't one more thing I knew to do except get my clothes together for leaving the next day, then go for a ride with Glenna and Jake.

Saturday afternoon we drove up to Lake Jordan and enjoyed sunlight glinting on water. I asked Glenna to point out Nora's house—a nice cedar home set back from the road right on the water. It told me nothing except what I already knew: Nora had both taste and money. Glenna also pointed out a place she and Jake had their eye on if the owner ever decided to sell. We stopped for ice cream on the way back and got home in time for all of us to take a long nap. None of us are as young as we used to be.

Bloodthirsty men hate a man of integrity and seek to kill the upright. *Proverbs 29:10*

Twenty-Eight

While Mac and her family were enjoying a lazy weekend, I—Josheba—was getting madder and madder. Morse hadn't gotten back, and my big dance was Saturday night.

I spent Saturday morning getting my hair freshened up, and the afternoon fetching my dress from the cleaners and buying a new pair of shoes. I called the rental place to see if Morse had picked up his tux. He hadn't. I dropped by the house several times to see if he'd left a message on my machine. He hadn't. He finally called about five.

I had come a long way that past week. Formerly I would have fallen all over him, glad to hear his voice. I guess I'd been that needy for love right after Mama died. Now I was annoyed and didn't mind if he knew it. "When did you get back?" I demanded.

"Uh, baby, I'm not back yet. We—"

"How far away are you? We've been invited to join some people for dinner—" I stopped, a sinking feeling in my stomach. "You are coming, aren't you? You promised."

"I know I did, baby, but you just wouldn't believe how great the river is right now. Why don't you drive up tomorrow and spend a day or two?" His voice was as coaxing as if inviting me to join him was his sole purpose for calling.

"You mean you aren't coming? Why didn't you call sooner?"

"Now don't whine, baby. You know I hate whiners."

"Don't keep calling me 'baby,' Morse. It's not making me any less mad. And I'm not whining, I'm asking for information. If you'd called yesterday, I could have asked my cousin to take me. I don't know if he can go this late."

"You mean to tell me you'd go out dancing with somebody else, sweet thing?" His voice was still jovial, but with an edge I'd learned to dread.

Some habits are hard to break. Automatically I tried to calm him down—but my laugh sounded false even to my own ears. "He's my cousin, for goodness sake! Two years younger than me, and more in love with racing cars than with women. A good dancer, though."

"I don't like to think of you dancing with anybody but me, Josheba. You just stay home until I get there."

"Not if I can help it." I hung up. The phone rang almost immediately and at intervals for the next hour. I let it ring.

Meanwhile, I called my cousin, but he was off racing somewhere. I was about to settle down for a long dull evening when I remembered Lewis talking about his days as a hot-shot attorney. I dialed the teen center.

"Lewis, do you have a tux?" I blurted as soon as I heard his voice.

"Hey, Josheba! Sure I do. Want to borrow it?"

"It and you in it. I've been stood up for an important party tonight, and—" I stopped, realizing what I was doing. *The man proposed to you, Josheba,* I told myself fiercely, *and here you are using him like a hired escort!*

I burned with shame.

"Oh, Lewis, I'm sorry. I called before I thought. Listen, forget I said anything about a tux. But has Mac called you?"

"From a tux to Mac in one breath? Slow down, girl. First, what about Mac?"

"We were over at Kateisha's on Thursday, and she said some dudes are planning to meet at the center early tomorrow morning. Six-thirty, I think she said."

"As a matter of curiosity, how do they plan to get in—did she say?"

"No, but she said something about cookies or biscuits—something like that."

"Biscuit. Thanks, Josheba. I'll take care of it. Now, what was that about a tux?"

I sighed. "Morse isn't coming back today after all, and a club I belong to is having a dance tonight. I wondered if maybe—"

He laughed. "Wonder no more. Morse's loss is my gain. I'd even like to make that permanent. What time?"

"I'll pick you up," I said faintly. "About seven-thirty? It's dinner and a dance."

I still felt faint when I hung up, but then I started humming. As I dressed, it seemed like the time couldn't pass fast enough. I found myself humming the whole time I was getting ready, and I seemed to be humming inside the whole evening.

Lewis wore a tux like he'd worn one all his life. I loved the way my friends looked at him—and at me—when I introduced him. I loved dancing against his shoulder. Dancing with Morse was always a bit like dancing with a bulldozer—he shoved me around the floor, and I let myself be shoved. Dancing with Lewis was like—dancing. If this was the last time I ever saw Lewis Henly (and it certainly ought to be, the way I was beginning to feel), I would at least have something worth remembering.

In spite of getting home late, I woke early Sunday morning. The clock said not quite six. I wondered if Lewis had done anything about that six-thirty meeting over at his club. It would be just like him to think he could handle it without help.

I couldn't lie there any longer. I could at least drive by and see if anything was going on. I pulled on the gray knit shorts, green T-shirt, and shoes I usually run in.

Like I planned, first I drove slowly past the center without stopping. The front door was closed and the street deserted except for one man out jogging with a Doberman. I drove around the block and back, intending to head home. Now the door was a little bit ajar.

My heart pounding, I parked around the corner and walked toward the center as inconspicuously as anybody could at that hour on a deserted street. At the door I gave a quick look around and darted quickly up the five shallow steps into the front hall.

I heard voices in Lewis's office, so I slipped into the lounge and pushed the door slowly shut, hoping it wouldn't squeak. It didn't. I left just enough of a crack to peep out of and hear through.

A voice I didn't recognize said, "They got Dré, man. What if he talks?"

"He ain't gonna talk. Not if he knows what's good for him." That sounded like Ricky Dodd. "Say, where's Z-dog? I ain't waitin' much longer. I got stuff to do, man."

"Z-dog will be here when he gets here," the first voice answered. "We wait till he does." The front door closed with a bang. "Maybe that's him now."

It wasn't. I had known those light footsteps just long enough to recognize them. Lewis's voice rang out, cheerful and normal. "Hey, fellows. What's coming down? What you doin' here at this hour, Biscuit?"

"Uh—we got a meetin'. We ain't botherin' nothin', and I'm gonna lock up real good."

There was a short thud, as if someone had lunged forward, then a grunt. Lewis spoke again. "Try that once more, Ricky, and I'll break your neck. Now, clear out, both of you. This place is clean, and it's going to stay that way as long as I have anything to say about it."

Ricky's reply was low—low enough for me to catch the slight sounds of the front door slowly opening and stealthy footsteps moving down the hall.

Putting my eye to the crack, I caught a glimpse of a stocky young man with very dark skin. His hair was cut short around his ears and snarled on top of his head. I recognized him at once: the youth at the library who stole Mac's purse and her car. In spite of the heat, I shivered. The very air around him seemed poisoned.

My eyes darted from where I stood to the telephone on the desk. Could I reach it and call 911 without being heard? I tiptoed toward it.

"What have we here? A little friendly conference between homies?" The newcomer's voice was about as friendly as a cobra's.

"Z-dog!" Ricky exclaimed. "We were waitin' for you."

"What's he doing here?"

"I run this place," Lewis said, "and I object to meetings being held here that I haven't called."

Z-dog gave a short, deep laugh. "I hold meetings when and where I please, man."

Lewis spoke evenly. "Not in my club you don't. I don't want any trouble, so why don't you all find another place for your little conference?"

Z-dog laughed again. A more unpleasant sound I never hope to hear. "Think you got things under control, don't you, Mr. Henly? But you know what? Your being here just makes things easier for me. I've been wantin' to terminate my relationship with Ricky here—"

Ricky squealed.

"No, Z-dog!" Biscuit begged.

"Shaddup," Z-dog barked.

"Put down the gun, Z-dog," Lewis ordered.

Urgently I pushed the phone buttons and held my breath. As soon as a dispatcher answered, I muttered, "Hurry! Send the police at once. There's somebody here with a gun and I think he's about to shoot!" I gave the address as quickly as I could, straining to hear what was going on in the other room. I couldn't hear a thing. "Please hurry!" I repeated.

"Right away," the dispatcher said crisply.

I put the receiver down silently and tiptoed back to the door to listen.

". . . beautiful setup," Z-dog was congratulating himself. "Kid killed by director of youth club, who kills himself in remorse." Ricky was blubbering. "Too bad, homie!"

Again Z-dog laughed. I felt the hair on my neck rise.

I heard Lewis shout "Run, Rick!" as a shot rang out. Running feet thundered down the hall, and out the front door. I clung to the doorjamb, wondering what to do. Where were the police?

Someone groaned.

Someone else retched.

"You didn't have to shoot him, man!" Biscuit blubbered. "He didn't do nothin'."

"Shaddup, or I'll do you next. I gotta think. Who knew we was comin' here?"

"Nobody, 'cept you, me, Dré, and Ricky. You didn't have to shoot *him*, man!" Biscuit's voice rose to a scream. "You didn't have to *shoot* him!" I heard a thump, a thud, and something skid into the hall. Then I heard another thud, and someone hit the floor.

I peeked out. Just outside my door lay the gun. I dashed out and snatched it up, marveling at how easily it fit my hand. In an instant the stocky young man turned in the office doorway to face me. I leveled the gun at him.

Beyond him, out of the corner of my eye, I saw Lewis sprawled on the floor against a filing cabinet, with Biscuit crumpled beside him. I dared not look at them longer. I had to concentrate on Z-dog until the police came.

Oh, God, where are they? I begged. *Hurry, God, hurry!* I was praying and didn't care.

"Give me that gun!" Z-dog reached out, fixing me with the coldest eyes I'd ever seen.

I took several steps back toward the lounge. "One more step and I shoot." I was ashamed of the quiver in my voice and the way my hand was shaking.

He gave me a cocky grin. "I don't think so." He moved an inch closer.

I took a deep breath, aimed for his lower belly, and fired.

He reeled, clutched his groin, and fell, screaming oaths. In what must be incredible pain, he rolled over and started edging my way.

My hands were trembling so hard I knew I could not aim again. "Keep coming and I'll fire again. I'll probably kill you." To my horror, I knew I'd do it.

He must have known, too, for he collapsed groaning onto the floor. I peered over him toward Lewis. Lewis's shirt was covered with blood, and I heard his breath coming in short gasps. "Hang on, baby!" I urged him. "Hang on. Help's coming. Hang on!"

Z-dog continued to groan, Biscuit to sob, and Lewis to gasp for air. The sounds were a ghastly trio that filled and overwhelmed me. How long could I stand, aiming a gun at two men while the only one I cared about bled to death a few feet away? Time stretched until I felt my nerves would snap. "Oh, God, help," I found myself whimpering. "Oh, God, help!"

After what seemed like an eternity, I heard a shout behind me. "Lady, freeze!"

I turned. A police officer filled the front doorway, gun drawn.

"Thank God," I breathed, tears of relief running down my cheeks. "These are the men you want, officer. I'm the person who called for help." I shakily handed over the gun and ran to kneel on the floor beside Lewis. "Hang on, baby. Help is here. Hang on!"

Suddenly the center was full of police. One called for an ambulance. Another bent over Z-dog, who was still swearing and moaning in pain. A third handcuffed Biscuit, who sat on Lewis's desk chair and blubbered like a baby. "He took the bullet for Rick. Z-dog hadn't ought to shoot Lewis. He never done nobody any harm!"

"Shaddup!" an officer told him.

"Don't be rough on him," I said angrily. "If he hadn't knocked the gun out of Z-dog's hand, we might all be dead."

The officer helped Biscuit up and out to a squad car with a bit more respect.

Lewis gasped for air. His head lolled to my shoulder, and his eyes looked into mine pleadingly. "Oh, baby— "

"Don't talk," I said urgently. Tears streamed down my cheeks, but I did not want to take my hands from his hair to wipe them away. "Save your strength. Oh, Lewis, I love you."

"Too late." He reached out and clutched my arm. "Sorry, baby," he said clearly, then his voice faded and his head lolled to my arm.

I screamed.

One of the officers touched my shoulder gently. "Okay, ma'am, the rescue unit is here. Can we just ask you a few questions in another room?"

I stared at him, not quite comprehending. He put one hand gently under my elbow and helped me to my feet. I wiped my cheeks with both hands, then bent and touched Lewis's shoulder in farewell. He was past knowing or caring.

"Is he dead?" I asked, terrified.

"We need to examine him," said one of the rescue people. "Let us by, please."

The officer had to almost drag me across the hall to the lounge. "I want to know if he's all right," I begged.

"I'll ask them to let us know." He went back out and returned very soon. "His vital signs are faint, but he's still breathing. Now, suppose you tell me what happened."

Sometime while I was talking, I looked down and saw that my clothes were smeared with blood. They seemed to belong to somebody else.

He took notes without comment until I had finished, then asked, "Tell me again how you happened to be in this building this morning. I don't quite understand."

I didn't want Kateisha or Mac involved, so I weighed my answer very carefully, eyes on a tissue I was wadding between my hands. It, too, was smeared with Lewis's blood. "I . . . I was driving by and saw the door ajar. I know — " I stopped. Should that be "knew"? "I *know* the director," I said with emphasis, "so I came in to see if something was wrong." I brushed my hand over my forehead. "Sorry, officer, I'm not thinking too clearly. When I got here, I heard Ricky Dodd . . ."

His head came up, instantly alert. "Dodd was here this morning?"

I nodded. How had I forgotten to tell him that? "He ran, right after Lew — Mr. Henly — was shot. From something Biscuit said, I think the bullet was meant for Ricky, but he didn't stick around to find out." I suddenly started shaking all over. "Officer, I'm not quite myself just now." My head felt heavy enough to fall off, and while I had stopped crying, there was a waterfall where my heart used to be. "I'm not doing too well. Could we talk later?"

He patted my shoulder. "Sure, ma'am. You've had quite a shock, and you're doing real fine. I'll have somebody drive you home. We'll have you sign a statement later."

I stood up, feeling like a ghost or something. "I have a car, thanks." I heard myself talking, but couldn't feel a thing. "I'll be fine. Do you know where they've taken Mr. Henly?"

"No, but I can find out." He came back and tried to tell me the hospital, but I couldn't hear what he was saying. Finally he wrote it down on a piece of paper and stuck it in my hands. "Now let me send you home," he said again.

"I'll be fine. Thanks." I walked steadily down the steps and out the door.

It wasn't really me doing the walking. I was somewhere up in the air, watching that calm woman who had just almost killed a man and maybe lost the only man she would ever love. She walked to her car, got in, and started the engine. I watched her drive away. That's the last thing I remember until nine o'clock, when I looked out my windshield, saw the small triangle park across from the Fitzgerald house, and wondered how I got there.

It looked so inviting! A fountain splashed in the center, surrounded by pink and white flowers Mac would know the name of. I didn't care about the name, just that they were pretty. A little bench circled one granddaddy of a pine tree. I parked and walked directly across the lawn toward it, inhaling the scent of new-mown grass. I sat down carefully on the bench, feeling its warmth on my thighs below my shorts. That was the first I knew how cold I was. Stretching my arms along the back of the bench, I basked in the sunlight, eyes closed.

Memories washed over me. Lewis in black turtleneck and pants, like a tall slim priest. Lewis speaking gently to Ricky even when Ricky was sullen and proud. Lewis laughing. Lewis saying he wanted to marry me. Lewis's slender shoulder beneath my cheek as we danced. Lewis gasping in pain. "Oh, God, save him!" I wailed.

Frantically I tried all my pockets, but somewhere I had lost the piece of paper saying which hospital he'd gone to. I didn't know where he was.

How long did I sit there, listening to birds calling in the trees and two poodles barking across the street? I was so still that a bold crow pecked the grass just beyond my feet. Gradually the peace of the place began to penetrate my numbness.

I stood and ambled about. For the first time I noticed a small monument to F. Scott and Zelda Fitzgerald. Zelda was raised in Montgomery. She met her future husband at a dance there, and after their marriage and years away, she brought him back to live in a house just across the street from this little park. What griefs had they known in their six months in that house? Was her mind already slipping into the darkness from which he would be unable to save her? Their park was a good place to grieve.

With one finger, I traced words on the plaque: *It was like the good gone times when we still believed in summer hotels and the philosophies of popular songs.*

The quote meant nothing to me, but it made me remember the second night Lewis and I went out to dinner. The band played the same awful tune again and again, until he joked, "If we're not careful, this is going to become our song."

Finally, tears flooded my eyes. I welcomed their release.

Listen to advice and accept instruction, and in the end you will be wise. *Proverbs 19:20*

Twenty-Nine

This is MacLaren again.

Jake wasn't quite up to sitting through an hour's service yet, so I stayed home Sunday morning and packed, while Glenna went to church. "Don't cook, we've got tons of food," she reminded me as she left. As if I needed telling. There wasn't a square inch of empty kitchen counter space, and the refrigerator was bowlegged.

Packing presented a challenge. I had all the clothes I'd bought as well as the ones I'd taken to Albuquerque a hundred years ago. Finally, I had to borrow a suitcase from Jake. Sweet thing, he hated being the cause of my having to buy new clothes so much, he offered to pay for them.

"I'd love to take your money, Jake," I told him, "but honesty compels me to admit I needed them anyway, and Hopemore doesn't have stores anywhere near as nice as Montgomery's. In a way, you did me a favor by having a heart attack. But you can put a check for a couple of hundred dollars in the collection plate next time you come to visit."

When I finished packing, I set the table for three and chose several casseroles that might go together. By then Jake was napping, so I sprayed myself with mosquito repellent and slipped out into the backyard for a few minutes of prayer and quiet on my own.

I was just about to go back inside when I heard a familiar voice. "Dangnation, I know somebody's here! Jake shouldn't be going to church quite yet."

I jumped up and ran across the backyard faster than I'd moved in years. "Joe Riddley? Is that you? Honey! I'm in the back!"

I'd barely gotten through the gate and into the drive when I was swept up in an enormous bear hug. "I decided to come get you, Little Bit. Couldn't wait any longer. Besides, I wanted to see how old Jake is bearing up under so much attention."

"How'd you get here so early?"

"Gained an hour with the time change, and sprayed my right foot with some of that lead my wife uses when she drives. Come get me a Co-cola. I haven't had a thing to eat or drink since breakfast, and these last fifty miles, my stomach's thought my throat was cut."

As we headed into the kitchen, he added, "If you have any ideas about us sharing that little biddy double bed in Glenna's guest room, you can think again. I robbed the till before I left. We're going to the Marriott."

Joe Riddley and Jake were exchanging insults and I was sitting there thinking how fond I am of both of them, when the doorbell rang. Josheba stood there looking pretty as a picture in a yellow and white dress, but with her face practically washed away with tears. When I told her to come on in, she managed a watery smile, but her lower lip quivered. "I'm sorry to come right before lunch, Mac, but something has hap . . . hap . . . Oh, Mac! I'm so scared he's dead!" She collapsed into my arms, sobbing.

I helped her into the living room.

"What on earth—?" Joe Riddley asked. Jake waved him to be quiet.

"Come on in, honey," I told her, "and wash your face. Then tell me all about it."

A splash of cold water and a few deep breaths, and Josheba felt as ready as she'd ever be to tell us what happened that morning.

When she finished, her big dark eyes were pitiful. "I've lost the paper telling me where they took him, Mac, and even if I knew, I'm scared to death to call and find out he's—he's—" She couldn't go on.

"Let me find out for you, honey." I called the police station and told them who I was and what I wanted, but they weren't giving out information to a woman calling from who knew where, for who knew what.

I was about to give them a piece of my mind when Joe Riddley took the phone. "This is Judge Joseph Yarbrough from Hopemore, Georgia, son. The woman you've been talking to is my wife. She needs that information, and she needs it quick." He handed me back the receiver. Less than a minute later, I knew where Lewis was.

I also knew that Josheba had touched Joe Riddley's big heart. Otherwise, he'd never have pulled rank like that.

My next call was scary, for I was almost as reluctant as Josheba to know if Lewis had died. The woman at the hospital information desk, however, said he was there and in critical condition. We comforted each other that he was still hanging on.

"You come in here and get a little bite to eat, then you go right down there and be near him," I told Josheba. "Give him every reason to live. You want me to come along?"

She shook her head. "Not right now, Mac. But if—if—"

"As soon as lunch is done here, Josheba, I'll be there. Count on it."

While she nibbled on some cold chicken and potato salad, I asked gently, "Do you want to talk about Lewis, dear?"

Josheba closed her eyes. "I wouldn't know what to talk about."

"Do you love him?"

"I don't know, Mac," she whispered. "I like talking to him, dancing with him, being with him—"

"What on earth do you think love is, honey?" I cast a look back into the living room, where the two dearest and most ornery men on earth were arguing about who was going to win the Auburn-Georgia game next fall.

"But I'm engaged to Morse! Besides, I don't understand Lewis sometimes, Mac. Today, he took that bullet for Ricky. For Ricky! Worthless as he is. I can't stand even the thought of that. How could somebody as fine as Lewis take a bullet for somebody like Ricky? And how would I know he wouldn't do it again?"

I shook my head. "You don't. That's who Lewis is, and what he believes in, and when you live with somebody, you also have to live with what they believe in. At some point you'll have to decide whether you'd rather live with what Lewis believes in, or what Morse does. For now, though, get down to that hospital and give Lewis something to live for. I'm gonna be praying for you both."

I expected a protest, but she just nodded. "We need it, Mac. We really need it."

Once she left, I left the armchair quarterbacks to their discussion and went to my room. There, as I had promised, I prayed for Josheba and Lewis. I also prayed for Ricky, Dré, Biscuit, and even Z-dog.

However, I couldn't help remembering a prayer our older son said one night when he was ten: "Lord, you know I am grateful for many things, but this day is not one of them."

The phone rang in the silence like a fire alarm.

I answered it in Glenna's room, ready to explain to one of Jake's friends that he was doing real well.

The voice on the other end was hoarse, choked with fear. "It's me, Ricky. Listen, I gotta talk to you. Can you meet me somewhere? I gotta talk to you bad."

"Can you come to my house?"

He hesitated. Maybe he was remembering, as I was, that the last time he'd been there it had been very late and he had not been welcome. "Who else is there? Police?"

"No, just my husband and my brother. But Ricky, if you're planning any funny stuff—" I was about to tell him Joe Riddley was a magistrate, but he interrupted.

"I ain't gonna try nothin'!" he protested desperately. "Lady, you're my only hope. You gotta help me. You just gotta." He added a word that only terror could have wrung from him: "Please!"

It took Ricky over an hour to get there. Meanwhile, Glenna came home and we ate dinner. Jake asked the blessing. As you can imagine, with all that was going on, that took awhile.

During the meal, I filled the other three in on every single detail of what had been happening. I wound up, "I don't know what Ricky wants, but I know he's in big trouble. He's been dealing drugs, I think, and I don't know what he was planning with Z-dog and Biscuit, but I doubt it was legitimate. He's also still out on bail for killing Myrna." I held one palm to my cheek, suddenly worried. "Are we harboring a fugitive when he comes?"

Joe Riddley shook his head. "Not unless his court date is past. But it sounds like this young man needs a good talking to."

Jake had taken a fork in the road way back in my story. "Kateisha's been having toothaches?" he asked me. "How long?"

"I don't know, but it must be a good while. It was swollen and looked like it pained her a lot, but she said it would go away, that it always does."

He turned to Glenna. "Honey, think you could go by this next week and see if she and her mother would let our dentist take a look at her? You may have to promise her a new dress or something before she'll go."

"A new CD," I corrected him. "Have you ever seen Kateisha in a dress?"

He poured himself another glass of tea. "No, but there's always a first time. You thinkin' what I'm thinkin', Joe Riddley? Talking with this Rick sounds like men's work to me, not women's work."

"I guess women's work is washing the dishes?" I asked, miffed.

"No, I thought women's work was getting yourself down to that hospital to make sure Josheba and Lewis are all right."

"The only thing it is *not*," Joe Riddley added with emphasis, "is getting any more involved in trying to find out how that little girl died. We'll talk to Carter later—all four of us," he added, knowing full well I was going to protest again, "to get him to stir his stumps on that, and you and I'll stick around a couple of days to be sure he does. But you've done enough—" I expected him to say "meddling," but he swallowed it and merely said, "already."

"Before anything else"—I reached over and rubbed his jaw, which was gleaming silver in the sunlight—"I think you might want to shave."

He rubbed his cheek and grinned ruefully. "I left Georgia so early, I plumb forgot."

As I watched him head to the bathroom, it sure felt good to have all four of us together, helping each other out. I forgot to tell Josheba, but that's what love's about, too.

I left for the hospital before Ricky got there and spent the afternoon sitting with Josheba. Surgeons had stitched Lewis together as best they could. Now everybody was sitting tight to see if he would come back from wherever his spirit had fled.

When I got home, I didn't get a full report about Ricky's visit from the menfolk, of course. You know men—they never tell you everything you want to know. What I did learn was that Joe Riddley talked real straight to Ricky about what his chances were if he kept going like he'd been going, and suggested that he offer to turn state's witness against the drug dealers he knew, in exchange for some kind of protection. Jake persuaded Ricky to let them call Carter, so Carter came over and talked to all of them, then took Ricky away.

Jake's hoping Ricky will wind up in the army. I hate to think our national safety might ever depend on Ricky Dodd, but Glenna insists, "We don't know what God and a little discipline could do for that boy."

Glenna was troubled about one thing Ricky said, though. Joe Riddley asked him before he left if he knew anything at all about Harriet's death. Ricky swore he didn't—nor her mother's, either—but said we ought to ask William. "That boy said William was paying Harriet not to tell that he had—oh, Clara, I can't even say it. Not William, with his own niece!"

We looked at one another soberly. "Harriet told Kateisha that William was paying her ten dollars a week not to tell Dee something," I admitted.

"Well, I don't believe it," Glenna said firmly. "I just don't."

"There's something else that's been bothering me," I told Glenna. "William said the other morning that he couldn't have a peroxide blonde working for him, but Myrna had brown hair when she left Montgomery. I think he must have seen her pretty recently."

I could hardly stand the pain in Glenna's eyes. It wasn't going to get any better until all this was over.

A kind man benefits himself, but a cruel man brings trouble on himself.
Proverbs 11:17

Thirty

Josheba's story continues . . .

I went home from the hospital after the five o'clock visit just long enough to shower again and get a bite to eat. It would be my second shower of the day, but I felt like I needed to wash the hospital smell out of my pores. Then I planned to go over to the police station and sign my statement.

When I got home, Morse's red Grand Am was parked at my curb.

"Where you been?" he greeted me, rising from the porch chair. "I come home from two weeks out of town, and you aren't even here to welcome me." He grabbed me and pulled me close.

I pulled back. "Morse, we've got to talk."

"Talk nothing, sweet thing. I didn't drive all day to talk."

"Well, we gotta talk anyway." I spoke quickly, knowing I might never get up this much courage again. "While you were gone, I started thinking. I'm not sure we're right for each other. I want—"

His jaw dropped. "You're that mad I missed your dance?" He swore. After two weeks of not hearing them, his obscenities poured over me like filth. I tried to recall. Had I ever heard Lewis utter a single one?

You can't spend your life comparing Morse to Lewis, a voice whispered in my brain.

But I turned angrily away from Morse, "Don't talk to me like that!"

"Like what, baby? Now I can't even talk? Man, you are *mad!* Come on, give me a kiss and say you missed me."

"I didn't miss you," I told him bluntly. "Not after a while. And I got someplace to go. Call me tomorrow." I started for the door.

He grabbed my arm. "Don't you walk out on me, sister! Nobody walks out on Morse." I tried to pull away, but his fingers pressed hard into my arm. "I said nobody walks out on Morse. Did you hear me?"

I stood absolutely still. For the first time I was actually afraid of him. Physically afraid. "I heard you, Morse. I'm not going anywhere. Let go."

"I'll let go when I feel like it, baby, and not one minute before. Now let's get one thing straight—"

I tensed. He'd never hit me, but I knew now it was only a matter of time. Then—

"Hiya doin', Josheba? Everything all right?" That was Miss Sadie, my next-door neighbor. She's older than God and twice as nosy, and I have to admit that in the past, I've said some pretty nasty things about her butting into other people's business. That Sunday afternoon, I could have kissed her.

"Hiya, Miss Sadie!" While he was distracted, I gently pulled my arm away from Morse and took a couple of steps back. "You doin' all right?"

"I'm fine, thank you very much. That your young man?" She stood right on the edge of her yard and peered nearsightedly across my lawn. "I thought he was taller and thinner, somehow."

"Who's she talking about?" Morse demanded. "Who's taller and thinner?"

"She's half blind, Morse," I pointed out quietly. "Now, look, I've got to go down to the police station and sign some papers. I witnessed a crime this morning, and a friend got hurt, so I've got to go by the hospital on my way back. Call me tomorrow, all right?" I hurried inside and dead bolted my door.

Morse no doubt wanted to take me apart limb from limb, but with Miss Sadie perched on the grass like a little biddy nosy-bird, he decided to stomp to his car and roar away.

"Thank you, God, for nosy old women," I breathed. Looked like I sure was getting back in the praying habit.

Plans fail for lack of counsel, but
with many advisers they succeed.
Proverbs 15:22

Thirty-One

Mac wraps it up . . .

By Monday morning, there was again good news and bad news. The good news was, Jake was daily growing stronger, Ricky was maybe heading in some new directions, Z-dog was painfully recuperating under police guard and officially accused of stealing Jake's car and using it in several burglaries, and Carter had agreed to talk with William Sykes about how he knew Myrna was a peroxide blonde if he hadn't seen her for fifteen years.

The bad news was, Lewis was still unconscious, and Carter still insisted that Harriet's case was closed. Have you ever seen two English bulldogs eye to eye? Glenna said that was the picture she got when Joe Riddley tried to convince Carter to reopen Harriet's case.

It was now two weeks since I had come to Montgomery, and it looked like finding out how we lost Harriet could take forever—except Joe Riddley wanted to go home now. I asked him for one more day, so I could think things over and talk to everybody one more time.

I decided to begin with Julie and Dee. I called to see if they were home, and Dee said Julie had spent the night with Rachel and they'd probably be around the pool all morning. A pool seemed like a nice place to start. I wouldn't mind spending the morning in one, myself.

Rachel's mother came to the door with a portable phone to her ear. When I introduced myself as a friend of Dee looking for Julie, she immediately said, "Julie went somewhere this morning with some other girls, but Rachel's out by the pool." She waved her hand toward the gate in the back fence. "Do you mind if I don't come with you? I'm on long distance."

Rachel was indeed by the pool, listening to rock music and improving her tan. Not that a tan would improve her much, poor dear. She was a large lumpy girl with small dark eyes too close together. Apparently Princess Julie preferred less attractive ladies-in-waiting.

When I told Rachel I'd hoped to find Julie, she got a sulky look. "She's gone shopping with some of the other *cheerleaders.*" Clearly Rachel had not been invited.

"I'm sorry. I'm investigating Harriet Lawson's death, and I had a few questions to ask her." I waited a minute, hoping she'd fall for the bait.

Rachel tugged her bathing suit down over her large backside and swung around to sit up on her towel. "That was really awful, wasn't it? I mean, you don't think something like that could happen to anybody you know."

"You knew Harriet, too?" I sat in one of the white plastic chairs that circled the pool.

Rachel brushed back a strand of long lank hair and said doubtfully, "Sort of. I mean, she was a year younger than us, and she hadn't been at Julie's long, but sometimes when we were listening to music, or going to the mall or something, she'd like, you know, be with us."

I nodded. "I understand. She wasn't exactly a friend, but you knew her."

Rachel nodded earnestly.

"Well, I'm trying to get a picture of the last day anybody saw Harriet. Tuesday, June fourth. Was Julie with you that day?"

Rachel's eyes flickered, then she lowered them and reached for a tube of sunscreen. Slowly she started rubbing it into her thick calves.

"Was she?" I prodded.

"That's a long time ago," Rachel muttered without looking up. "I don't know if I can remember that far back."

"It was the first week school was out," I prompted. "That first Tuesday."

Rachel shrugged. "I really can't remember. We probably hung out together."

"Up at the lake," I said, as if reminding her.

"How'd you know?" she demanded. "Who saw us?"

I'd been guessing, but I know guilt when I see it. "Never mind that. Were there boys with you?"

Rachel jumped, then nodded reluctantly. "A couple. From school. Just friends, like."

"Did you go to Julie's grandmother's house?"

"No." Rachel sounded glad to change the subject. "We go up there all the time, but not that day. Have you been there?"

I shook my head. "Just to drive by. Now, Rachel, I have a very serious question."

She went pale and swallowed. Tears filled her eyes. "I can't tell. I promised! Okay? I can't tell!" She leaped to her feet and dove into the pool.

I went to the poolside and knelt to meet her when she surfaced. "Rachel, listen. I—"

She submerged and swam to the deep end with long, sure strokes. I started to head around the poolside to meet her when she needed air, but we could play that game all day.

I cast a quick look at the house. Her mother was not in view. Quickly I kicked off my shoes, knelt on the side of the pool, and toppled in. The water felt so good I could have stayed all day, but I wasn't there for fun. I started toward her with long sure strokes. Rachel watched me with astonishment. I guess it never occurred to her that grandmothers can swim.

As I got closer, she opened her mouth. "Don't you shriek," I told her grimly. "I don't give a darn where you and Julie were that day—although it sounds like it's something you're pretty ashamed of. What I want to know is, did either of you see Harriet that Tuesday?"

"Harriet?" It wasn't at all what she expected. "No, ma'am! I didn't see Harriet after school was out. And I know Julie didn't see her that day. She was with me the whole time."

I heard a sliding door open. "I was on the side of the pool talking to Rachel, and fell in," I explained sheepishly to Rachel's mother as I pulled myself up a ladder. I accepted her offer of a towel, refused an offer of dry clothes, and drove thoughtfully home. On June fourth, Harriet hadn't been the only missing child whom nobody knew was gone.

On my way home, I thought over everything I knew. As I put things in order, I saw I might have had something backwards all along. If I turned it around, one thing was frighteningly clear. I knew who could most likely have killed Harriet. And if I was right, given the way she'd been found, I knew how.

"What on earth happened to you?" Glenna exclaimed when I dripped in through the back door.

Joe Riddley heard, and left Jake and ESPN in the den to join us. "Looks like she decided to swim and couldn't wait for her suit. That right, honey?"

I glared at him. "I was talking to a child who kept insisting on swimming away from me. There was nothing to do but follow her. And you had the motel key, so I couldn't get in our room for dry clothes." I held out my palm. He fumbled in his pocket and handed it over.

Glenna fetched me a dry towel. "At least take this. Oh—Carter called. They talked to William, and now they've taken him downtown for questioning."

"What did you find out about Julie?" Jake called as his game broke for a commercial.

"Rachel says they didn't see Harriet all day, and I believe her. The two of them were up at the lake that day with some boys from school, doing something they don't want their parents to know about. From the looks of poor Rachel, it was more likely drugs than sex."

"So that's one down and how many to go?" Joe Riddley inquired. "Or have you decided who killed Harriet yet, Little Bit?"

"I'm afraid so. I'm not absolutely positive, however, so I won't tell you yet. And I don't know how to prove it if I'm right. I just have one idea. Let me see what you all think about it, then I'll go change my clothes."

Glenna pulled up another chair, Jake turned off the television, and I told them.

"It might work," Joe Riddley admitted when I was done. "If Carter cooperates."

"Leave Carter to me," Glenna said, a look in her eye I had never seen before.

"We'll tackle Lou Ella, too," Jake offered. "Glenna can call and tell her to get herself over here to see me."

"Do that," I told them. "Meanwhile, I'll go see Eunice, Dee, and Claire Scott."

"I'm going with you," Joe Riddley heaved himself up from the couch. "I don't want you driving my car again. You must've already soaked the driver's seat."

"We haven't even *seen* mine yet," Jake grumbled. "First it was getting Clara's dents out, then it was hauled down to the police station. Next thing we know they'll be putting it in the Smithsonian."

"You should be honored," I told him. "It's not everybody whose car is chosen for *three* burglaries."

Eunice Crawley was at work, scowling at a computer screen. "Good afternoon," she greeted us. "I got so far behind being out so much last week, I'll never get caught up. What can I do for you?"

I introduced her to Joe Riddley, then said, "I just wanted to give you the latest news on Harriet."

Eunice sighed. "Seems like I can't stop thinking about her and poor Myrna. Hadn't seen neither one of them for years, then suddenly they're all I think about. It's no wonder I don't get my work done."

"Well, there may be something happening about Harriet this evening or tomorrow. A Biloxi man has come forward who says he was in town and up in the cemetery when Harriet was—and he saw something!" I waited for her to react.

"Do tell," she breathed. "What was it?"

"I don't know, but he's coming back up to Montgomery this evening, and he'll talk to the police tomorrow. Maybe we'll know something after that."

She leaned forward eagerly. "He saw it? Why didn't he say anything 'til now?"

"Maybe he didn't realize what was happening, or maybe finding the body didn't make the Biloxi papers. Anyway, he's coming in late tonight and going straight to the Marriott, but he'll talk with the police in the morning."

I'd told myself and told myself I was making up a story, not lying, but my voice still shook. My son Walker, who took a lot of drama in high school and college, swears lying is just like pretending you are in a play. Given some of his shenanigans growing up, he ought to know. However, I never was in a play, so I added, "I'm sorry to sound so wobbly this morning, but a good friend of ours went to the hospital yesterday, and he's still unconscious." Forgive me, Lewis, for using you like that.

"I'm real sorry to hear it." Eunice rested on her forearms. "What about Myrna—did this man who's coming kill her, too?"

"He didn't kill anybody," I explained again, exasperated at having to lie some more. "I think he just saw something." I took a scrap of paper out of my pocket and laid it down on Eunice's desk so I could see it without my reading glasses. "All I know about him is his name, Thomas Wilson, and that he'll be staying in room 214 at the Marriott."

Eunice looked at Joe Riddley and said in a voice that, in other circumstances, would have made me proud, "Your wife sure does beat all. Where does she get the energy to run around in all this heat? It's not like Harriet was her kin or anything." She turned back to me. "But I know how you feel. I keep thinking I ought to be doing something, too, but I wouldn't know where to start."

I stood up. "Well, maybe we'll know something after they've talked to this man."

We conveniently forgot the paper on her desk.

Next we drove up to Claire Scott's. "I don't have to actually see Claire," I told Joe Riddley. "I just need to leave the paper for her."

Claire's mother was watering her black-eyed Susans, wearing the same pink print dress she'd worn the first time I saw her. "Looks like a feed-sack dress," Joe Riddley said out of one side of his mouth as he pulled close to the curb, "just like our mamas wore."

"My mama never wore dresses made from feed sacks," I protested.

"Your mama's husband didn't own a feed store. Howdy, ma'am." He raised his hat. "I'm Mr. Yarbrough, and this is my wife. We came—" He stopped and let me take over.

"We've come about Harriet again."

The old woman tucked a wisp of white hair into her straw hat and contemplated us with her light blue eyes. "I heard she was dead. Will they be having a memorial service, do you know? I feel I kinda owe it to Bertha Lawson to go, being as she left Harriet in Claire's care, so to speak."

"I haven't heard about a memorial service," I told her, "but I did hear that the police have a good lead on the person who killed her."

The woman flung her head up, surprised. "Killed her? I thought she caught flu or something, sleeping out. Ran away from Dixie, I heard."

"Yes, she did run away from home, but we're pretty sure she was killed on purpose."

"Lordy, who'd do a thing like that?"

I shook my head. "The police aren't sure, but they think they have someone who can help them, a witness who was up at the cemetery that afternoon." I fished in my purse for a second scrap of paper and held it out far enough to read. "Here's his name, Thomas Wilson, from Biloxi. I think he actually saw or heard something. He's staying at the Marriott tonight in"—I peered at the paper—"room 214, and he'll talk to the police in the morning. I thought Claire might like to know. Would you give her the message?"

"A man's coming up from Biloxi to talk to the police. I surely will. And I hope they catch whoever it was." She splashed water angrily onto a bed of begonias near the walk. "It ain't right to take the life of a child."

As I headed back to the car, I accidentally dropped the paper on the grass.

"She picked it up and put it in her pocket," Joe Riddley informed me as he got in. "But stick to the nursery business, Little Bit. You'd never make it on Broadway. Where next?"

When we parked on Dee's driveway and crossed William's soft lawn, a curtain moved slightly at the living room window. Dee came to the door as pretty as ever in a blue flowered skirt and white top with a long string of gold add-a-beads around her neck. Her lipstick was blurred, though, and her mascara had run when she cried.

She stood back to let us in without even asking who Joe Riddley was, then quickly shut the door behind us. "Laura, you just won't believe the terrible thing that's happened. They've taken William down to the police station for questioning! They think he's been in touch with Myrna sometime recently, and I'm terrified they . . ." Her voice broke. She was obviously frantic. Poor William wasn't pretty, and he might not always be strictly honest, but his wife loved him. "And then reporters started calling—even the television people. I'm so glad you're here!" She collapsed on my shoulder.

She wouldn't be so glad later, I thought sadly, giving her an awkward hug. I hoped she'd never learn how many of their notions the police were getting from me.

"How're you holding up?" Joe Riddley bent down and asked kindly.

"Just barely," Dee moaned. "The television reporter was downright rude. Wondered if she could put me on the evening news. When I didn't recognize your car, I almost didn't answer the bell. Are you Laura's brother?"

When I introduced them, her surprise wasn't a bit flattering. Apparently it hadn't occurred to her I was married.

Especially not to such a nice, handsome man. And as worried as she was, Dee couldn't help turning on the charm for him. Her blue eyes widened pitifully. "Nothing this awful has ever happened to us. Those reporters are just ghouls!" She led the way to the sunroom. "Thank God, Julie's over at Rachel's. I can't decide about calling her to come home. I don't like to worry her, but it will be awful if she hears it from somebody else. I don't know what to do."

I was tempted to suggest she call. Miss Slyboots could stand to be found out once in a while. In fact, it would probably be good for her. I felt a twinge of unexpected compassion. Maybe Julie's main problem was that nobody ever told her mother on her. Dee wasn't such a doting parent that she'd refuse to discipline the child, nor was Julie really bad—just used to getting away with things.

However, no matter what Joe Riddley might tell you, I don't always jump into other people's lives with both feet. I knew this was neither the time nor the place to worry Dee with anything else. She had enough on her plate without having to call all over town trying to find her daughter.

For one thing, she had suddenly remembered she was a Montgomery hostess. "Please sit down. Can I get you all a Coke or something?"

"No, thanks." I took a chair, and Joe Riddley sat down gingerly on the love seat, perching on the front of his cushion as if afraid the wicker couldn't stand up to his two hundred pounds.

"How could anybody think William . . ." Dee's voice trembled and stopped. She settled herself on the chaise, arranged her skirt, and looked at us with eyes brimming with tears.

"Have you talked with a lawyer?" I asked matter-of-factly.

She nodded. "He said he'd go down to the station at once."

"Well, I hate to ask this, but do you think William killed Myrna?"

"Of course not! He didn't even *know* Myrna. I don't think they'd met more than two or three times. Besides, William wouldn't kill *anybody*." She fiddled with her beads.

A car roared up the drive. A door slammed, and a key rattled in the kitchen lock. "Dee? Dee! Are you here?" Nora started talking before she reached the sunroom. "What did you mean by that message you left on my machine about William?"

I waited a bit nervously to see what Dee would say, since it had been me who left the message—holding my nose and sniffing to sound like I was crying. However, Nora went right on talking without waiting for a reply. "And why should he—Oh! I didn't realize you had company." She stood in the doorway, slim in pale white slacks and an orange and yellow top. Why hadn't that woman's hips slid south when the rest of ours did?

And whom did she think Joe Riddley's silver Town Car belonged to—the yard man?

"Hello, Nora," I said. "I came by to give Dee some news, and she's been giving us some instead. This is my husband, Joe Riddley Yarbrough." I almost said "Judge Yarbrough." There was something about Nora that made me want to impress her. Perhaps those hips, or the way her hair still looked so naturally red. I realized just in time, however, that if I said "judge," Nora and Dee might expect things of Joe Riddley he couldn't deliver, and he'd practically kill himself trying. He can be hard on our boys, but pretty women make putty out of him.

Dee sighed. "I was just telling Laura and her husband, Nora—William's been taken to the police station to answer questions about Myrna, and I've been perfectly besieged by reporters. You can't imagine how tacky some of them were."

Nora sat down suddenly in a straight chair. "What on earth do they think William knows about that woman?"

Dee shook her head. "I have no idea. He didn't call me, his secretary did. She said the police asked him some questions about his trip to New Orleans last spring, then asked him to come downtown with them." Her voice trembled. "You know what that means. It means they think William ki—ki—killed her!" She burst into tears. Joe Riddley reached for a tissue and handed it across to her, although she could easily have gotten it herself.

I thought we'd better get on with our business and leave. I could tell by his expression what he was thinking: *Little Bit, how could you even think one of these delightful ladies could kill anybody?* I've always said it's a good thing he's a magistrate and not a trial judge. No woman in Hope County would ever get convicted except the loud, the rude, or the ugly.

I reached into my pocketbook, pulled out a scrap of paper, and repeated what I'd told Eunice and old Mrs. Scott. Nora, who is no dummy, pooh-poohed the whole idea of somebody coming forward after all this time, but Dee snatched up the paper and looked at it like she'd like to memorize what it said.

She didn't need to do that. I left it on her wicker coffee table.

When we got home, Glenna poured us each a glass of tea and got us settled in the den, then she and Jake sat down with us to compare stories.

"Carter called," she told us. "William admits running into Myrna down in New Orleans in early May, and telling her that Harriet's grandmother and father had both died and left Harriet—to quote Carter—'a bundle.' William said he figures Myrna came back to get her hands on some of it. He swears he didn't kill her, though, and has employees at his store who can testify he was there the day she got shot. Carter also asked him about why he was paying

Harriet, and he says he never touched her—that one day they were in the kitchen and he just bumped into her, but she accused him of trying—you know. Anyway, he says he wasn't, but he gave her an allowance because he felt sorry for her. I was so *glad* to hear that."

"Yeah, right," Joe Riddley muttered under his breath.

Jake rubbed his hands together, a sure sign he was nervous. "We had a good visit with Lou Ella, too, but we can't tell you everything she said. It boiled down to this: she found out on Monday, June third, how bad William's business is doing, and she got real upset."

"She cried!" Glenna marveled. "She sat here and cried to think her grandson had gotten in such a financial bind and she never suspected. 'I've been too busy with outside things and not kept watch over my family,' she said."

"But what does that have to do with where she was on June fourth?" I asked whichever one of them wanted to tell me.

"She was with our preacher all morning. Lou Ella grew up Catholic in New Orleans—her real name is Lourdes Elaine. She changed it in college. Anyway, she said that was the first time in years she'd wished she had a priest to confess to, so she called the preacher and asked if she could talk to him. She was just *stricken* to think how much William had suffered without her knowing a thing about it. After she'd talked to the preacher, she had William over for a late lunch to, as she put it, 'Make things right.' I don't know exactly what she meant—"

"But we figure it had something to do with writing a check for Julie's education," Jake finished. "We didn't call the preacher to check that alibi, Clara, but we could if necessary."

I shook my head. "At this point we don't need to verify any alibis. All we need to do is eat supper and see if a bird comes to our bait this evening."

What the wicked dreads will overtake him; what the righteous desire will be granted. *Proverbs 10:24*

Thirty-Two

"It was a dark and stormy night," I murmured.

Joe Riddley turned from the TV movie he was watching. "What did you say?"

"Nothing. I was just trying to set the mood—and pass the time." I nestled against his shoulder and wiggled to get the pillows more comfortable behind my back. "What if this doesn't work?" I wiggled some more. "Or what if the person I'm expecting does come, but I'm wrong about who killed Harriet?"

"I still wish you'd tell me who you suspect—and stop worrying," Joe Riddley growled. "If nobody comes or we don't get a confession, we've lost a night's sleep and watched a good movie—if you'll hush and let me see it."

It was well past eleven, and by now my bottom was numb and there was no comfortable position left to sit. We were propped, of course, on our bed in room 214 at the Marriott watching *Midway* – an old World War II movie Joe Riddley's already seen a hundred times and never passes up a chance to see again. Carter, hopefully, was standing guard by the peephole in his room across the hall.

Thunder rumbled beyond the windows. I got up and padded across the floor to pull back the drapes. Outside our windows, Nature was just beginning another spectacular performance. Lightning flashed. Thunder rumbled. Even as I watched, rain began sheeting down.

"If nobody's come by now, we wasted our time," I complained. "Nobody in their right mind, even a desperate mind, would come out now in that storm."

"Little Bit," Joe Riddley said in exasperation, "if you don't stop talking I am going to call down and rent you another room. Hush! Here come the American dive bombers! Watch what happens."

I knew what was going to happen. Aircraft carriers were going to blow up. People were going to die. America was going to win. I'd lived the book.

"I wish we'd gotten some Co-colas." I climbed off the bed for a glass of water.

"Go get some," Joe Riddley told me, intent on his movie. "My wallet's on the dresser." I knew he wasn't thinking about what he was saying, but I was bored enough to go. Nobody was going to come this late and in all that rain.

I took the ice bucket and some dollars from his wallet and left with the feeling I was being let out of jail. Waiting has never been my strong suit. Unfortunately, the ice machine was slow, and the drink machine kept spitting back my dollars. I smoothed out all the wrinkles and ran them through four times each before going to the office for some change. Nobody will ever convince me that machines aren't conscious beings. They always know when you are in a hurry, and do all they can to hold you up.

Finally, carrying two canned Co-colas and a bucket of ice, I hurried back to our room. Rounding a corner, I saw ahead of me down the hall, almost at our door, the killer of Harriet Lawson. Nora Sykes. With a gun.

It was a small silver gun. It gleamed very prettily in the hall lights, then slid nicely into the pocket of that lovely full green skirt I'd admired at the hospital. With it, Nora wore the marvelous green and purple top I liked so much. She even had on her pretty green shoes.

She raised her hand to knock at the door. In the next two seconds, I had approximately a million thoughts, all jumbled together. One was a very clear picture of Joe Riddley opening that door and getting a bullet plumb through him. Another was to wonder if it would help if I screamed and swooned. I didn't know how to swoon. Besides, chances were good that Nora would shoot me and then turn to shoot Joe Riddley as soon as he showed the whites of his dear, familiar eyes.

A third thought was to wish I'd gotten training in karate or jujitsu, one of those fancy methods of sneaking up on somebody and knocking them cold before they suspect a thing—except, given my agility in other sports, I'd have been maimed for life during training.

A fourth thought was to wonder if I could throw a canned drink and knock her out. Since I can't throw a round baseball straight at close range, the very best I could hope for at that distance with a canned Co-cola was that it would hit the ground, spew all over, and distract her for a second.

I am ashamed to admit I even wondered if I'd get to find out where she got those shoes before she shot me.

Finally I remembered something my mama always said: *Use the gifts the good Lord gave you, girl. That's what they are for.*

At that moment, the only two weapons that stood between Joe Riddley Yarbrough and a small silver gun—

besides two cold Co-colas and a full ice bucket—were Southern charm and a carrying voice.

"Why, hello!" I called brightly and very loudly down the hall, hurrying toward her. "Were you looking for me, Nora?"

She turned toward me, startled. Do you know, she was so well trained by her mother that she actually smiled? I kept walking. Having read somewhere that a moving target is harder to hit, I wove back and forth across that wide hall, hoping I looked either drunk or very sleepy.

"I'm so sorry," I called, sounding as apologetic as if I'd stood up Rosalynn Carter when I'd invited her to tea. "I got very thirsty and ran down for some drinks, but I got lost coming back. I don't stay in hotels very often, and I plumb forgot my room number. Wasn't that silly? I've written it on every scrap of paper I could find all day long, and I still forgot."

From a moment's uncertainty in her white still face, I thought I'd scored with that. I hoped she was thinking *Maybe the number on that piece of paper wasn't the out-of-town visitor's room after all.*

She still hadn't said a word as I came nearer, but I pretended not to notice.

"I had to go ask the desk clerk," I babbled on. "I hope you haven't been standing there too long." I got within handing range. "Here, if you'll hold these for a second, I'll get the key out of my pocket." I stuck out the two drinks, and she automatically put out both hands to take them. I tucked the ice bucket in my left elbow and fumbled with my right hand in my pants and then my jacket pocket.

Come on, Carter! I was silently urging. *Where are you? Get your eye to that peephole and get yourself out that door before this dadgum killer turns around and sees you! Now, while we've both got our backs to you and her hands are full! And Joe Riddley, don't you dare open our door.*

Both doors remained obstinately shut.

Since I kept my eyes fixed on Nora's face, I sensed rather than saw when she stuck both Cokes in one hand and lowered her other hand back toward her gun pocket. *Come on, Carter!* I thought, trying to send a louder silent message through the door across the hall. He must not have on his listening ears.

"Oh, no!" I exclaimed, louder than before. "I've left my key inside on the dresser. I'll have to — "

At least I'd gotten the attention of a man next door. "What's going on out there?" A very large and irate head stuck out his door. "People are trying to sleep around here."

"Sorry!" I put a finger to my lips and gave him my silliest smile. "I've locked myself out of my room."

"Go ask for a key at the desk." He was about to go back inside, leaving us alone in the hall.

"Could you just call and ask them to bring one?" I pleaded, hoping I could still bat my lashes when my whole face felt frozen. "Tell them poor Mrs. Yarbrough is standing right here waiting, with her guest, Nora Sykes. Please!"

He slammed the door behind him, hard. I doubted, somehow, that he was going to call for my key, and I had run out of clever things to say.

I've never been good at a poker face, anyway, and I'd spoken too desperately and too deliberately. Nora slid her hand back in her pocket. With the entire world to choose from, I was going to die in this hall.

I had to know one thing before it happened. "Why did you kill Harriet, Nora?"

She raised her eyebrows in surprise. "For the money, of course. Julie needs it for college. Poor William's just not a businessman. I doubt if he'd be able to pay for more than a year at a *quality* college."

I thought for a second about trying to distract her with a discussion of the American university system, but she'd already made me too mad. People who assume that some colleges are automatically better than others always get my dander up. I sit on the board of our local community college, and if it's not quality, I don't know what is. "Surely you've got enough money to send her yourself," I said, with just that little edge to my charm that any Southern woman worth her salt knows how to use.

Her eyes flashed. "Of course I have enough, but that's not the point. Julie deserves that money. Harriet didn't. She'd have wasted her whole inheritance. That's probably the only thing in history that Dee and I have ever agreed on."

"You can't kill people just because they don't spend their money the way you think they should," I pointed out, stalling for time and wondering where the dickens Carter was.

"I didn't want to kill her. For nearly a week I kept trying to persuade her to sign a paper, but Harriet wouldn't listen to reason. Very foolish." Her green eyes glittered in the light. She held out the cans. "Please take these drinks. They are very cold."

I ignored her request. "From what I've heard about Harriet, you can't have had an easy time with her for nearly a week."

A small and very unpleasant smile flickered on her lips. "I drugged her soft drinks. That child drinks more of them than you would think possible. The poor dear thought she had a touch of the flu. And I kept telling her we were going to see her mother as soon as she felt better. It wasn't as hard as you might think. Now take these drinks, please." Again she thrust them at me.

I shook my head. "Put them down if you don't want them."

She bent her knees and tumbled them from her arm onto the carpet, watching me every second. If I gave one quick thought to shoving her while she was distracted and trying to get away before she could shoot, I was too spineless to try.

"So you had Harriet up at your lake house all week?" I asked as she stood erect, right hand still in her pocket. She didn't answer. Desperately, I kept talking. "I know it's true, Nora, just like I know you killed her. I even know how. Nicotiana, wasn't it? Out of William's flower beds. The tobacco family is so deadly in any form."

I'd startled her. "How did you guess?"

"We're in the nursery business. If the cigarettes under Harriet were supposed to make forensics think she was a smoker, you could have saved yourself the trouble. A medical examiner I called this afternoon told me they routinely find nicotine in everybody these days. We've all got it, even rabid nonsmokers like Harriet. He said they don't even bother to report it a lot of the time. They didn't for Harriet, but he's going back to check their findings."

Over her shoulder I saw a movement. Carter, far down the corridor, edging along the wall. Where in heaven's name had he been? Terrified I'd give a sign I'd seen him, I willed myself to look straight at Nora. At the edge of my vision, Carter crept closer and closer. Would he get to her before she got me? And how could I stall her until he did?

Your mind does the strangest things sometimes. I found myself once again admiring Nora's pretty green and purple sweater. "I know it's changing the subject, Nora, but would you mind telling me where you got those shoes? I've been wanting some that very shade of green."

Her eyes flickered toward her feet, but the instant was too short for me to run. "Dillard's, honey. They're soft as gloves. You can try them on in the car. Don't look surprised. We're going for a little ride. Now I have a gun in my pocket, so don't make a scene. Would you please turn around and lead the way to the ele—"

She stopped, diverted by something over my shoulder. "Oh, dear. Your husband is out looking for you." Her forehead puckered in a worried frown.

I whirled. That fool Joe Riddley was getting off the elevator! I tried to shoo him back, but the dummox just waved back and started loping up the long hall.

"Such a nice man," Nora murmured, almost to herself, "but he's made things very difficult." Slowly and deliberately she pulled the little gun from her pocket. "I doubt I can shoot both of you and get away, but as my daddy used to say, we never know what we can do until we try."

"No!" I gasped. "He doesn't know a thing. Really! Run, Joe Riddley! Run!" You find out how much you really love somebody when you're about to lose them.

Nora wasn't listening to either one of us. She was raising the little gun until it was aimed directly at my chest. "No!" Joe Riddley yelled, pounding up the hall.

Over her shoulder, Carter was still one room away.

I didn't take time to think. I threw my whole bucket of ice in her face.

Startled, she staggered backwards. Carter sprang forward. As he pinned her arms to her side, I saw her finger tighten on the trigger.

I flung myself face forward onto the scratchy carpet as the shot rang out. Heard it whiz over my head. "Watch out, Joe Riddley!" I screamed.

I heard him throw himself to the floor. "What in tarnation . . . ?"

Carter struggled with Nora for what seemed an hour but was probably seconds. She was stronger than she looked. I reached for her ankle and tugged. She shook her foot trying to loosen my grip, and toppled backwards. Carter wrested the gun from her as she fell and dropped it to the carpet near my head. Then he held her down while she wriggled to get free.

I grabbed the gun and clutched it close to my chest. Doors up and down the hall flew open and cautious heads popped out.

"Go back to bed. It's okay, folks, go back to bed," Joe Riddley climbed to his feet and flapped his hands. For all the world he sounded like he does on Wednesday nights, quieting the church supper crowd before the program. He bent and peered down at me. "You okay down there, Little Bit?"

Mama often said no experience is ever wasted. Since that moment, I've known how to swoon.

The LORD works out everything for his own ends—even the wicked for a day of disaster. *Proverbs 16:4*

Thirty-Three

Jake shifted himself on his pillows and pulled the covers up around his chest. "All right, now, begin at the beginning and tell us everything."

"Do you think you are up to this?" Glenna reached out an anxious hand to touch him. She was perched awkwardly on the bed at his waist. Joe Riddley sat leaning up against the footboard, and I leaned against him. Ever since I fainted, I'd needed him real close by.

"Nora pulled a gun on my big sister," Jake said indignantly. "I want to know why."

"Because MacLaren had to have one of her Co-colas." Joe Riddley put his arm around me and squeezed, then left it there. "I was so involved with my movie, I didn't think about what she was doing until she was out of sight. I called Carter, and he pointed out that she could be in danger if she ran into somebody out there alone, so he said we ought to go after her. By the time we got to the vending room, though, she'd gone to the lobby. We went back to the room, thinking she'd gone back a different way, and when she wasn't there, we panicked and started combing the halls. We got back just in time. You do beat all, Little Bit, for getting around!"

I laid my head on his shoulder. "You're a fine one to talk. Look at how much effort I wasted trying to keep you from opening the danged door. I'd have let Nora beat on it till she was blue in the face, if I'd known you were out gallivanting." I lifted my face for a kiss.

"You two can smooch later," Jake said grumpily. "What about the story?" I didn't blame him for sounding peeved. We'd roused him up from a sound sleep much too early, but Joe Riddley and I had been at the police station for hours. We'd decided to wake Glenna and Jake and tell them everything right away, then we could all go to bed.

"You are *certain* Nora killed Harriet?" Glenna twisted her hands in her lap.

I nodded. "Positive. She told me she did, then made a full confession to the police before William and her lawyer got there. Now they have persuaded her to take it back, of course, but Carter doesn't think they'll have much trouble proving it."

Her gray eyes were huge with pain. "*Why,* Clara? Why would she do such a thing?"

"Dee's mother's money. Nora knew—even if Lou Ella didn't—that William's business was in hot water. She wanted them to have enough to send Julie to what she calls 'a quality college.'"

I paused for Jake's predictable reply. Sure enough, "Send her to Auburn."

"It was William's insisting on sending her to Bama that started all this," I informed him. "Nora felt if they had more money, though, they'd be willing to send Julie to one of the colleges Nora planned to show her, and she was dead certain Julie would like one of them better than a big state school. Also, as we grandmothers tend to do, she felt her own granddaughter both needed and deserved that money far more than Harriet. She decided to get it for her. Nora insists she didn't set out to kill Harriet, though. She just wanted to pressure her into signing a paper giving her inheritance to Julie. So, on June fourth, Nora called Harriet at the club, pretended to be her mother, and set up an appointment in the cemetery. She met Harriet there and took her up to the lake house — promising that her mother would be waiting. All week she kept her there, insisting she sign the paper."

"Why didn't Harriet just run away?" Jake wondered. "She seemed to have plenty of gumption the one time I saw her."

"Nora kept her sedated," I explained, "and told her she had the flu. She also kept promising to take Harriet to her mother as soon as she felt better and signed the paper. Harriet, however, kept refusing to sign, and the Sykeses were supposed to leave for the mountains Friday afternoon. Finally, Friday morning, Nora poisoned her. When Harriet was nearly dead, she drove her to the cemetery and left her in the kudzu."

Jake was interested enough to wiggle up on his pillows. "Why not dump her in the lake, or in the country somewhere?"

"She didn't want it connected to her lake house, silly. Also, she needed Harriet found. Julie — or Dee, actually — couldn't inherit the money otherwise. Nora thought that when they got back from the mountains, William would call the police to report Harriet missing, the police would tell him they'd found a body, he would identify her, and it would be over. Instead, William refused to call. No wonder Nora kept after me to look for the child. She admitted tonight she made a prank call one night when it looked like even Lou Ella couldn't persuade William to report

Harriet missing. Nora wanted to spur me on to keep looking. I must have seemed like a godsend to her."

"I guess you were, honey," Glenna said sadly. "Just not the way she wanted."

That silenced even me for a minute.

Joe Riddley picked up where I'd left off. "No matter how much Nora tries now to say it didn't happen, if Harriet was at the lake house for several days, she'll have left evidence all over the place."

"Nora said the first time I met her that Harriet was never up there," I remembered.

He gave me an approving hug. "Good remembering, Little Bit. They may want you to testify to that. The poison made Harriet very sick, too, so they'll check Nora's car for traces of where Harriet threw up, or threads from the clothes she was wearing when she was found."

"But why didn't forensics find any poison?" From the eager way she leaned forward, and her tone of voice, I could tell Glenna still hoped it wasn't really true.

"She used a plant that's part of the tobacco family," I explained. "We've all been exposed to so much nicotine that forensics expected to find it. Even though her levels were a bit elevated, they didn't think it odd."

Joe Riddley shifted beside me, and I knew he was about to launch out into one of his antismoking diatribes. It was time to change the subject. "Ricky may be able to identify Nora's voice as the woman who called him to come to Myrna's, too," I told Jake and Glenna.

Jake sat bolt upright and stared at Glenna in disbelief. "We've known this woman all our married lives! She never acted like a mass murderer before."

"She's not a mass murderer," Glenna protested gently. "She's a very troubled woman."

"And although we're pretty sure Nora killed Myrna, Nora hasn't confessed to that," I pointed out. "Last night she insisted that for years she'd assumed Myrna was already dead. I suspect Dee was so embarrassed at having a prostitute in the family, she kept up the pretense that she died years ago. Nora certainly never expected Myrna to show up alive to inherit Harriet's estate. But William admitted to Carter that Myrna called to ask for a job. He must have mentioned that to his mother in his daily call, and Nora would have realized at once that Myrna, not Dee, was Harriet's legal heir. What a shock! She must have been frantic. Yet look at how quickly she planned to kill Myrna and set Ricky up as her killer. She's very bright."

"Don't sound so admiring, Little Bit," Joe Riddley warned.

"Will Dee get the money now?" Glenna asked.

I shrugged. "Eunice is Myrna's heir, and since Myrna died after Harriet—"

"A good lawyer ought to be able to get Dee *some* of the money. It was her mother's, after all." I could tell by Glenna's expression that she was wondering who she knew who might help. Then, because she was Glenna, her mind moved on to other people who would be needing help. "I really ought to call Lou Ella." Her hand reached for the phone.

"Wait until morning," I said quickly. "William and Dee decided not to tell her anything until then."

"Dee?" Jake growled. "That bag of fluff? You mean to tell me she came down to the police station in the middle of the night for Nora?"

"She's not as much fluff as Nora has made you think," I informed him. "And she will stand by William—and he by his mother—through whatever comes."

"Let's be sure to call Lou Ella in the morning," Jake told Glenna—as if she and I hadn't already discussed it. "She's a tough old bird, but she's going to take this hard. Just don't let on that Clara's meddling had anything to do with what happend." He settled back into his pillows.

"Now tell me one more thing, Sis. How'd Nora get the kid's gun?"

"She admitted that before William got down to the station. She found the gun in Harriet's drawer Tuesday, while taking clothes to make Dee think Harriet had come by the house. She took the gun up to the lake house and accused Harriet of planning to hurt William's family. Harriet told her it was Ricky's, that she was keeping it for him."

"Maybe having the gun gave her the idea of setting Ricky up," Joe Riddley added.

I nodded. "Maybe so. Anyway, what I think happened is this: she called Ricky pretending to be Myrna looking for drugs, and told him to meet her at Eunice's. Then she went to Eunice's, shot Myrna through Eunice's Polar Bear pillow, waited until she saw Ricky get off the bus a couple of blocks away, called 911, and left. They think they may be able to do a voice match with the 911 tape, by the way. Nora didn't know Myrna had called me, though, so she didn't expect me to surprise Ricky. She thought the police would find him there."

Jake turned around and gave his pillow a good punch-out. Then he challenged me. "Tell the truth, Sis. You didn't really know who it was until Nora showed up tonight with her gun, did you?"

I was torn between calming him down and bragging. It came out a little of both. "Yes, Bubba, after I talked to Rachel, I was pretty sure who it was. I'd already noticed that Nora always talked about Harriet in the past tense, from the very beginning. Everybody else mixed up the past and present, which was more natural. Also, Nora told William that Harriet's body had been found in Oakwood Cemetery, but she was in the kitchen talking to Julie when I told Dee exactly where it was found. I'd also done some thinking about how those clothes disappeared from Dee's. What if the last batch of clothes was taken to make people think Harriet was still alive Friday, so the family could get to the mountains and have a good alibi when the body was found? Nora certainly comes and goes in their house as she pleases.

"But Nora swore she'd been at the lake the day Harriet disappeared, and everytime I asked Julie in Nora's presence where she was that Tuesday, she acted real nervous. Once I knew that she'd been to the lake, I thought she was afraid her grandmother had seen her there. That seemed to give Nora a perfect alibi. After I talked with Rachel, though, I realized I might be thinking backwards. What if, instead, Julie had *not* seen her grandmother's car when she and her friends went past the lake house—even though Nora kept insisting she was there?

"That would certainly explain Julie's strange behavior about some silver earrings, too. I knew they were Harriet's and asked where she got them. She said her grandmother gave them to her—but she looked funny when she said it. I thought she was lying. I even wondered if she'd killed Harriet and taken them. But later I got to thinking that maybe, instead, she wondered where her grandmother got them. Nora never wears silver. From a couple of looks Julie gave Nora that morning out at Wynlakes, I think my asking about the earrings planted some serious questions in her mind."

It's a good thing I didn't expect congratulations from my brother. He looked at me like he still didn't believe I'd come to all those conclusions by myself, and growled, "I want to know one more thing. Who rammed my car?"

"With my wife in it," Joe Riddley added. Jake waved that away.

"That's something I don't know," I admitted. "Last night as we left the hotel, lightning flashed, and I realized that you don't really see colors in lightning, you see dark and light. In that light, Nora's hair looked as white as Ricky's. Maybe she borrowed William's truck to go pick up an oak tree and waited for me at the hospital. Maybe she bailed Ricky out and hired him to scare me—although I think that's highly unlikely. I think what probably happened is that William bailed Ricky out of jail and paid him to scare me, hoping I'd get off the case. He's certainly never been pleased I was looking for Harriet. He said he was even tempted to identify the wrong body to make me give it up."

"Now why would William do a thing like that?" Jake demanded.

I shrugged. "He says it was because he didn't want me bothering his wife."

"William was a very nice boy," Glenna repeated what she'd said days earlier. "I suspect he's grown up into a nice man."

"A nice man doesn't ram other people's cars," Jake informed her. He yawned. "There's probably more to be told, Clara, but it's time for smart people to sleep. You folks going back to the hotel, or are you going to lie down next door?"

"Like you said, it's time to sleep." Joe Riddley stood and pulled me up with him. "That means having room enough to stretch out. We're going back to the hotel."

That's all the story, except the two best parts. Josheba woke us up at noon to say Lewis had come out of his coma. We went to see him on our way out of town, and he looked pretty perky, considering. Of course, that could be because Josheba was holding his hand. The two of them looked like cats who've found a whole pot of cream.

The other best part was that Joe Riddley and I were finally free to head back to Georgia.

We had a great trip, riding along singing those old gospel songs he likes so much and just enjoying being back together. We worked our way through "Life Is Like a Mountain Railroad" and were halfway through "The Great Speckled Bird" when I saw blue lights in my side mirror. Since there wasn't any traffic on the road, neither one of us had been paying a whole lot of attention to how fast he was going, and we'd been too busy harmonizing to notice the trooper under a viaduct.

If Joe Riddley tries to tell you he could have talked his way out of that ticket if I hadn't butted in, don't you believe him for a minute. Sometimes he doesn't have the sense to know when he's been helped.

Besides, considering what was about to happen to us back in Georgia, that speeding ticket would soon be the least of our worries . . .